STRATFORD ZOO

MIDNIGHT REVUE PRESENTS:

ROMEO and JULIET

Written by Ian Lendler
Art by Zack Giallongo
Colors by Alisa Harris

First Second
New York

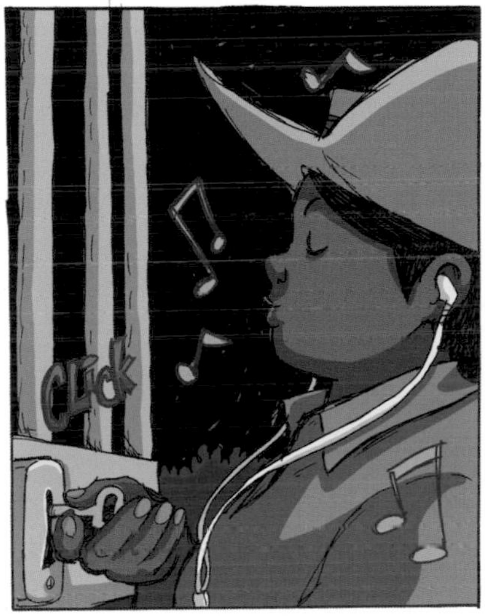
CLICK

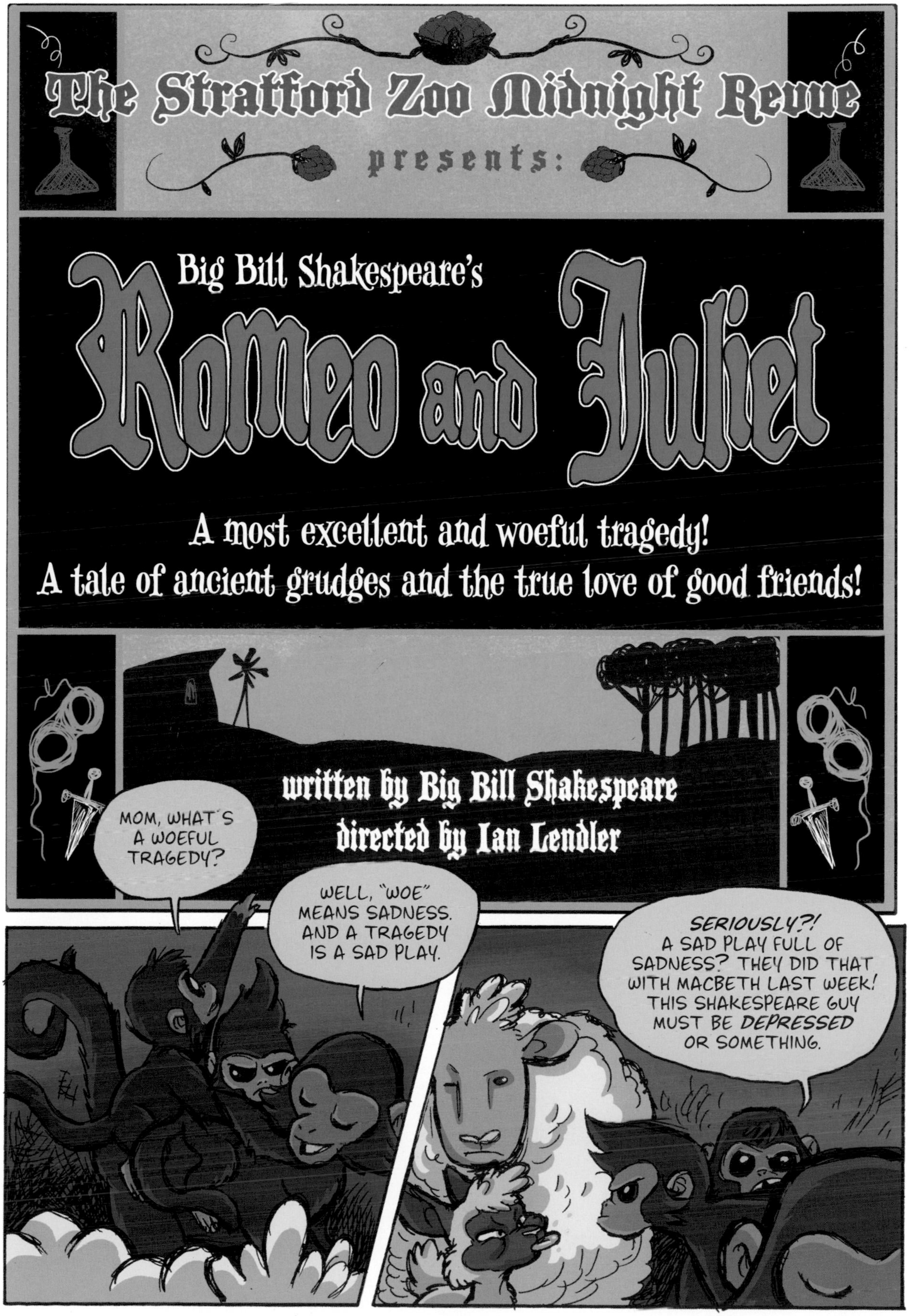
The Stratford Zoo Midnight Revue
presents:
Big Bill Shakespeare's
Romeo and Juliet
A most excellent and woeful tragedy!
A tale of ancient grudges and the true love of good friends!
written by Big Bill Shakespeare
directed by Ian Lendler
MOM, WHAT'S A WOEFUL TRAGEDY?
WELL, "WOE" MEANS SADNESS. AND A TRAGEDY IS A SAD PLAY.
SERIOUSLY?! A SAD PLAY FULL OF SADNESS? THEY DID THAT WITH MACBETH LAST WEEK! THIS SHAKESPEARE GUY MUST BE DEPRESSED OR SOMETHING.

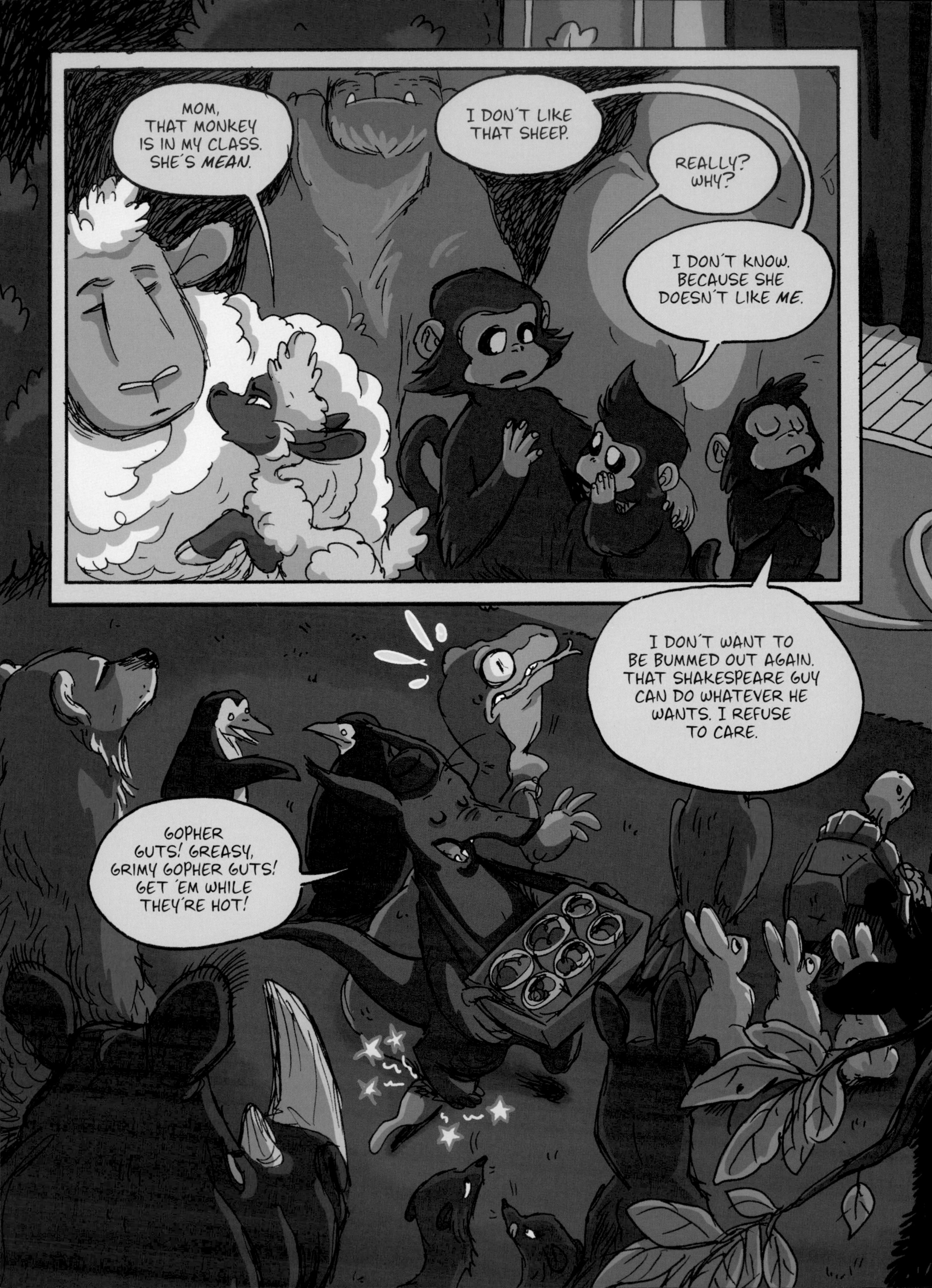
MOM, THAT MONKEY IS IN MY CLASS. SHE´S *MEAN*.
I DON´T LIKE THAT SHEEP.
REALLY? WHY?
I DON´T KNOW. BECAUSE SHE DOESN´T LIKE *ME*.
I DON´T WANT TO BE BUMMED OUT AGAIN. THAT SHAKESPEARE GUY CAN DO WHATEVER HE WANTS. I REFUSE TO CARE.
GOPHER GUTS! GREASY, GRIMY GOPHER GUTS! GET ´EM WHILE THEY´RE HOT!

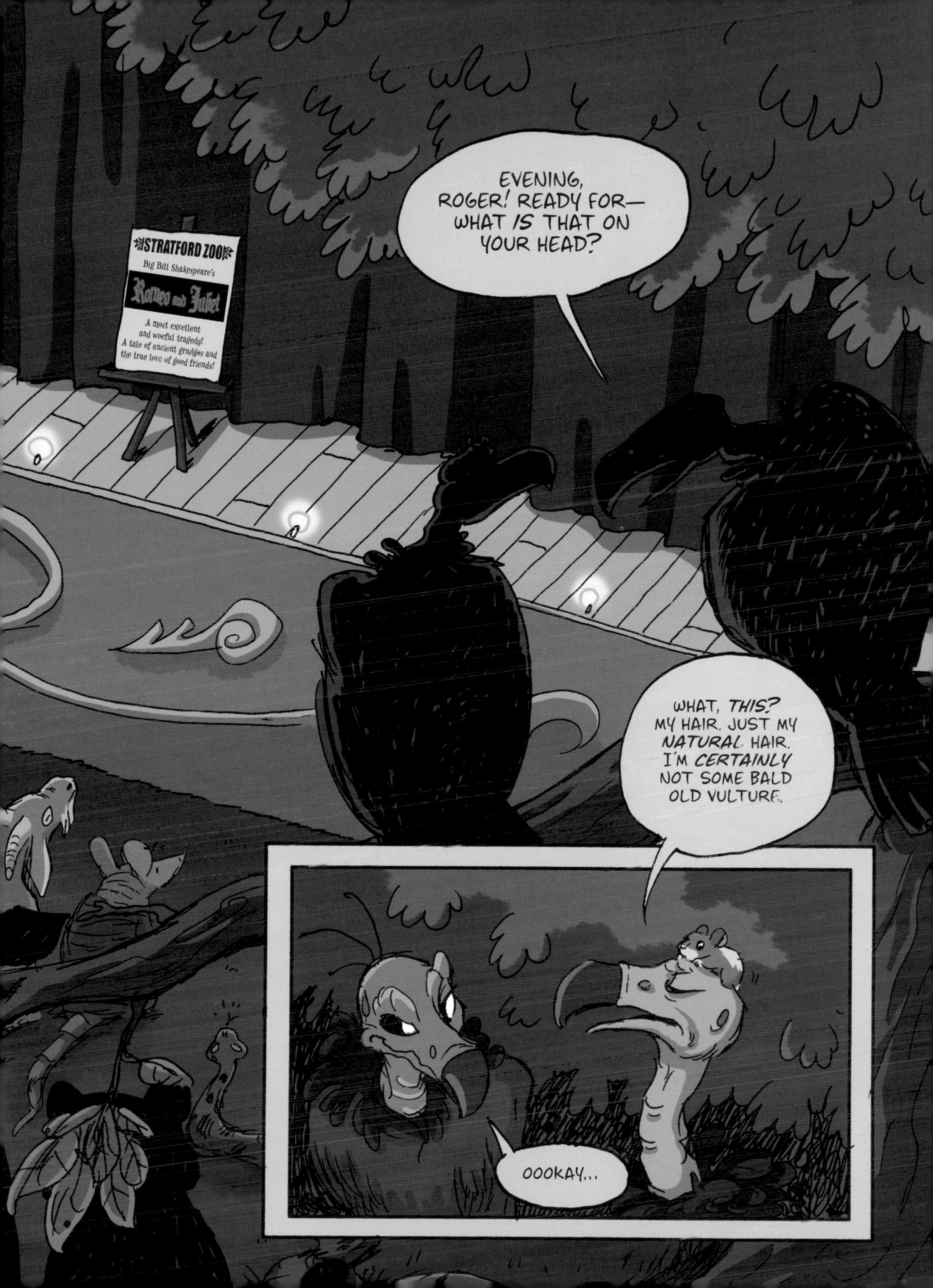
STRATFORD ZOO
Big Bill Shakespeare's
Romeo and Juliet
A most excellent and woeful tragedy! A tale of ancient grudges and the true love of good friends!
EVENING, ROGER! READY FOR— WHAT *IS* THAT ON YOUR HEAD?
WHAT, *THIS?* MY HAIR. JUST MY *NATURAL* HAIR. I'M *CERTAINLY* NOT SOME BALD OLD VULTURE.
OOOKAY...

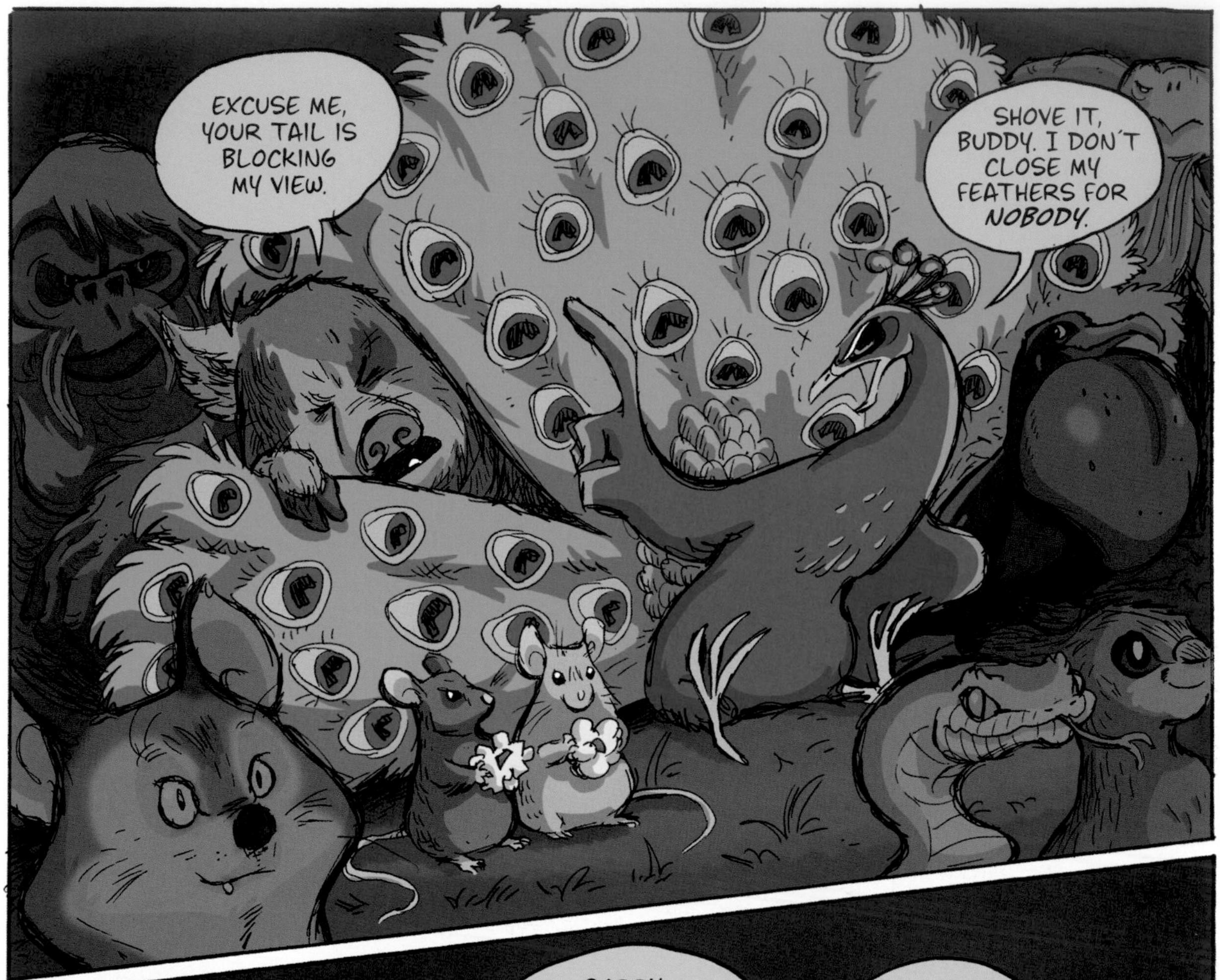
EXCUSE ME, YOUR TAIL IS BLOCKING MY VIEW.
SHOVE IT, BUDDY. I DON´T CLOSE MY FEATHERS FOR NOBODY.
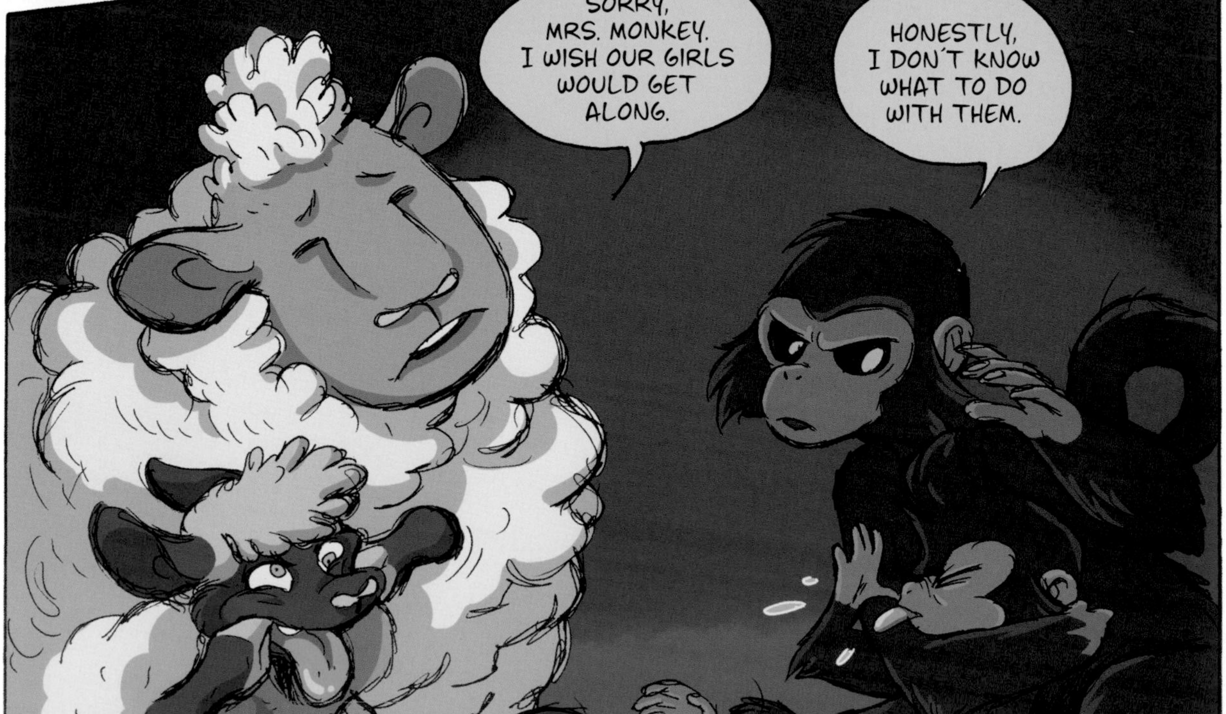
SORRY, MRS. MONKEY. I WISH OUR GIRLS WOULD GET ALONG.
HONESTLY, I DON´T KNOW WHAT TO DO WITH THEM.

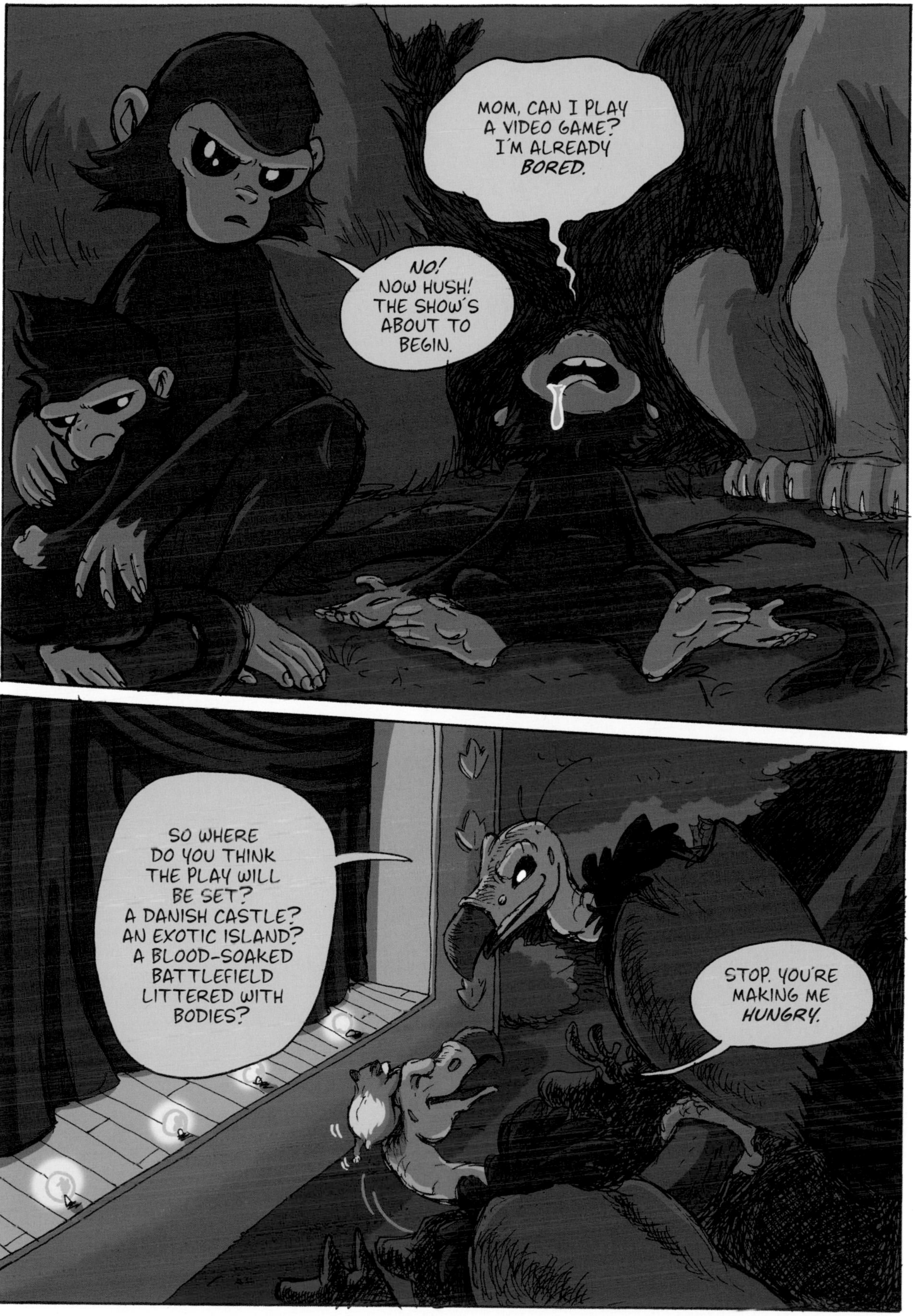
MOM, CAN I PLAY A VIDEO GAME? I'M ALREADY *BORED.*
NO! NOW HUSH! THE SHOW'S ABOUT TO BEGIN.
SO WHERE DO YOU THINK THE PLAY WILL BE SET? A DANISH CASTLE? AN EXOTIC ISLAND? A BLOOD-SOAKED BATTLEFIELD LITTERED WITH BODIES?
STOP. YOU'RE MAKING ME *HUNGRY.*

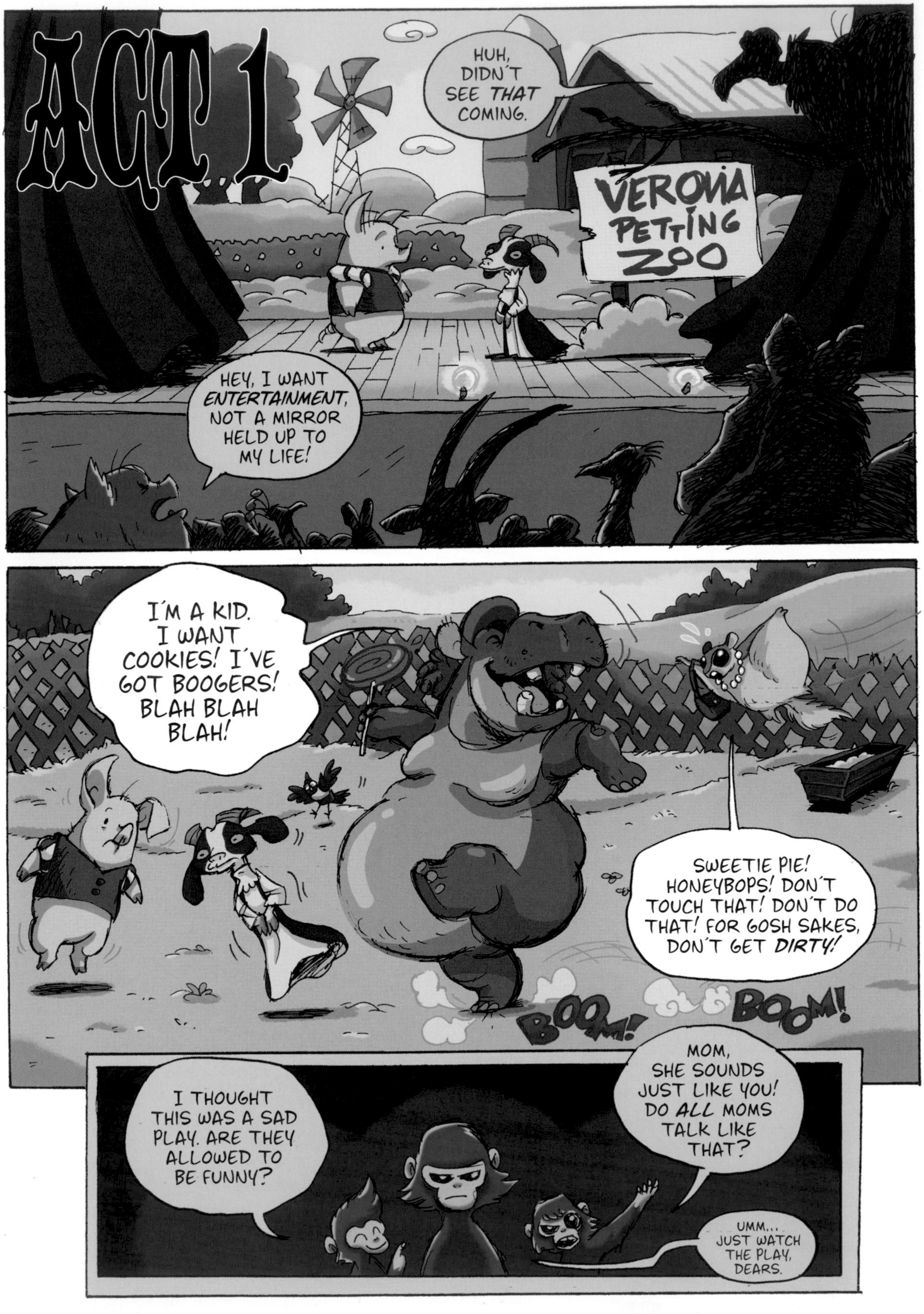
ACT 1
HUH, DIDN'T SEE THAT COMING.
VERONA PETTING ZOO
HEY, I WANT ENTERTAINMENT, NOT A MIRROR HELD UP TO MY LIFE!
I'M A KID. I WANT COOKIES! I'VE GOT BOOGERS! BLAH BLAH BLAH!
SWEETIE PIE! HONEYBOPS! DON'T TOUCH THAT! DON'T DO THAT! FOR GOSH SAKES, DON'T GET DIRTY!
BOOM! BOOM!
I THOUGHT THIS WAS A SAD PLAY. ARE THEY ALLOWED TO BE FUNNY?
MOM, SHE SOUNDS JUST LIKE YOU! DO ALL MOMS TALK LIKE THAT?
UMM... JUST WATCH THE PLAY, DEARS.

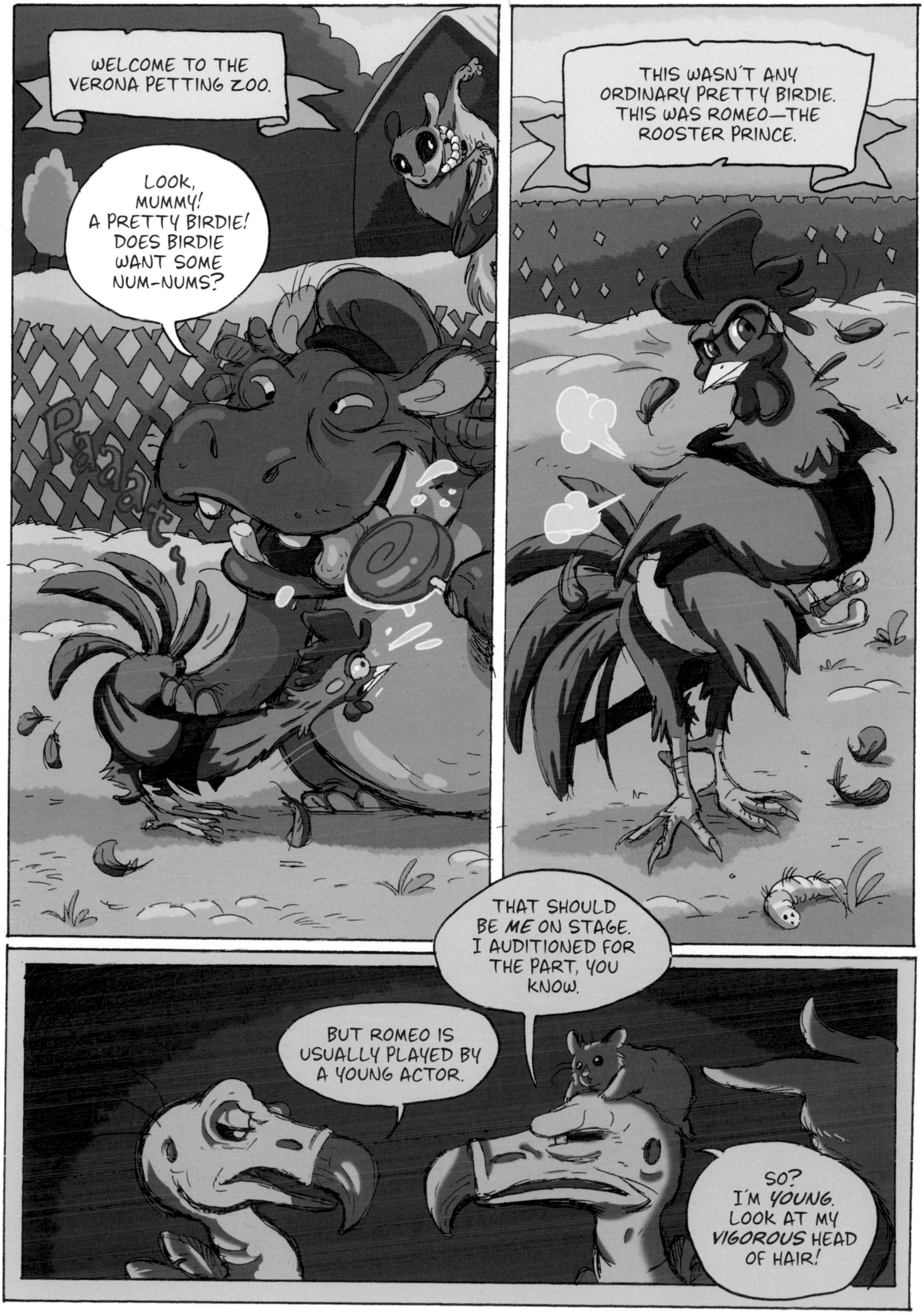
WELCOME TO THE VERONA PETTING ZOO.
LOOK, MUMMY! A PRETTY BIRDIE! DOES BIRDIE WANT SOME NUM-NUMS?
Paaat!
THIS WASN'T ANY ORDINARY PRETTY BIRDIE. THIS WAS ROMEO—THE ROOSTER PRINCE.
THAT SHOULD BE *ME* ON STAGE. I AUDITIONED FOR THE PART, YOU KNOW.
BUT ROMEO IS USUALLY PLAYED BY A YOUNG ACTOR.
SO? I'M *YOUNG*. LOOK AT MY *VIGOROUS* HEAD OF HAIR!

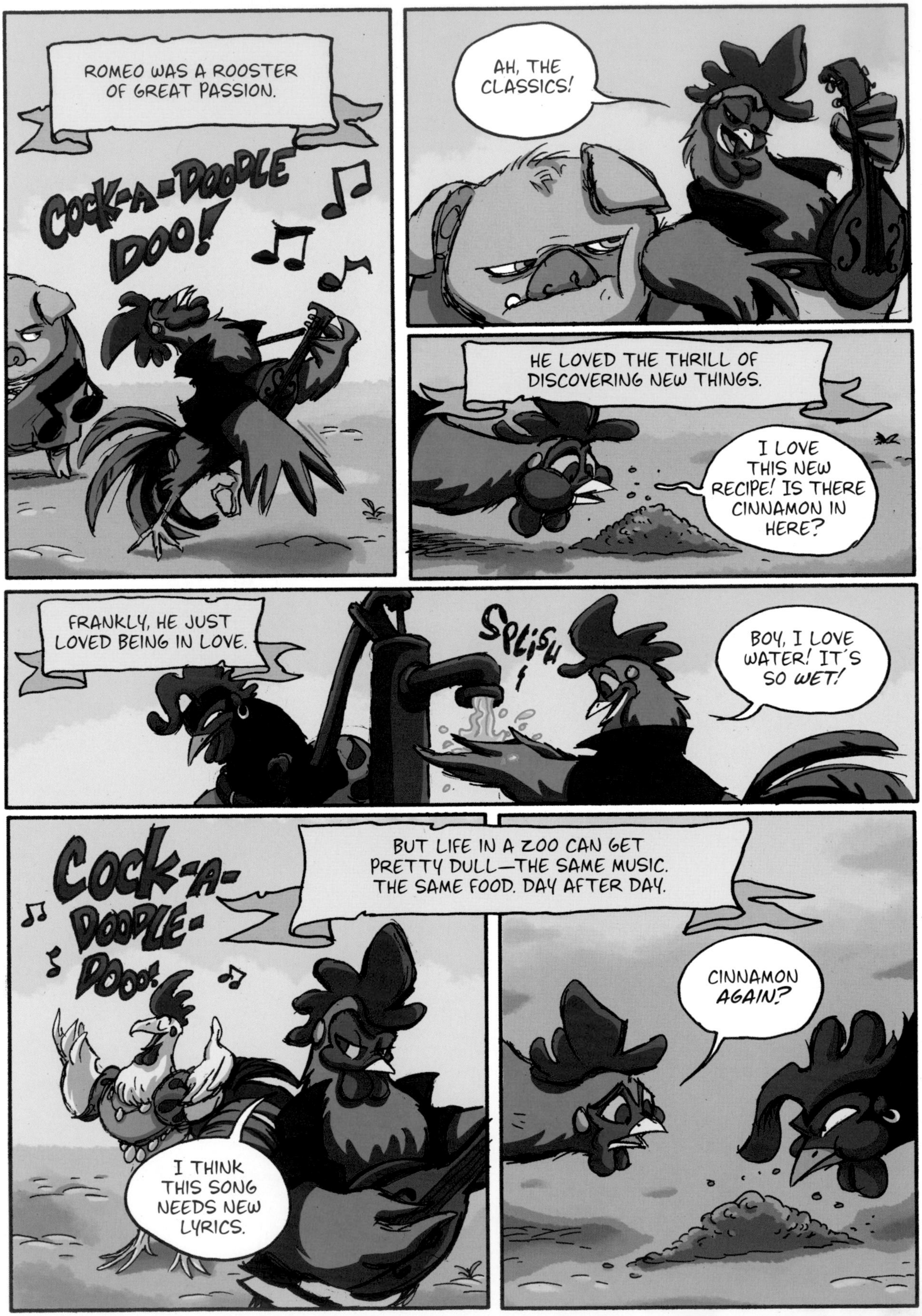
ROMEO WAS A ROOSTER OF GREAT PASSION.
COCK-A-DOODLE DOO!
AH, THE CLASSICS!
HE LOVED THE THRILL OF DISCOVERING NEW THINGS.
I LOVE THIS NEW RECIPE! IS THERE CINNAMON IN HERE?
FRANKLY, HE JUST LOVED BEING IN LOVE.
SPLISH
BOY, I LOVE WATER! IT'S SO WET!
COCK-A-DOODLE-DOOO!
BUT LIFE IN A ZOO CAN GET PRETTY DULL—THE SAME MUSIC. THE SAME FOOD. DAY AFTER DAY.
I THINK THIS SONG NEEDS NEW LYRICS.
CINNAMON AGAIN?

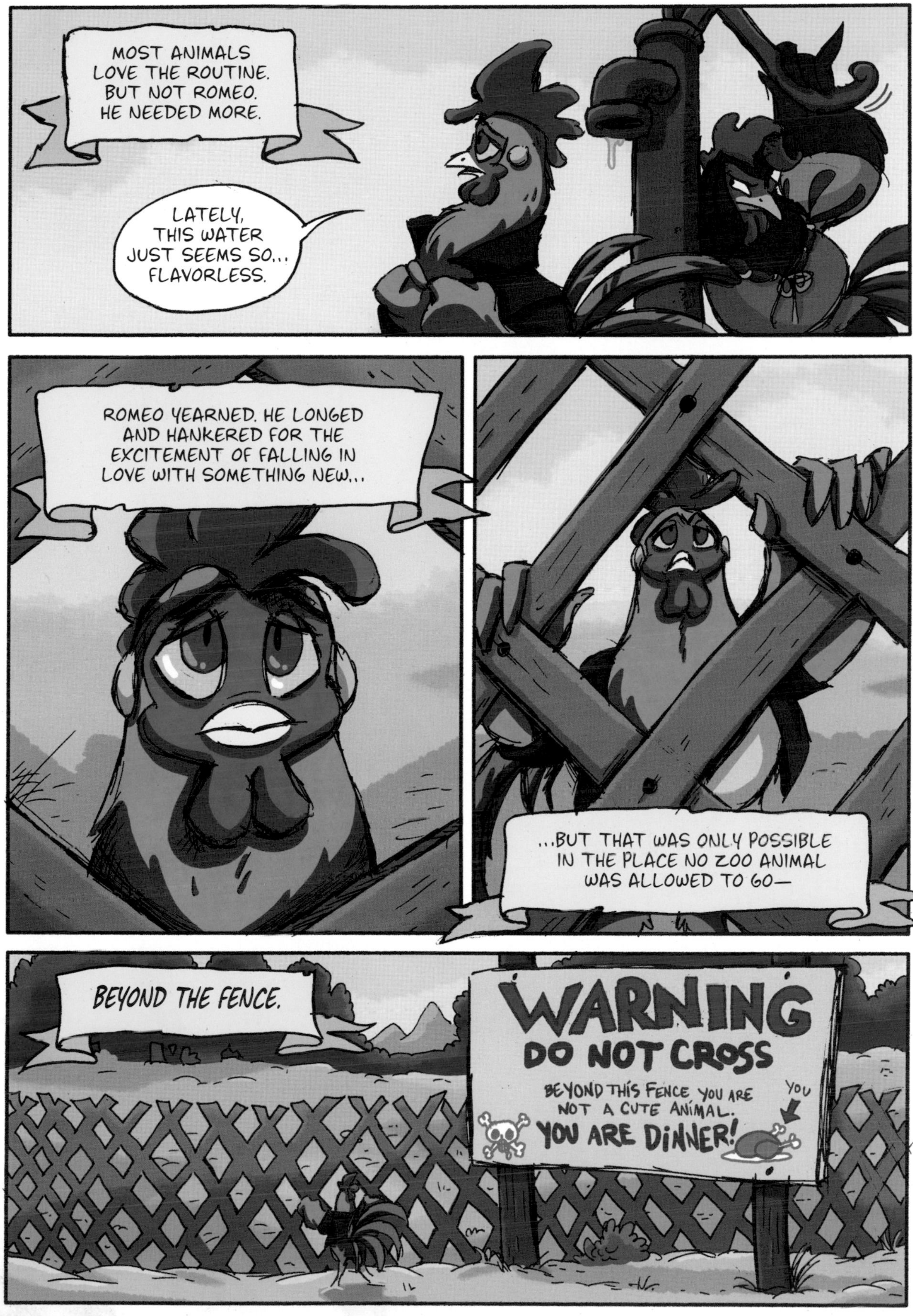
MOST ANIMALS LOVE THE ROUTINE. BUT NOT ROMEO. HE NEEDED MORE.
LATELY, THIS WATER JUST SEEMS SO... FLAVORLESS.
ROMEO YEARNED. HE LONGED AND HANKERED FOR THE EXCITEMENT OF FALLING IN LOVE WITH SOMETHING NEW...
...BUT THAT WAS ONLY POSSIBLE IN THE PLACE NO ZOO ANIMAL WAS ALLOWED TO GO—
BEYOND THE FENCE.
WARNING
DO NOT CROSS
BEYOND THIS FENCE YOU ARE NOT A CUTE ANIMAL.
YOU ARE DINNER!
YOU

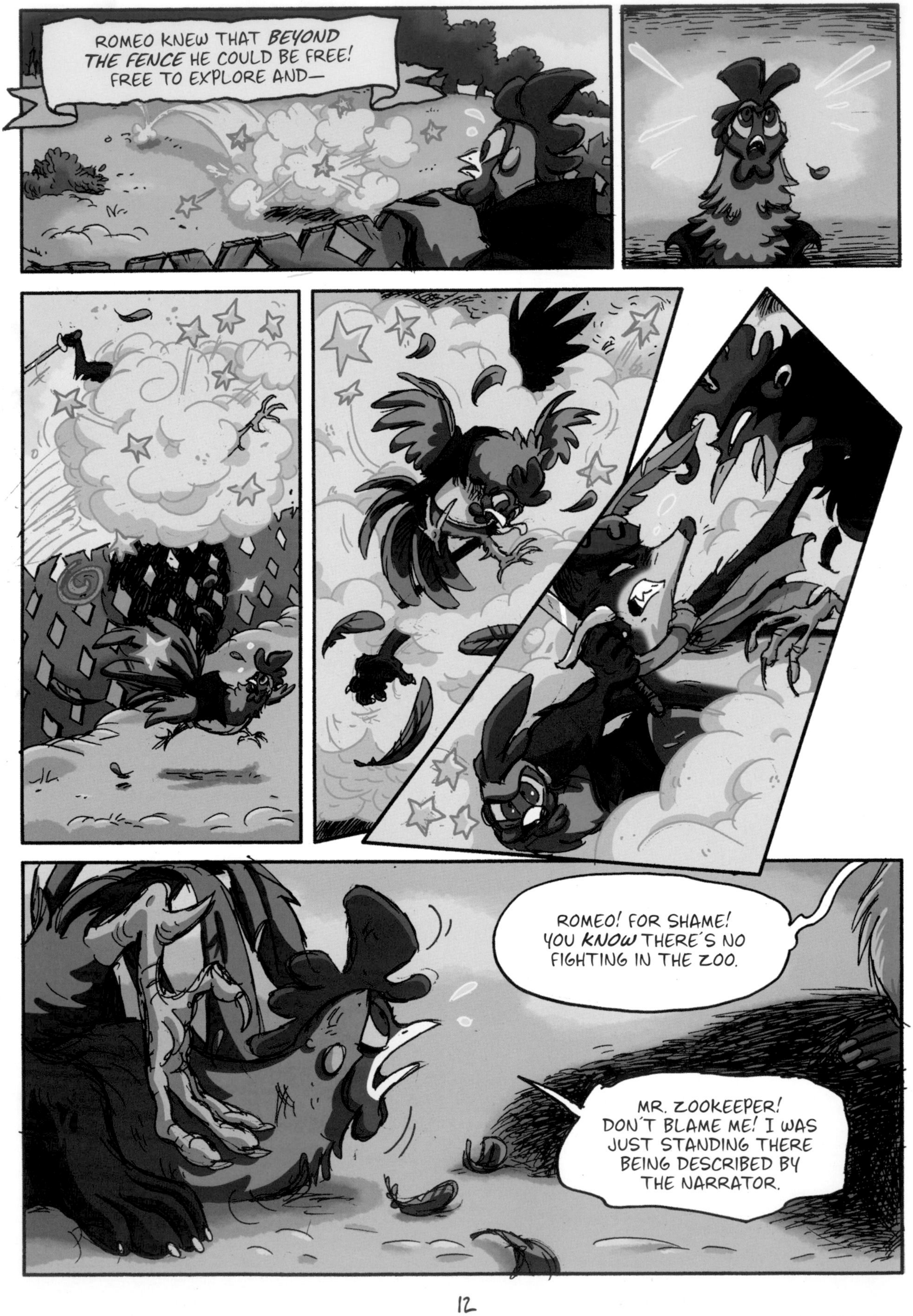
ROMEO KNEW THAT *BEYOND THE FENCE* HE COULD BE FREE! FREE TO EXPLORE AND—
ROMEO! FOR SHAME! YOU *KNOW* THERE'S NO FIGHTING IN THE ZOO.
MR. ZOOKEEPER! DON'T BLAME ME! I WAS JUST STANDING THERE BEING DESCRIBED BY THE NARRATOR.

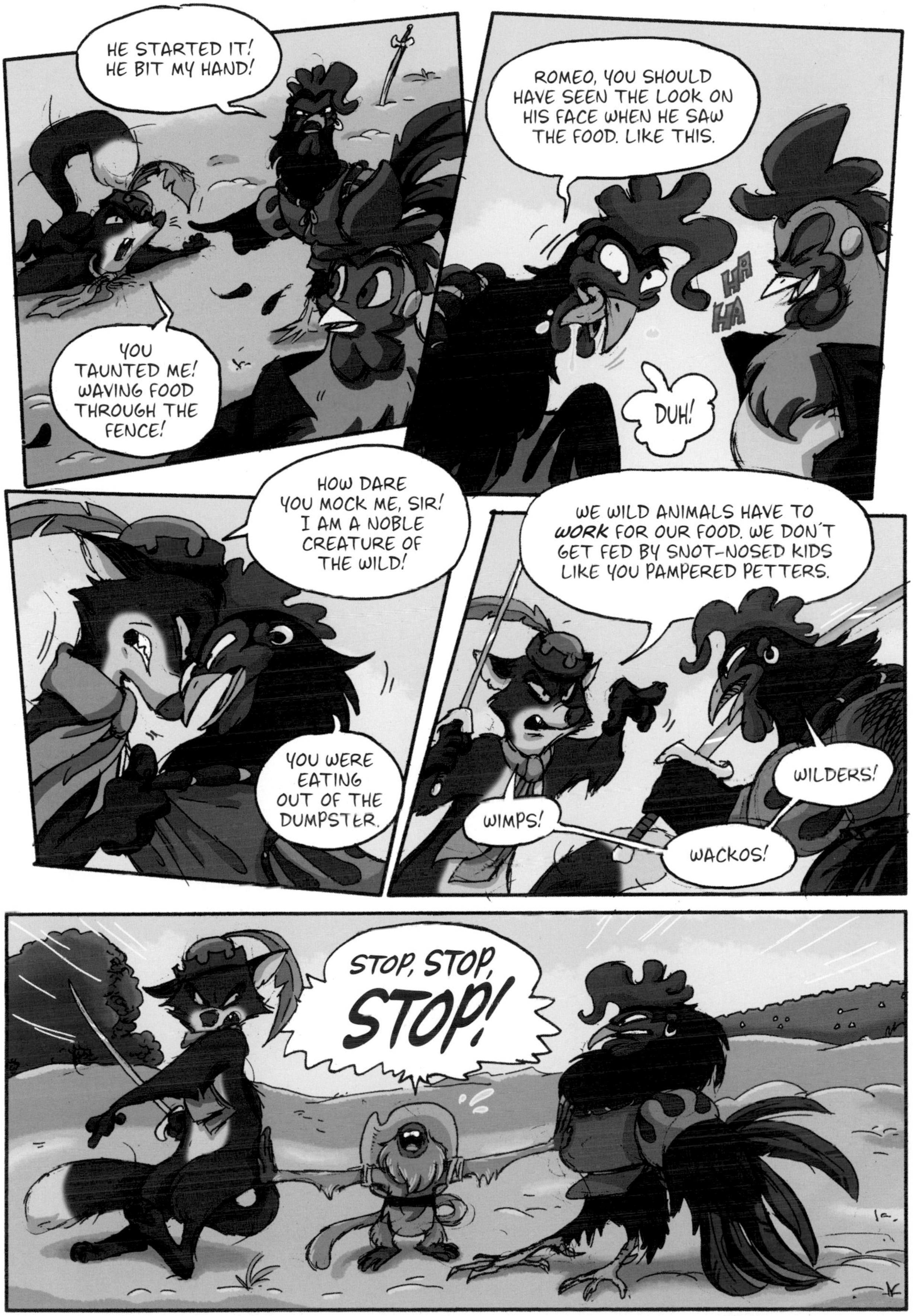
HE STARTED IT! HE BIT MY HAND!
YOU TAUNTED ME! WAVING FOOD THROUGH THE FENCE!
ROMEO, YOU SHOULD HAVE SEEN THE LOOK ON HIS FACE WHEN HE SAW THE FOOD. LIKE THIS.
HA HA
DUH!
HOW DARE YOU MOCK ME, SIR! I AM A NOBLE CREATURE OF THE WILD!
YOU WERE EATING OUT OF THE DUMPSTER.
WE WILD ANIMALS HAVE TO WORK FOR OUR FOOD. WE DON'T GET FED BY SNOT-NOSED KIDS LIKE YOU PAMPERED PETTERS.
WILDERS!
WIMPS!
WACKOS!
STOP, STOP, STOP!

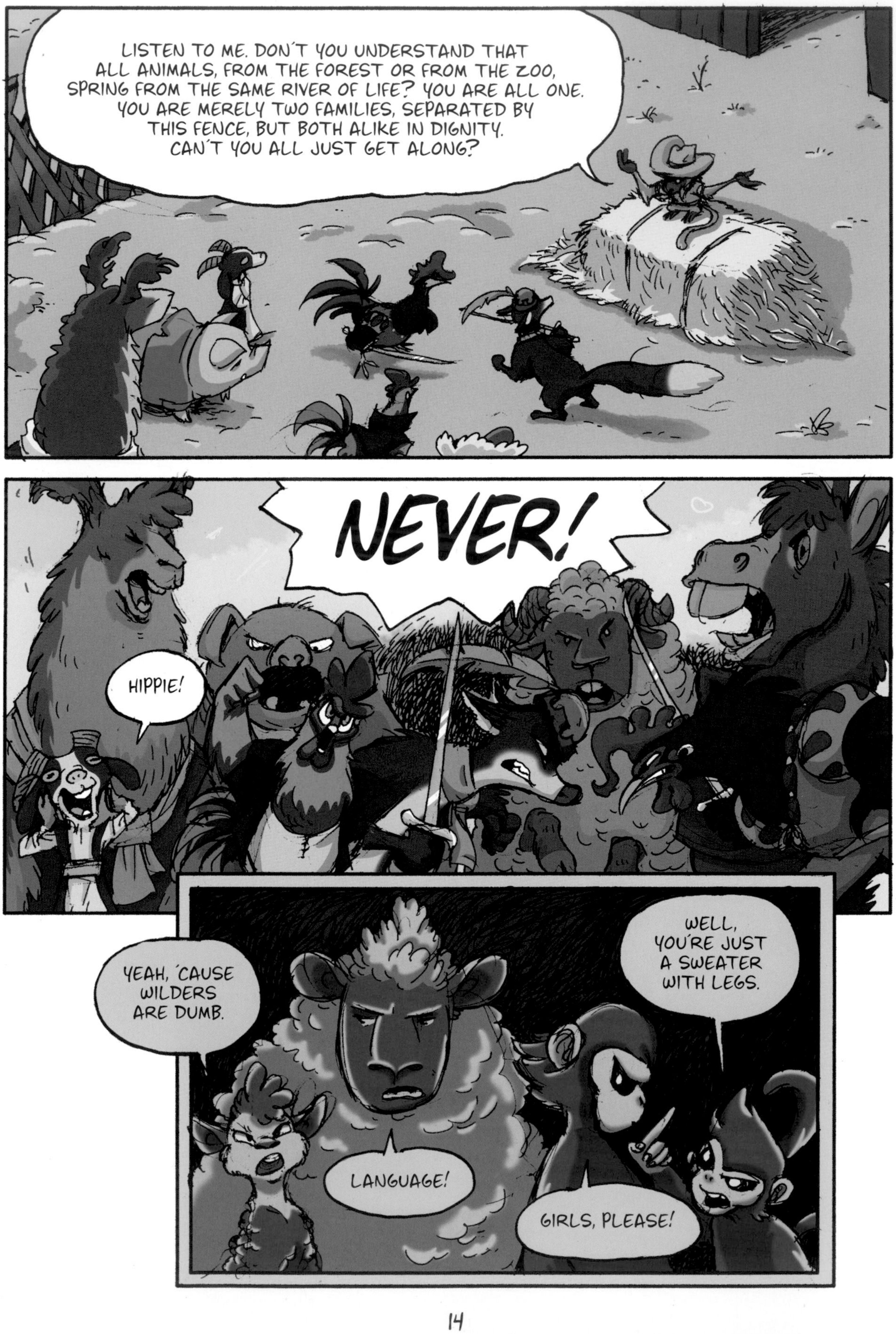
LISTEN TO ME. DON'T YOU UNDERSTAND THAT ALL ANIMALS, FROM THE FOREST OR FROM THE ZOO, SPRING FROM THE SAME RIVER OF LIFE? YOU ARE ALL ONE. YOU ARE MERELY TWO FAMILIES, SEPARATED BY THIS FENCE, BUT BOTH ALIKE IN DIGNITY. CAN'T YOU ALL JUST GET ALONG?
NEVER!
HIPPIE!
YEAH, 'CAUSE WILDERS ARE DUMB.
WELL, YOU'RE JUST A SWEATER WITH LEGS.
LANGUAGE!
GIRLS, PLEASE!

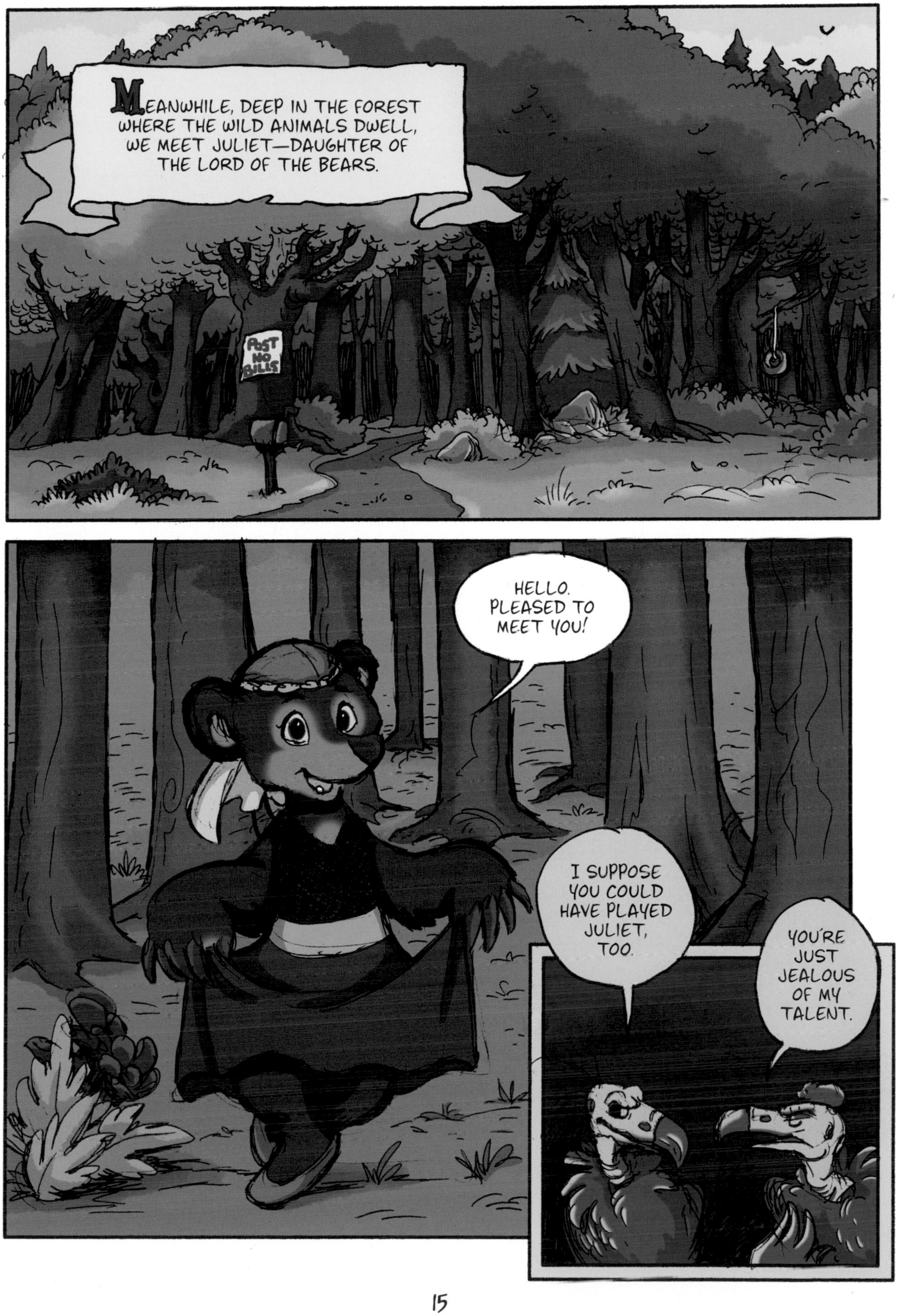
MEANWHILE, DEEP IN THE FOREST WHERE THE WILD ANIMALS DWELL, WE MEET JULIET—DAUGHTER OF THE LORD OF THE BEARS.
POST NO BILLS
HELLO. PLEASED TO MEET YOU!
I SUPPOSE YOU COULD HAVE PLAYED JULIET, TOO.
YOU'RE JUST JEALOUS OF MY TALENT.

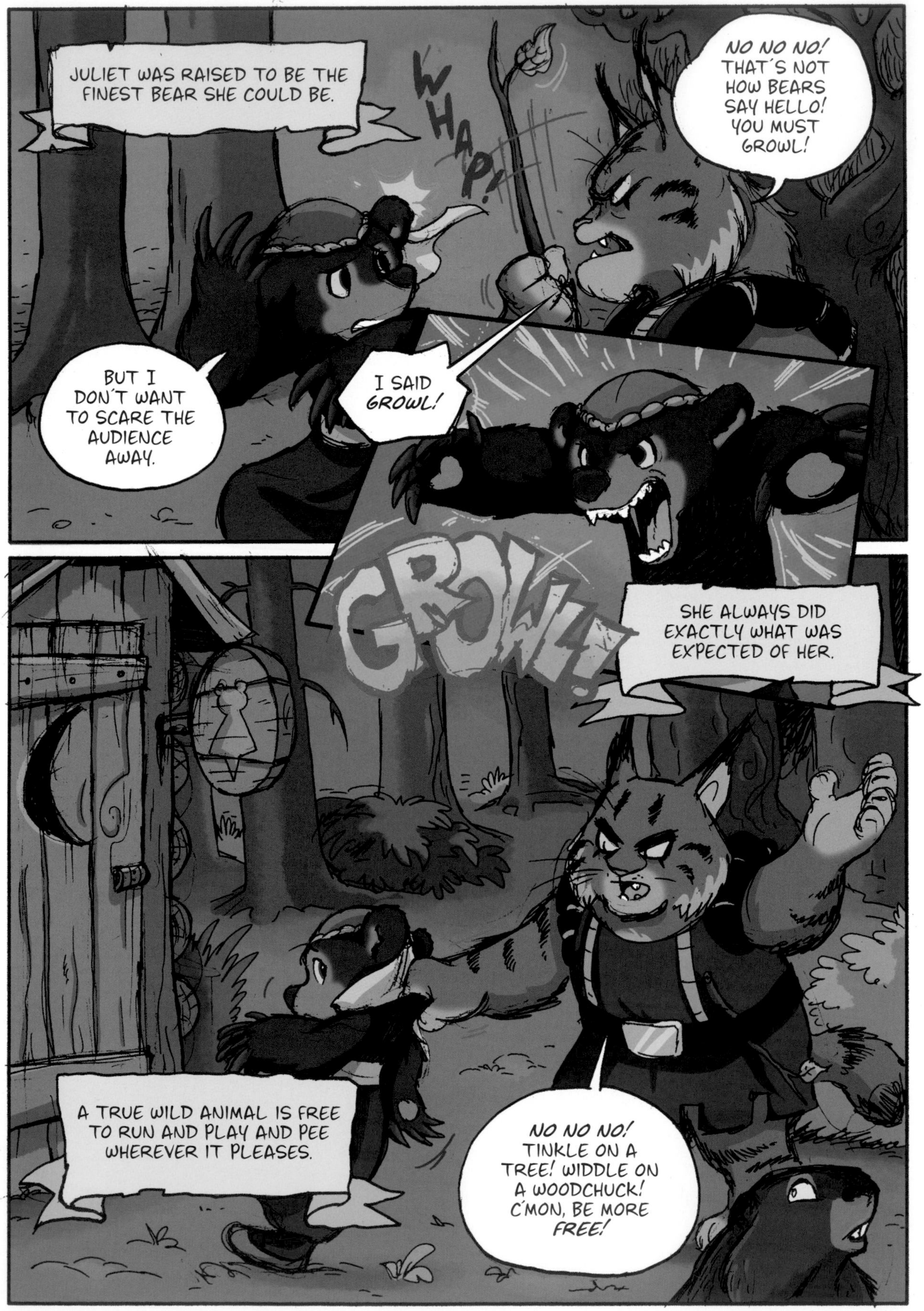
JULIET WAS RAISED TO BE THE FINEST BEAR SHE COULD BE.
WHAP!
NO NO NO! THAT'S NOT HOW BEARS SAY HELLO! YOU MUST GROWL!
BUT I DON'T WANT TO SCARE THE AUDIENCE AWAY.
I SAID GROWL!
GROWL!
SHE ALWAYS DID EXACTLY WHAT WAS EXPECTED OF HER.
A TRUE WILD ANIMAL IS FREE TO RUN AND PLAY AND PEE WHEREVER IT PLEASES.
NO NO NO! TINKLE ON A TREE! WIDDLE ON A WOODCHUCK! C'MON, BE MORE FREE!

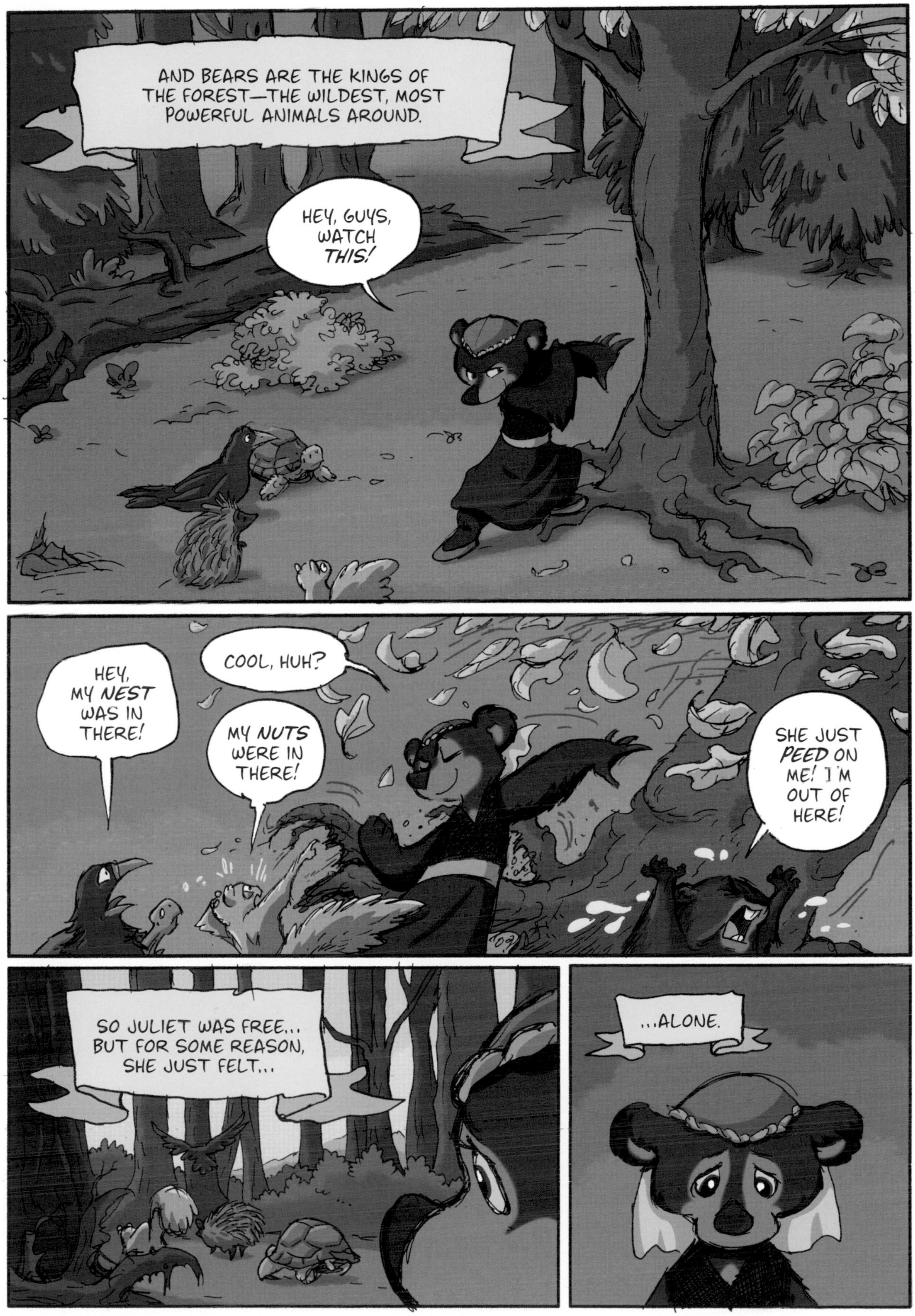
AND BEARS ARE THE KINGS OF THE FOREST—THE WILDEST, MOST POWERFUL ANIMALS AROUND.
HEY, GUYS, WATCH THIS!
HEY, MY NEST WAS IN THERE!
COOL, HUH?
MY NUTS WERE IN THERE!
SHE JUST PEED ON ME! I'M OUT OF HERE!
SO JULIET WAS FREE... BUT FOR SOME REASON, SHE JUST FELT...
...ALONE.

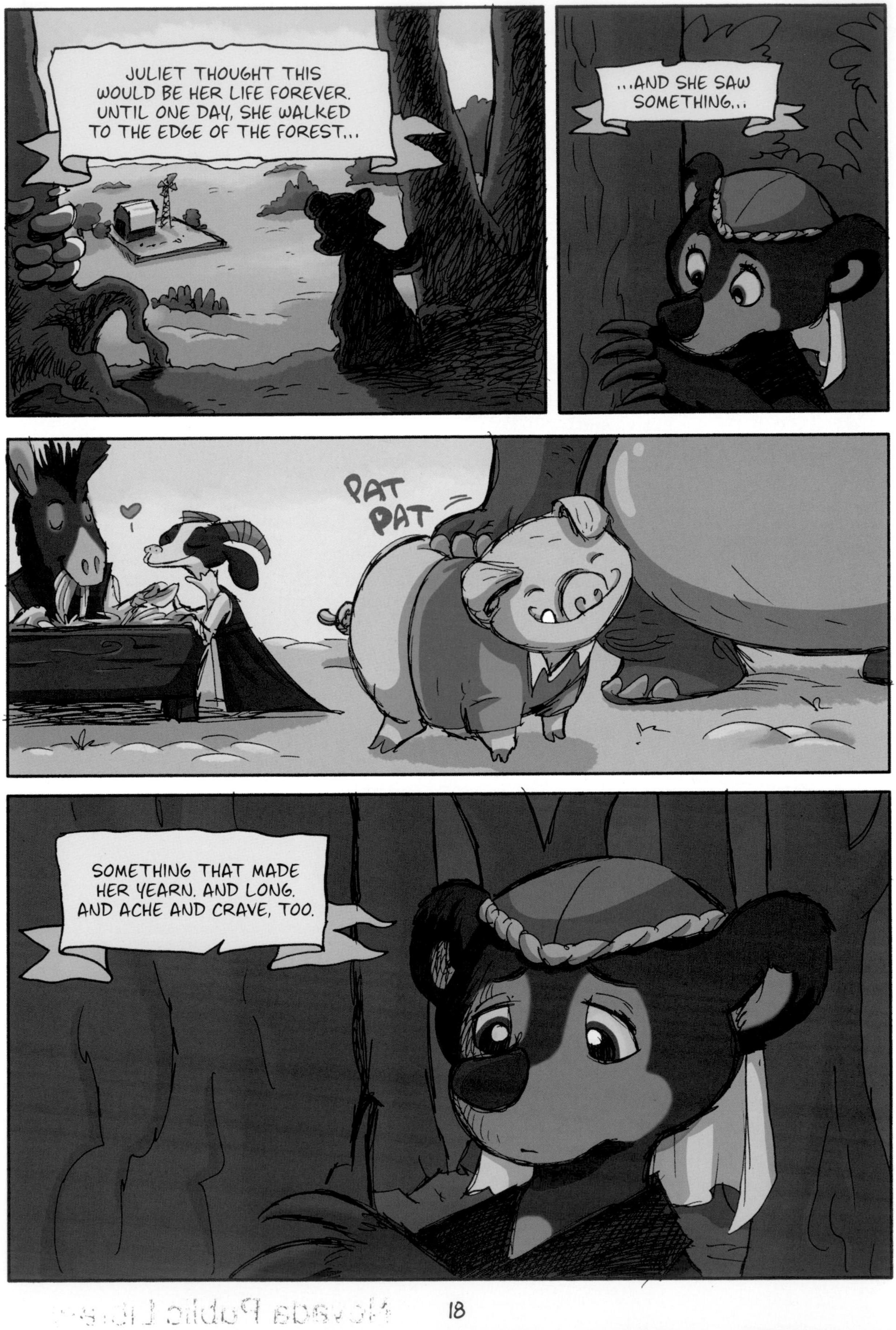
JULIET THOUGHT THIS WOULD BE HER LIFE FOREVER. UNTIL ONE DAY, SHE WALKED TO THE EDGE OF THE FOREST...
...AND SHE SAW SOMETHING...
PAT PAT
SOMETHING THAT MADE HER YEARN. AND LONG. AND ACHE AND CRAVE, TOO.

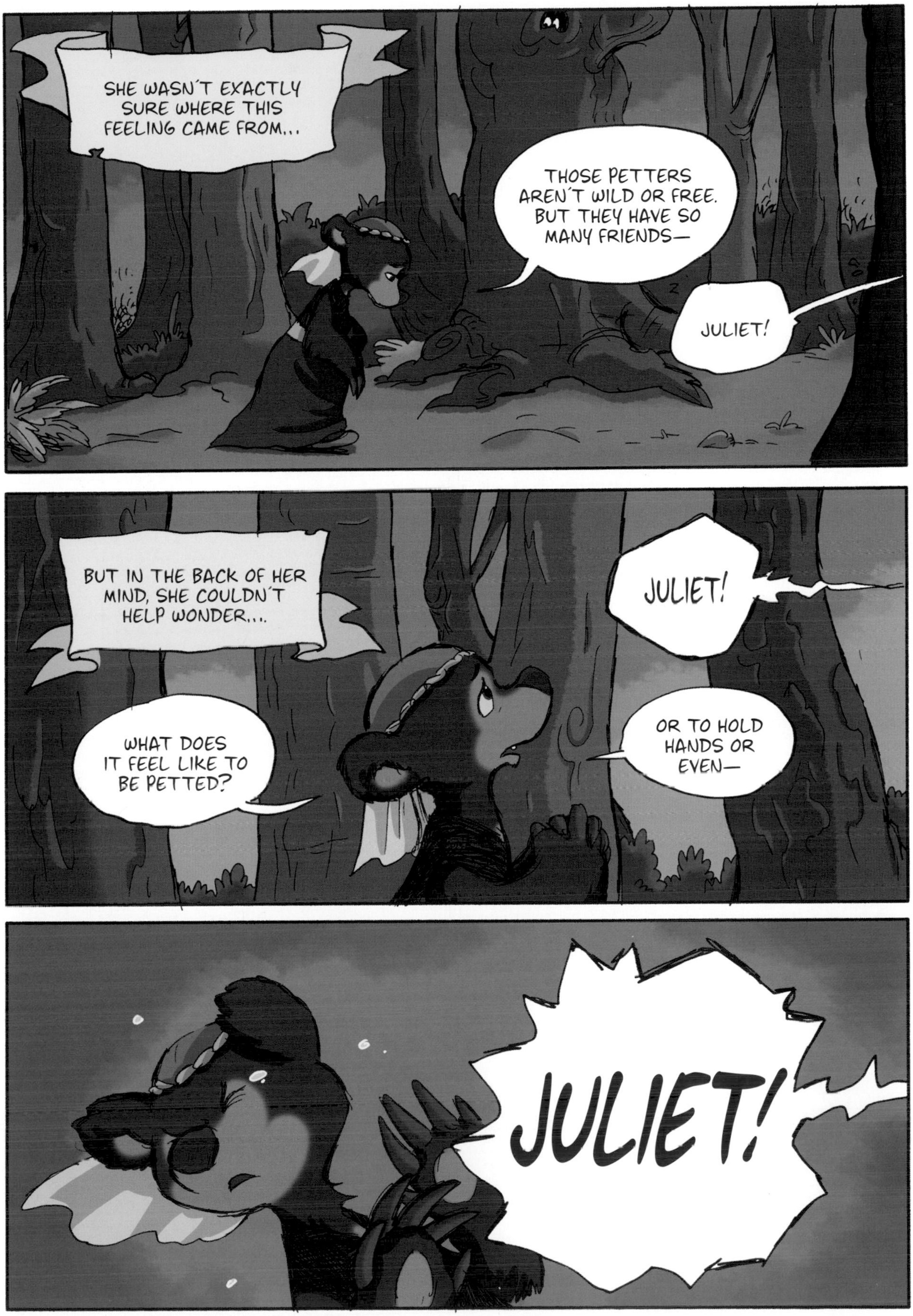
SHE WASN'T EXACTLY SURE WHERE THIS FEELING CAME FROM...
THOSE PETTERS AREN'T WILD OR FREE. BUT THEY HAVE SO MANY FRIENDS—
JULIET!
BUT IN THE BACK OF HER MIND, SHE COULDN'T HELP WONDER....
JULIET!
WHAT DOES IT FEEL LIKE TO BE PETTED?
OR TO HOLD HANDS OR EVEN—
JULIET!

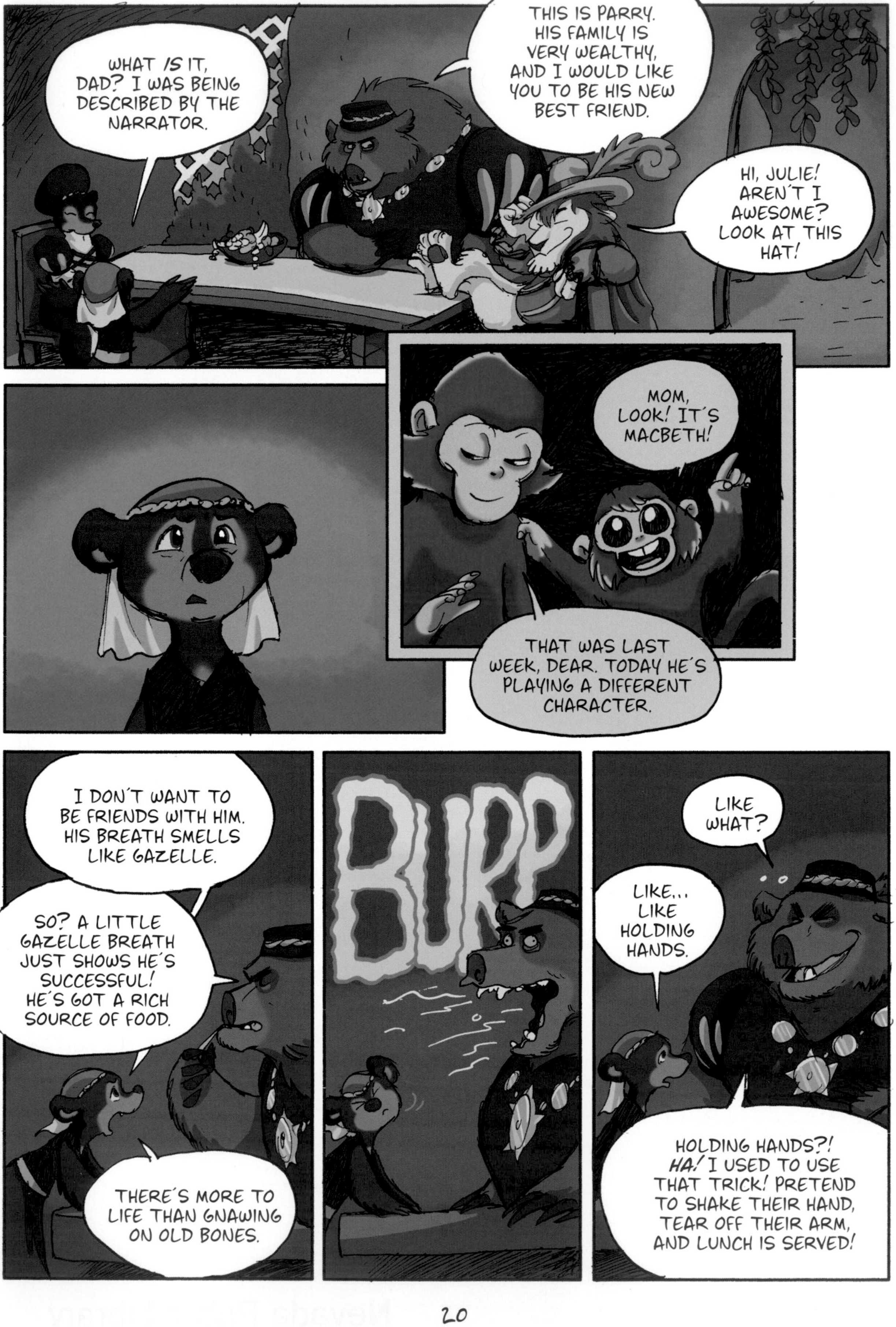
WHAT *IS* IT, DAD? I WAS BEING DESCRIBED BY THE NARRATOR.
THIS IS PARRY. HIS FAMILY IS VERY WEALTHY, AND I WOULD LIKE YOU TO BE HIS NEW BEST FRIEND.
HI, JULIE! AREN'T I AWESOME? LOOK AT THIS HAT!
MOM, LOOK! IT'S MACBETH!
THAT WAS LAST WEEK, DEAR. TODAY HE'S PLAYING A DIFFERENT CHARACTER.
I DON'T WANT TO BE FRIENDS WITH HIM. HIS BREATH SMELLS LIKE GAZELLE.
SO? A LITTLE GAZELLE BREATH JUST SHOWS HE'S SUCCESSFUL! HE'S GOT A RICH SOURCE OF FOOD.
THERE'S MORE TO LIFE THAN GNAWING ON OLD BONES.
BURP
LIKE WHAT?
LIKE... LIKE HOLDING HANDS.
HOLDING HANDS?! *HA!* I USED TO USE THAT TRICK! PRETEND TO SHAKE THEIR HAND, TEAR OFF THEIR ARM, AND LUNCH IS SERVED!

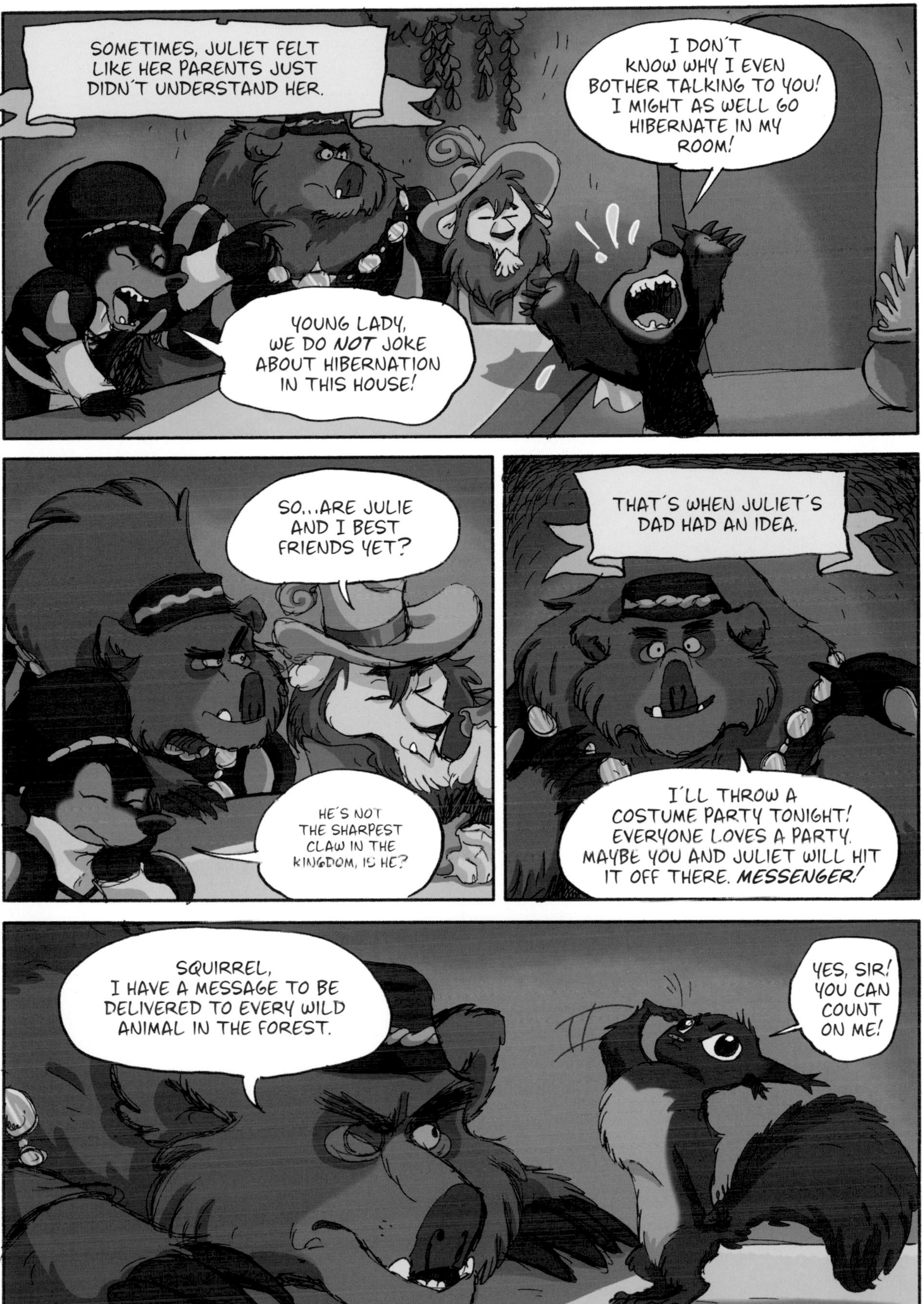
SOMETIMES, JULIET FELT LIKE HER PARENTS JUST DIDN'T UNDERSTAND HER.
I DON'T KNOW WHY I EVEN BOTHER TALKING TO YOU! I MIGHT AS WELL GO HIBERNATE IN MY ROOM!
YOUNG LADY, WE DO NOT JOKE ABOUT HIBERNATION IN THIS HOUSE!
SO...ARE JULIE AND I BEST FRIENDS YET?
HE'S NOT THE SHARPEST CLAW IN THE KINGDOM, IS HE?
THAT'S WHEN JULIET'S DAD HAD AN IDEA.
I'LL THROW A COSTUME PARTY TONIGHT! EVERYONE LOVES A PARTY. MAYBE YOU AND JULIET WILL HIT IT OFF THERE. MESSENGER!
SQUIRREL, I HAVE A MESSAGE TO BE DELIVERED TO EVERY WILD ANIMAL IN THE FOREST.
YES, SIR! YOU CAN COUNT ON ME!

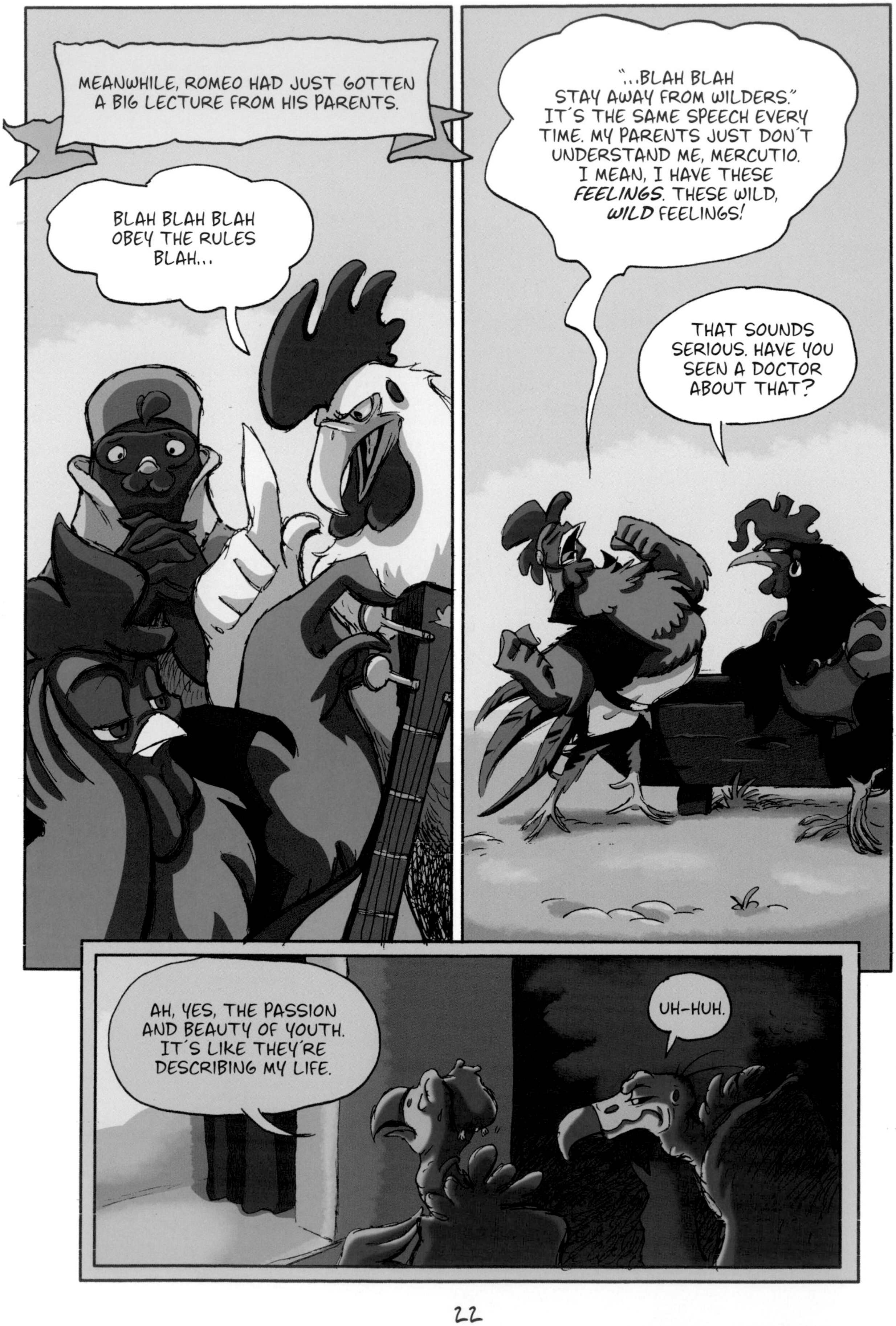
MEANWHILE, ROMEO HAD JUST GOTTEN A BIG LECTURE FROM HIS PARENTS.
BLAH BLAH BLAH OBEY THE RULES BLAH...
"...BLAH BLAH STAY AWAY FROM WILDERS." IT'S THE SAME SPEECH EVERY TIME. MY PARENTS JUST DON'T UNDERSTAND ME, MERCUTIO. I MEAN, I HAVE THESE *FEELINGS*. THESE WILD, *WILD* FEELINGS!
THAT SOUNDS SERIOUS. HAVE YOU SEEN A DOCTOR ABOUT THAT?
AH, YES, THE PASSION AND BEAUTY OF YOUTH. IT'S LIKE THEY'RE DESCRIBING MY LIFE.
UH-HUH.

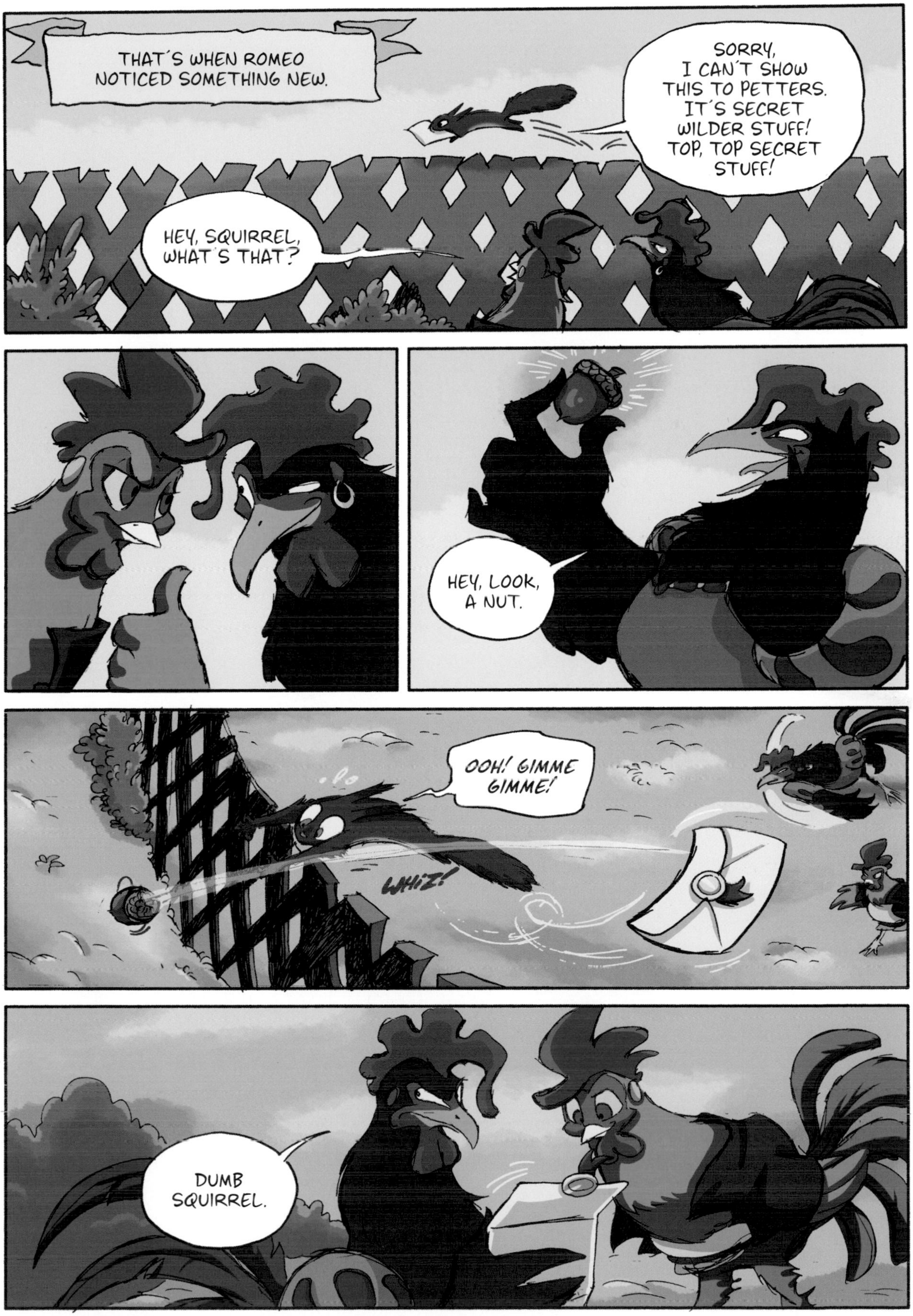
THAT´S WHEN ROMEO NOTICED SOMETHING NEW.
SORRY, I CAN´T SHOW THIS TO PETTERS. IT´S SECRET WILDER STUFF! TOP, TOP SECRET STUFF!
HEY, SQUIRREL, WHAT´S THAT?
HEY, LOOK, A NUT.
OOH! GIMME GIMME!
WHIZ!
DUMB SQUIRREL.

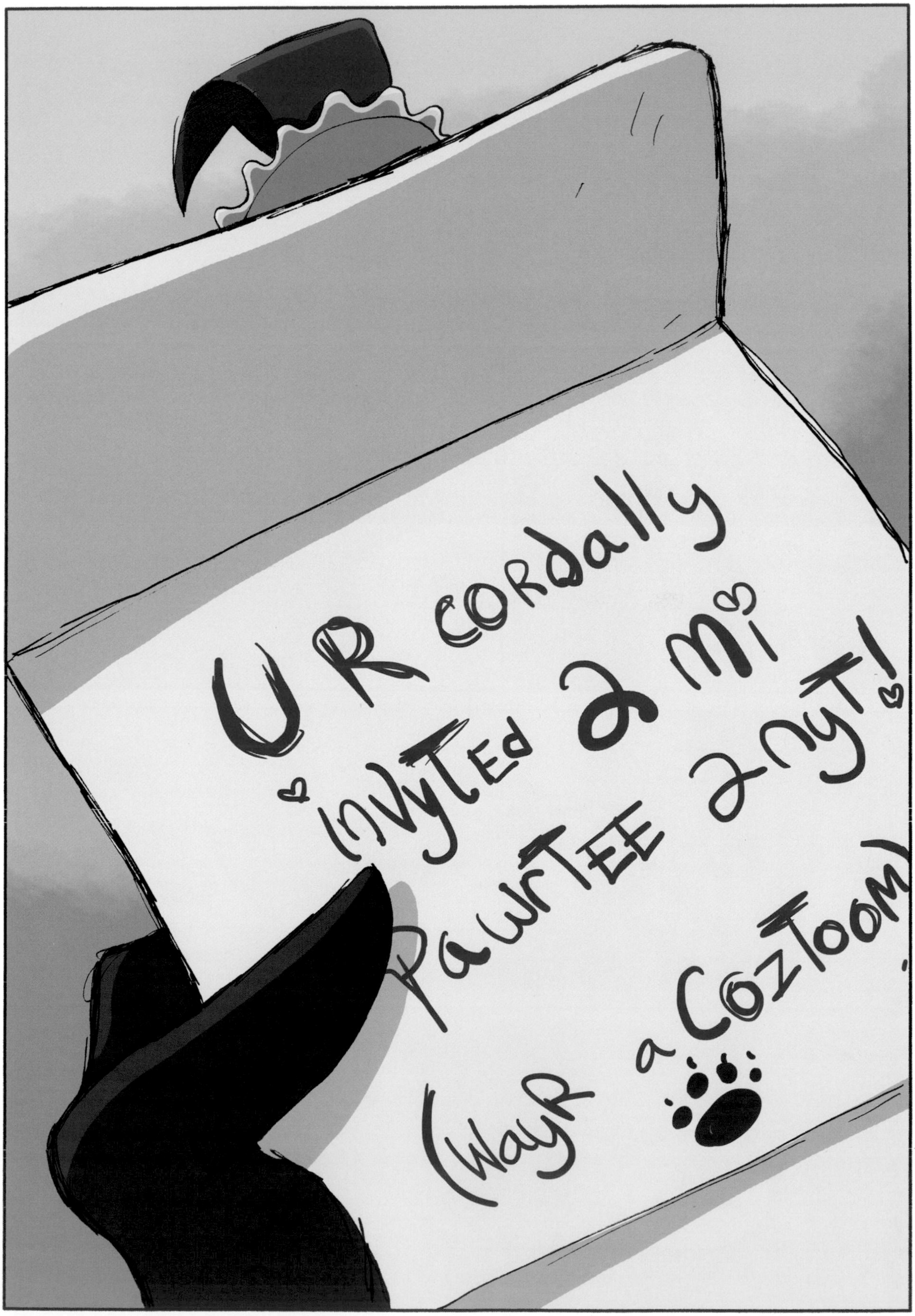
U R cordally invyted 2 mi pawrTEE 2nyT!
(WayR a CozToom)

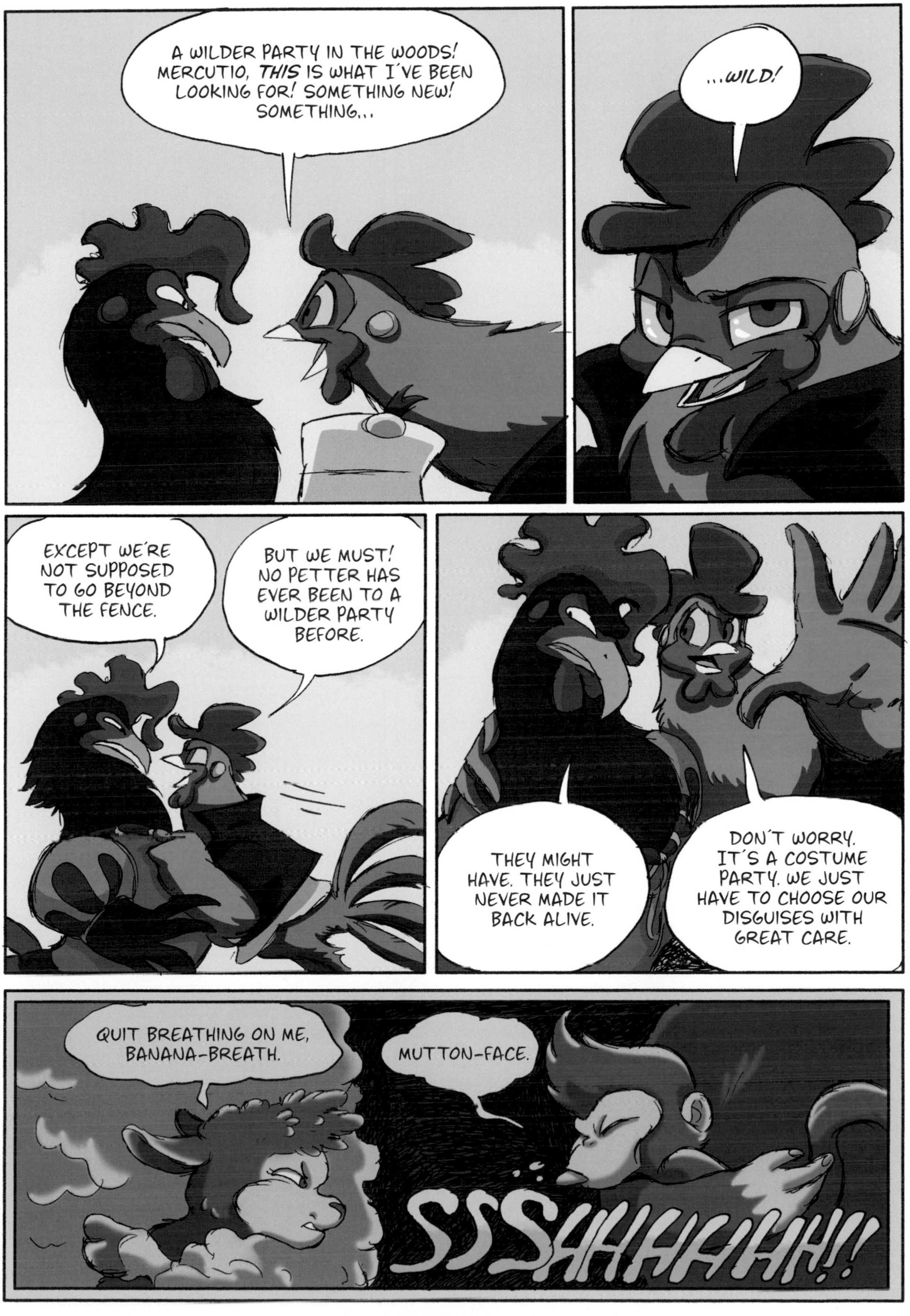
A WILDER PARTY IN THE WOODS! MERCUTIO, *THIS* IS WHAT I'VE BEEN LOOKING FOR! SOMETHING NEW! SOMETHING...
...*WILD!*
EXCEPT WE'RE NOT SUPPOSED TO GO BEYOND THE FENCE.
BUT WE MUST! NO PETTER HAS EVER BEEN TO A WILDER PARTY BEFORE.
THEY MIGHT HAVE. THEY JUST NEVER MADE IT BACK ALIVE.
DON'T WORRY. IT'S A COSTUME PARTY. WE JUST HAVE TO CHOOSE OUR DISGUISES WITH GREAT CARE.
QUIT BREATHING ON ME, BANANA-BREATH.
MUTTON-FACE.
SSSHHHHHH!!

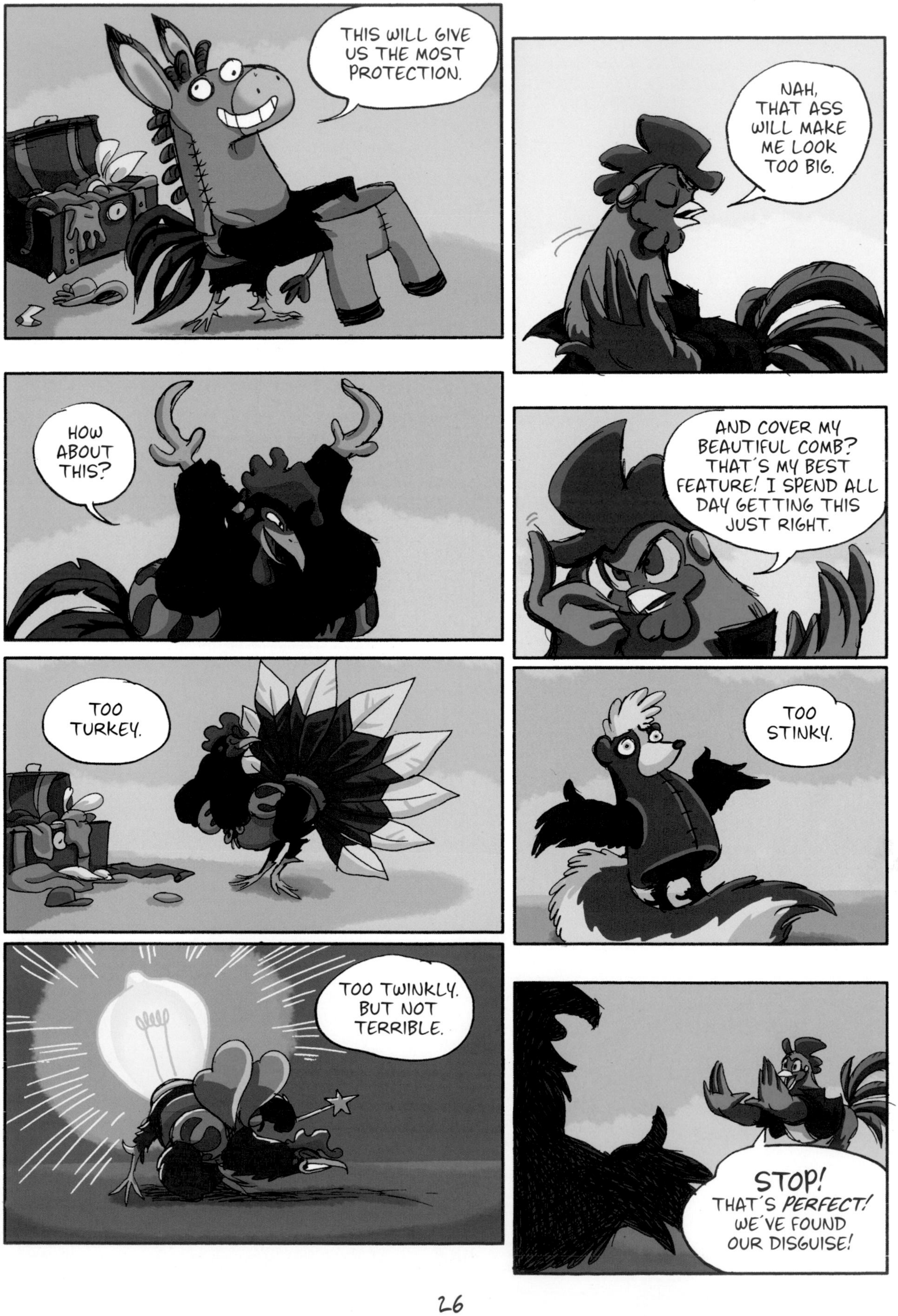
THIS WILL GIVE US THE MOST PROTECTION.
NAH, THAT ASS WILL MAKE ME LOOK TOO BIG.
HOW ABOUT THIS?
AND COVER MY BEAUTIFUL COMB? THAT'S MY BEST FEATURE! I SPEND ALL DAY GETTING THIS JUST RIGHT.
TOO TURKEY.
TOO STINKY.
TOO TWINKLY. BUT NOT TERRIBLE.
STOP! THAT'S *PERFECT!* WE'VE FOUND OUR DISGUISE!

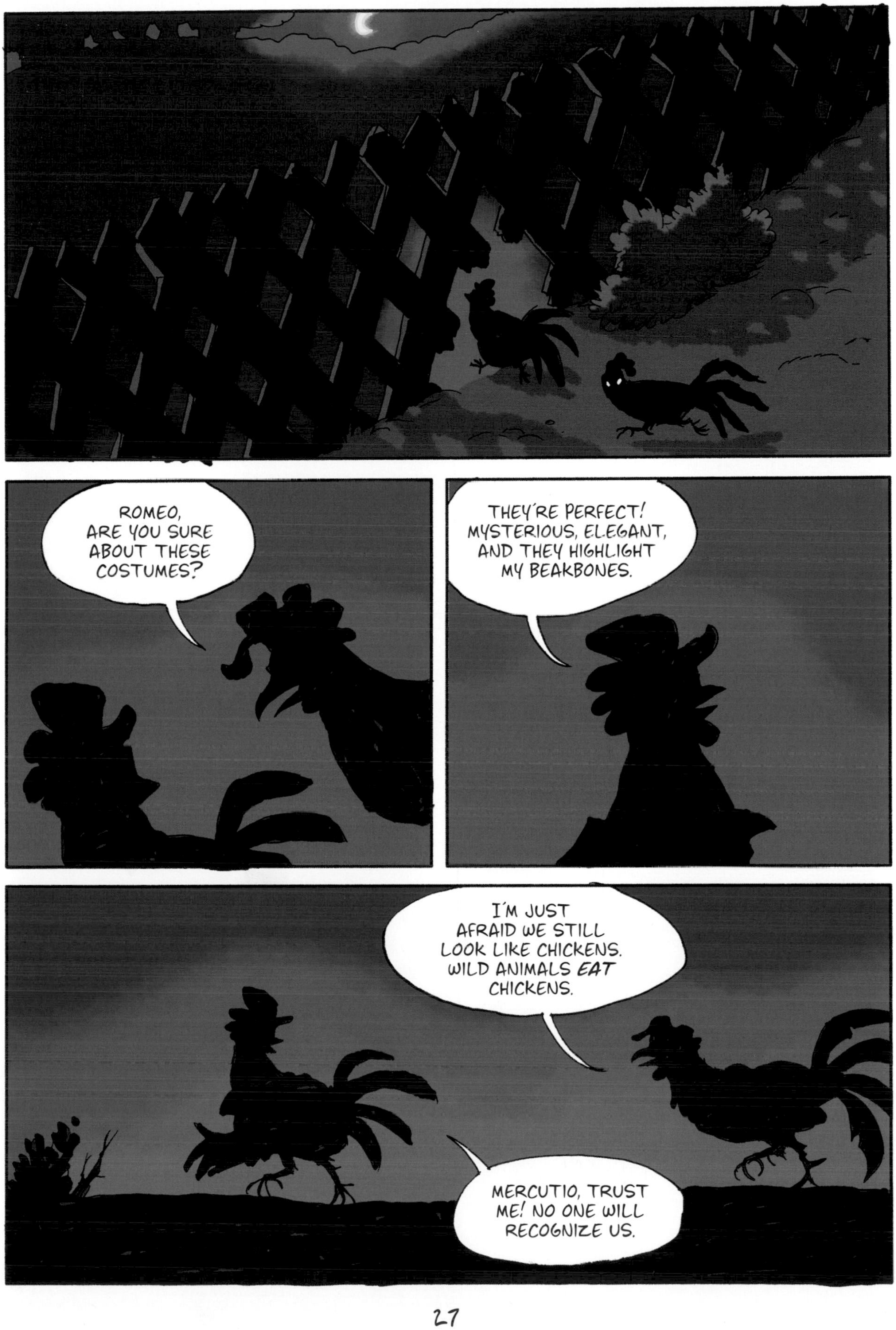
ROMEO, ARE YOU SURE ABOUT THESE COSTUMES?
THEY'RE PERFECT! MYSTERIOUS, ELEGANT, AND THEY HIGHLIGHT MY BEAKBONES.
I'M JUST AFRAID WE STILL LOOK LIKE CHICKENS. WILD ANIMALS *EAT* CHICKENS.
MERCUTIO, TRUST ME! NO ONE WILL RECOGNIZE US.

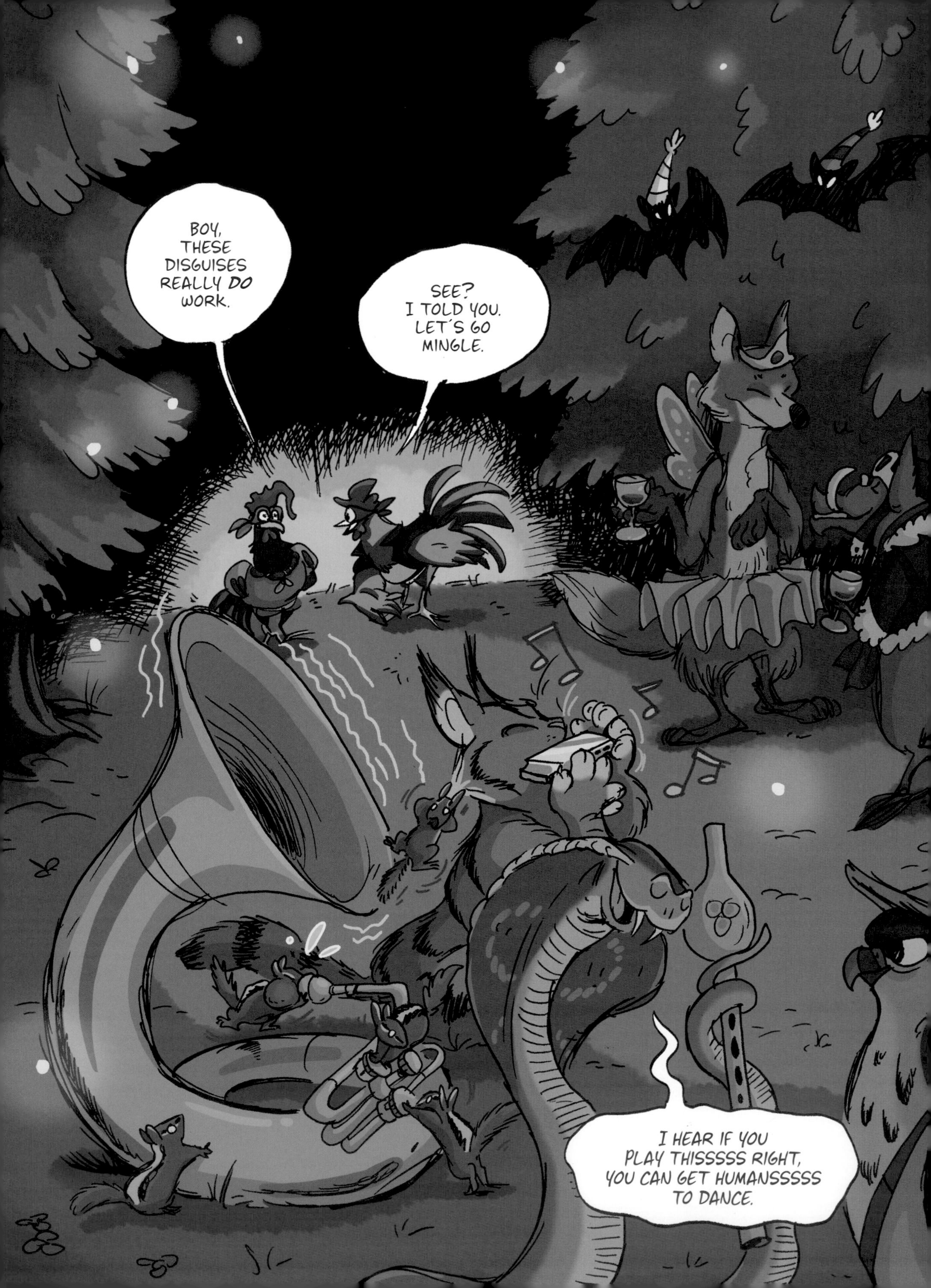
BOY, THESE DISGUISES REALLY DO WORK.
SEE? I TOLD YOU. LET'S GO MINGLE.
I HEAR IF YOU PLAY THISSSSS RIGHT, YOU CAN GET HUMANSSSSS TO DANCE.

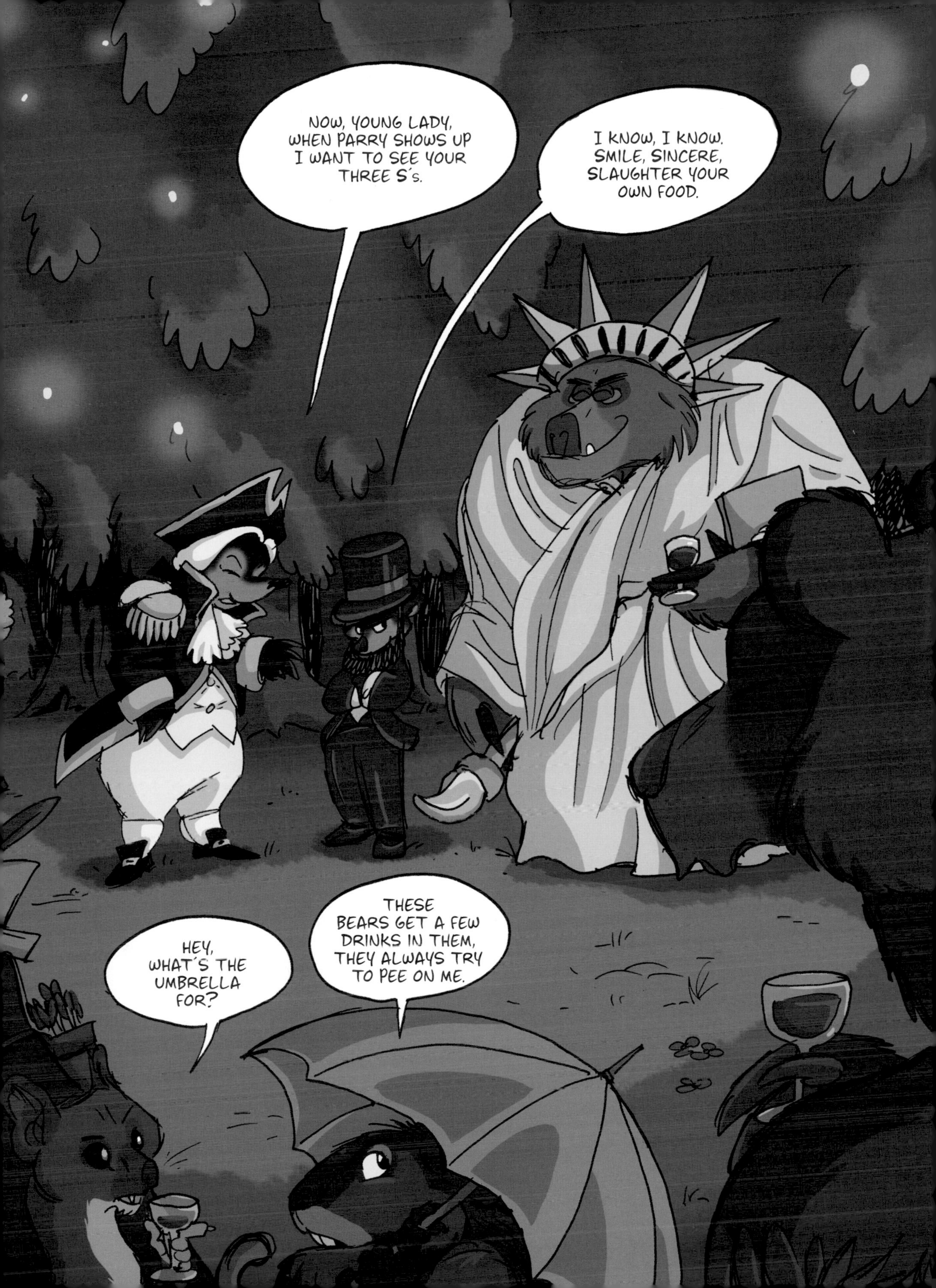
NOW, YOUNG LADY, WHEN PARRY SHOWS UP I WANT TO SEE YOUR THREE S´s.
I KNOW, I KNOW. SMILE, SINCERE, SLAUGHTER YOUR OWN FOOD.
HEY, WHAT´S THE UMBRELLA FOR?
THESE BEARS GET A FEW DRINKS IN THEM, THEY ALWAYS TRY TO PEE ON ME.

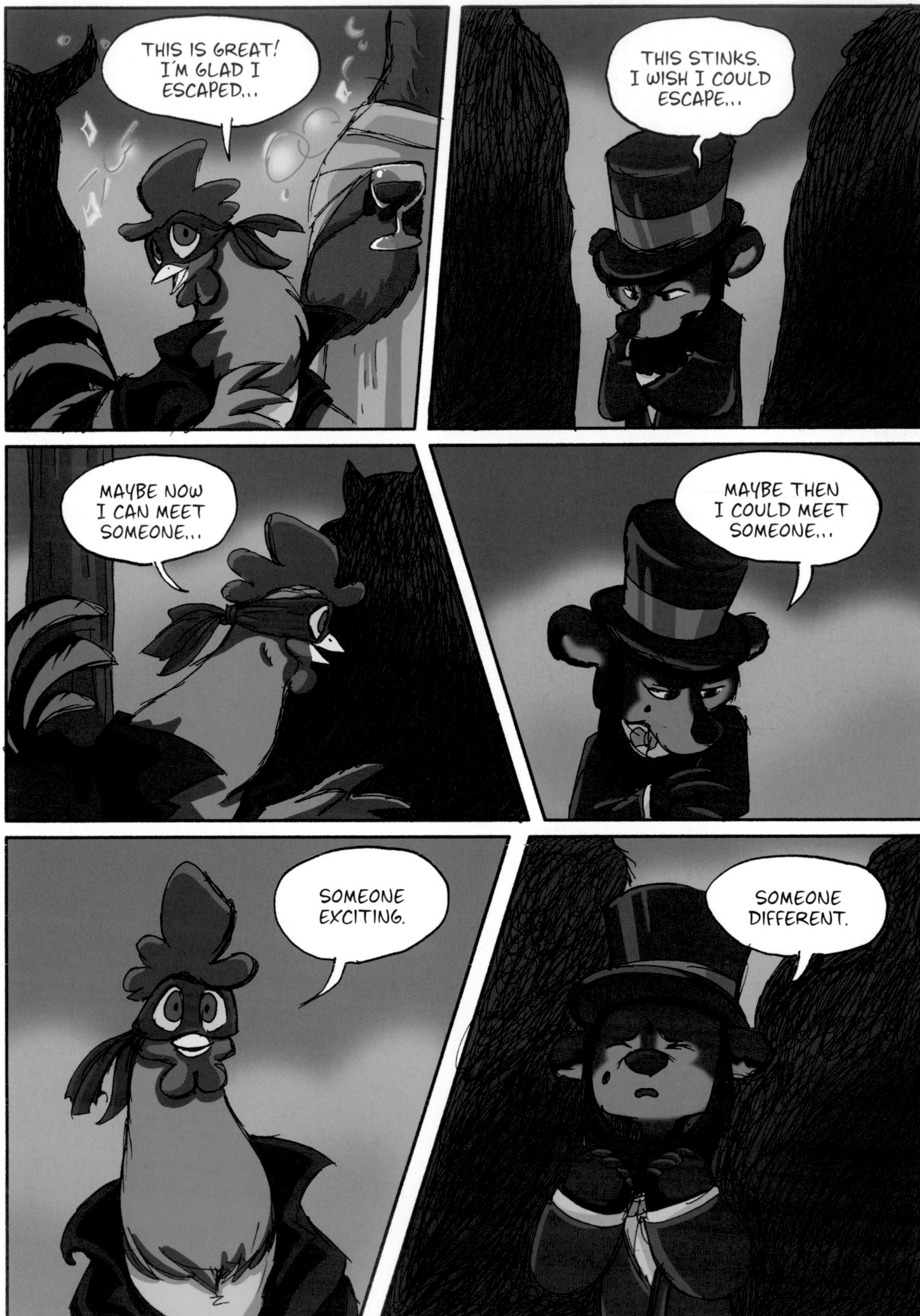
THIS IS GREAT! I´M GLAD I ESCAPED...
THIS STINKS. I WISH I COULD ESCAPE...
MAYBE NOW I CAN MEET SOMEONE...
MAYBE THEN I COULD MEET SOMEONE...
SOMEONE EXCITING.
SOMEONE DIFFERENT.

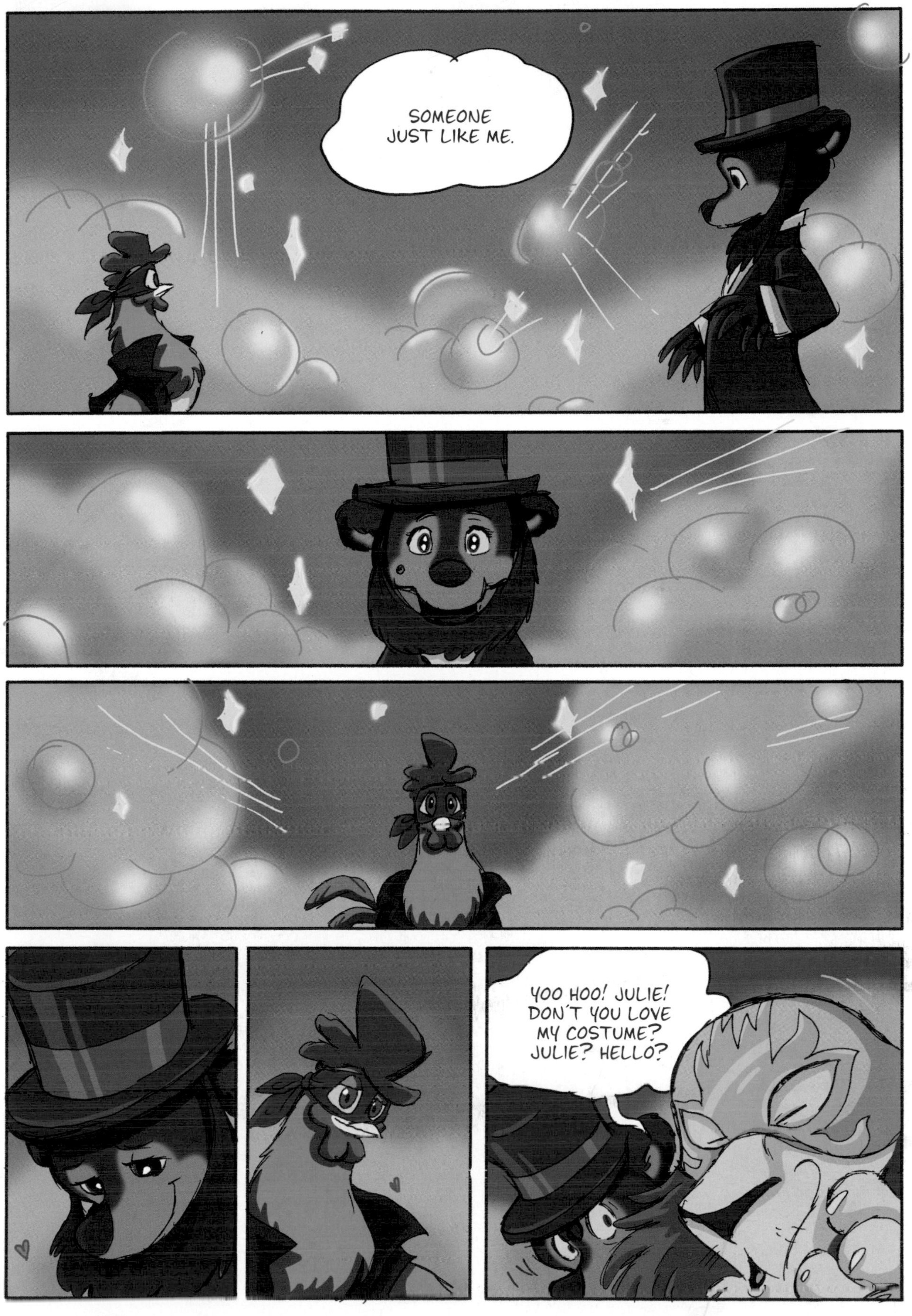
SOMEONE JUST LIKE ME.
YOO HOO! JULIE! DON'T YOU LOVE MY COSTUME? JULIE? HELLO?

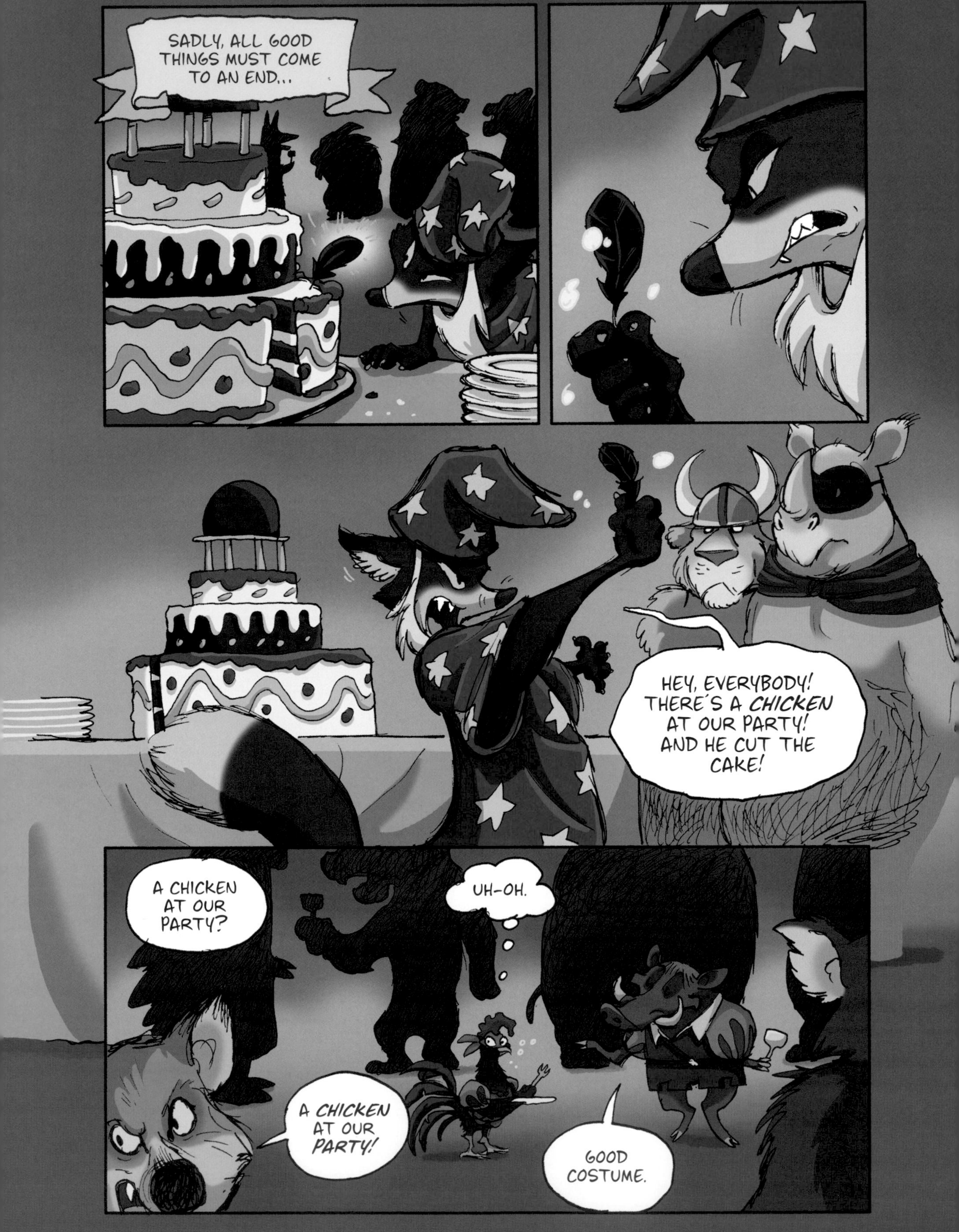
SADLY, ALL GOOD THINGS MUST COME TO AN END...
HEY, EVERYBODY! THERE'S A *CHICKEN* AT OUR PARTY! AND HE CUT THE CAKE!
A CHICKEN AT OUR PARTY?
UH-OH.
A *CHICKEN* AT OUR *PARTY*!
GOOD COSTUME.

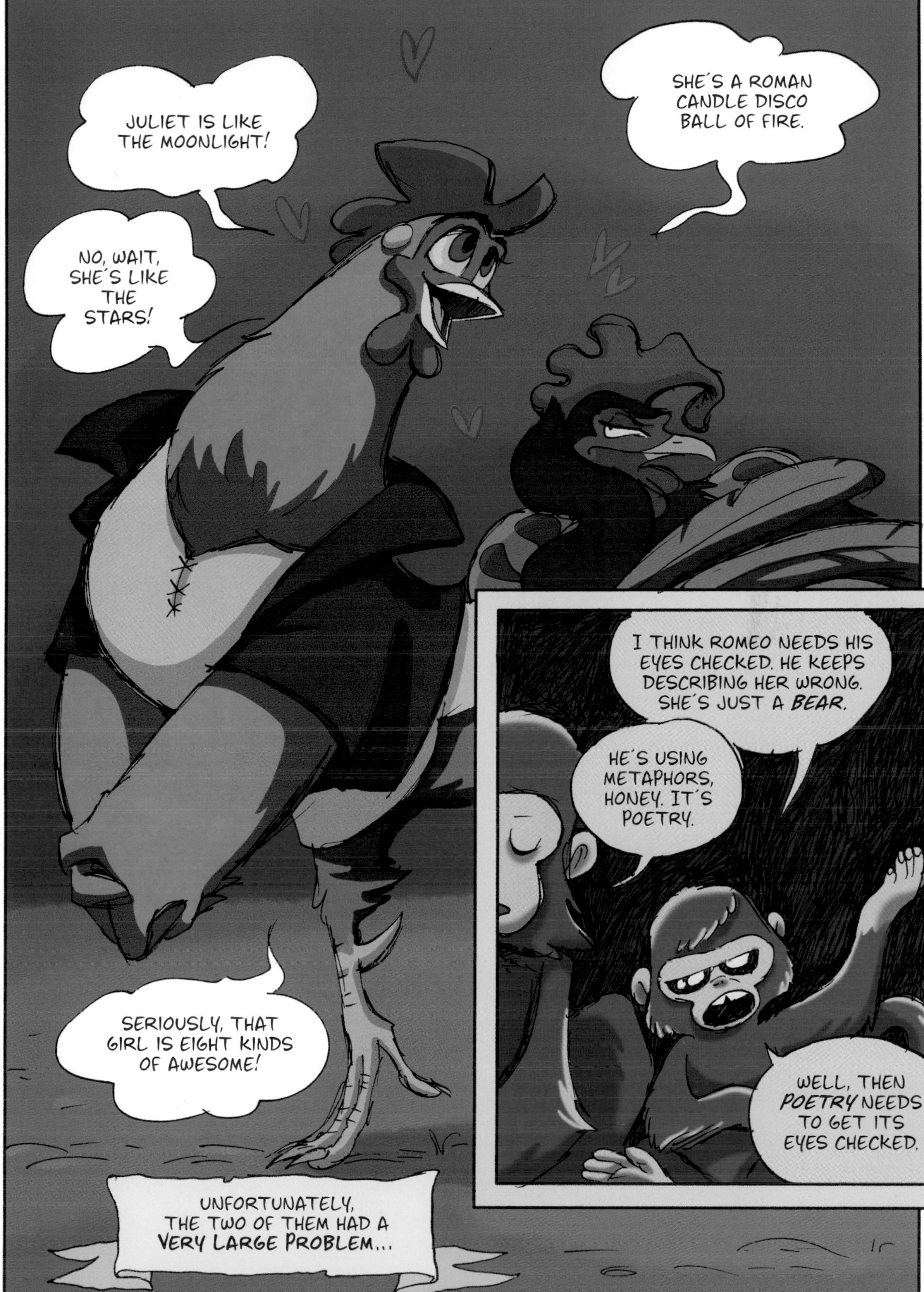
JULIET IS LIKE THE MOONLIGHT!
NO, WAIT, SHE'S LIKE THE STARS!
SHE'S A ROMAN CANDLE DISCO BALL OF FIRE.
SERIOUSLY, THAT GIRL IS EIGHT KINDS OF AWESOME!
UNFORTUNATELY, THE TWO OF THEM HAD A VERY LARGE PROBLEM...
I THINK ROMEO NEEDS HIS EYES CHECKED. HE KEEPS DESCRIBING HER WRONG. SHE'S JUST A *BEAR.*
HE'S USING METAPHORS, HONEY. IT'S POETRY.
WELL, THEN *POETRY* NEEDS TO GET ITS EYES CHECKED.

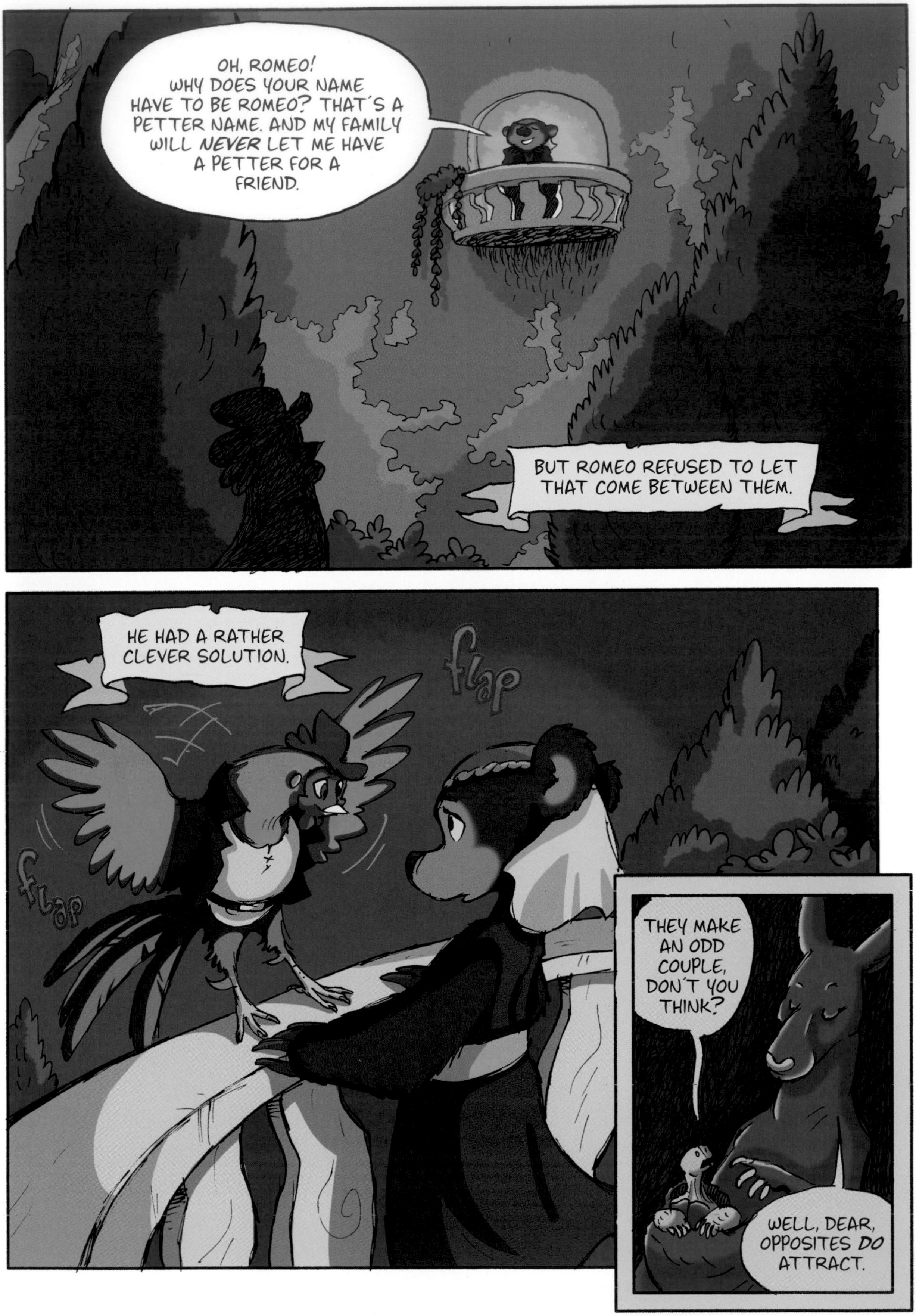

OH, ROMEO! WHY DOES YOUR NAME HAVE TO BE ROMEO? THAT´S A PETTER NAME. AND MY FAMILY WILL *NEVER* LET ME HAVE A PETTER FOR A FRIEND.
BUT ROMEO REFUSED TO LET THAT COME BETWEEN THEM.
HE HAD A RATHER CLEVER SOLUTION.
flap
flap
THEY MAKE AN ODD COUPLE, DON´T YOU THINK?
WELL, DEAR, OPPOSITES *DO* ATTRACT.

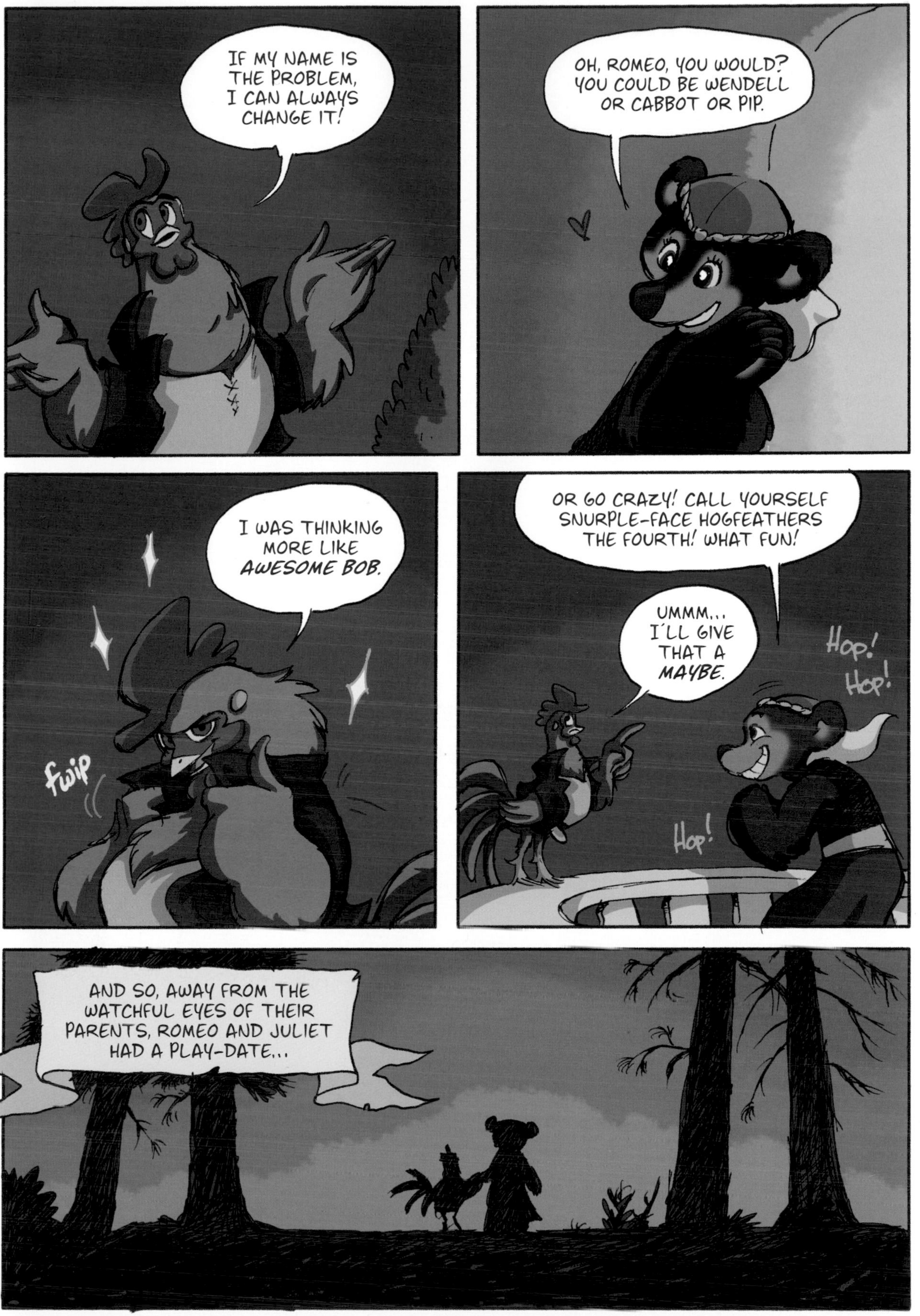
IF MY NAME IS THE PROBLEM, I CAN ALWAYS CHANGE IT!
OH, ROMEO, YOU WOULD? YOU COULD BE WENDELL OR CABBOT OR PIP.
I WAS THINKING MORE LIKE AWESOME BOB.
fwip
OR GO CRAZY! CALL YOURSELF SNURPLE-FACE HOGFEATHERS THE FOURTH! WHAT FUN!
UMMM... I'LL GIVE THAT A MAYBE.
Hop! Hop!
Hop!
AND SO, AWAY FROM THE WATCHFUL EYES OF THEIR PARENTS, ROMEO AND JULIET HAD A PLAY-DATE...

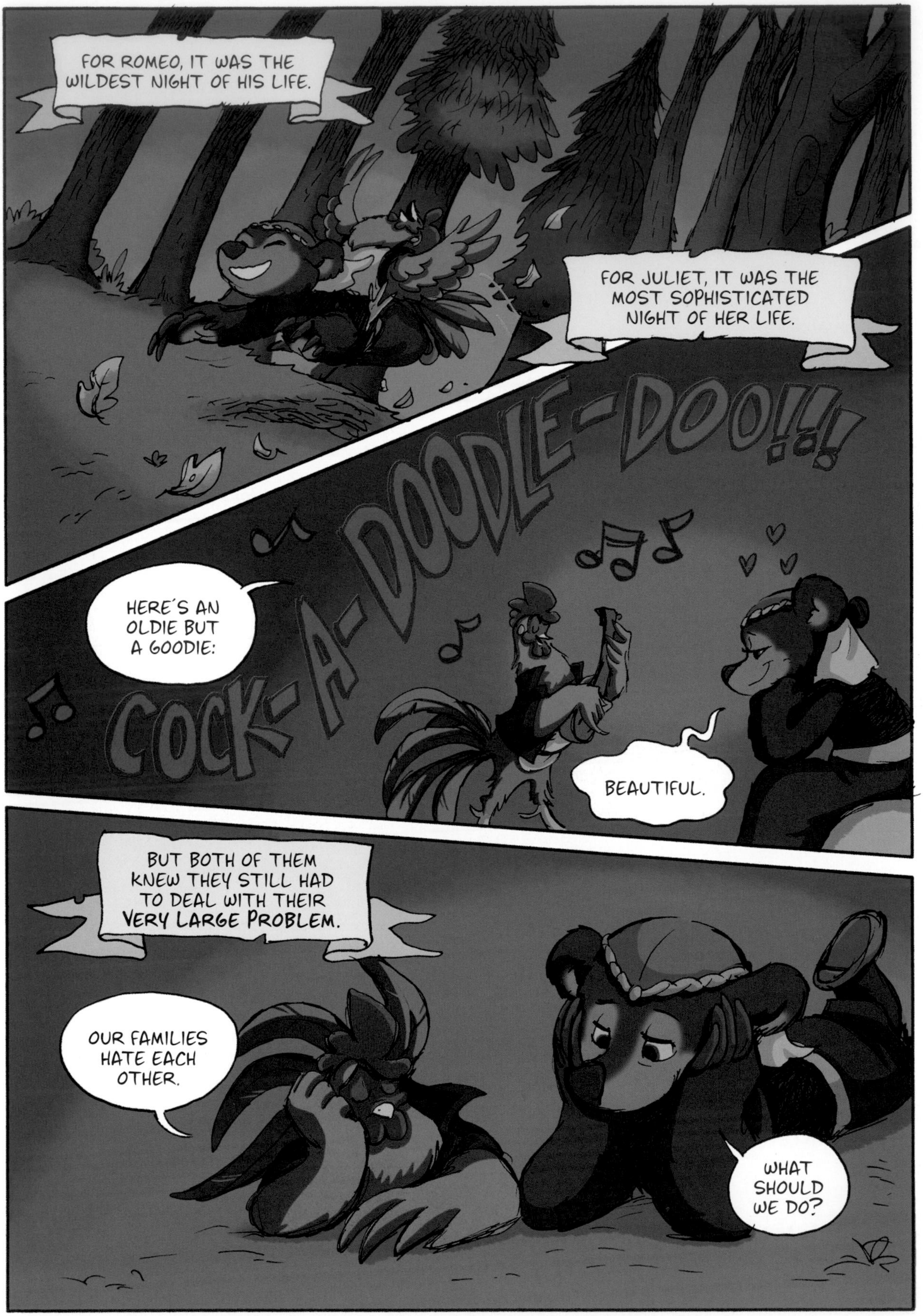
FOR ROMEO, IT WAS THE WILDEST NIGHT OF HIS LIFE.
FOR JULIET, IT WAS THE MOST SOPHISTICATED NIGHT OF HER LIFE.
COCK-A-DOODLE-DOO!!!
HERE´S AN OLDIE BUT A GOODIE:
BEAUTIFUL.
BUT BOTH OF THEM KNEW THEY STILL HAD TO DEAL WITH THEIR VERY LARGE PROBLEM.
OUR FAMILIES HATE EACH OTHER.
WHAT SHOULD WE DO?

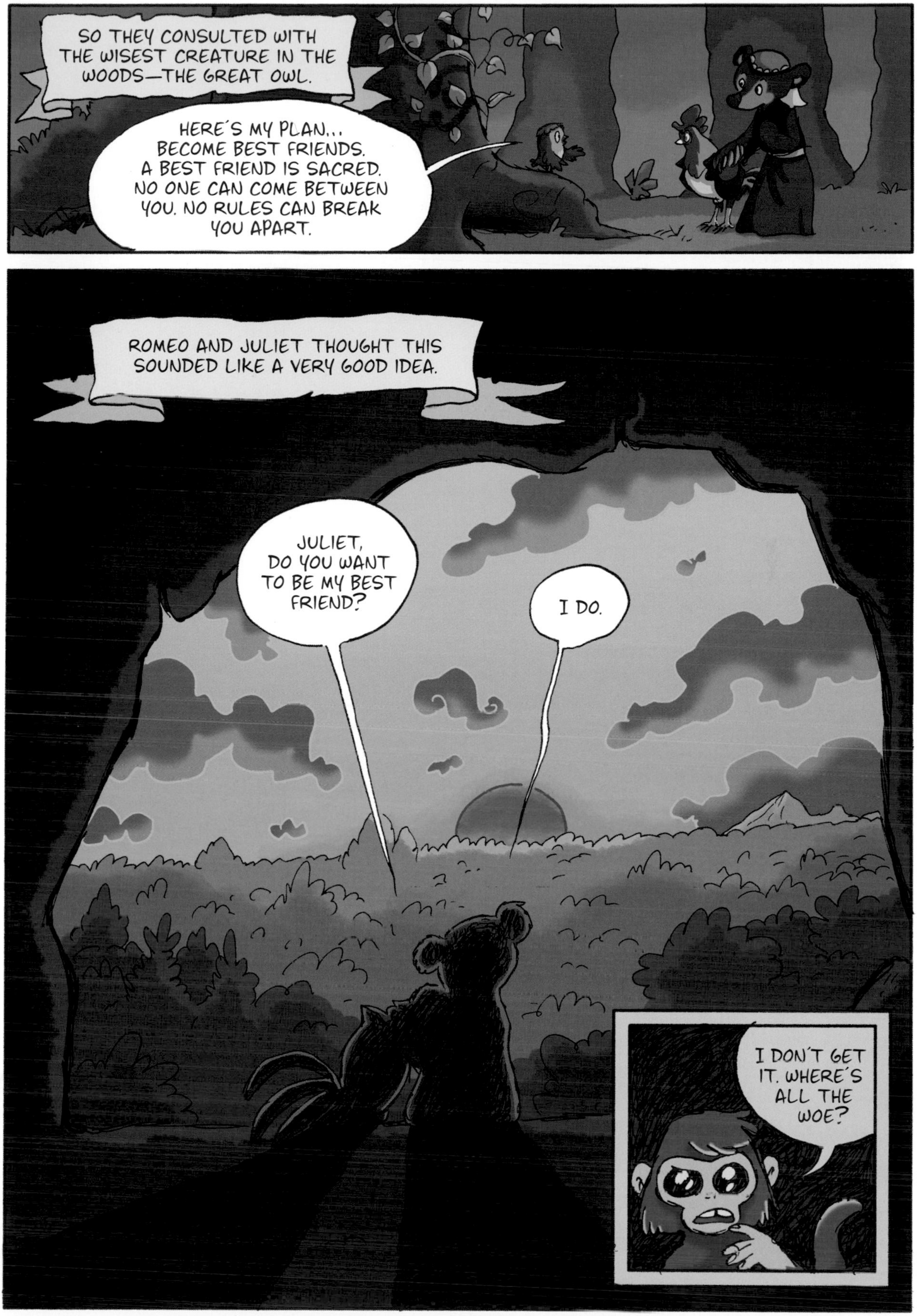

SO THEY CONSULTED WITH THE WISEST CREATURE IN THE WOODS—THE GREAT OWL.
HERE'S MY PLAN... BECOME BEST FRIENDS. A BEST FRIEND IS SACRED. NO ONE CAN COME BETWEEN YOU. NO RULES CAN BREAK YOU APART.
ROMEO AND JULIET THOUGHT THIS SOUNDED LIKE A VERY GOOD IDEA.
JULIET, DO YOU WANT TO BE MY BEST FRIEND?
I DO.
I DON'T GET IT. WHERE'S ALL THE WOE?

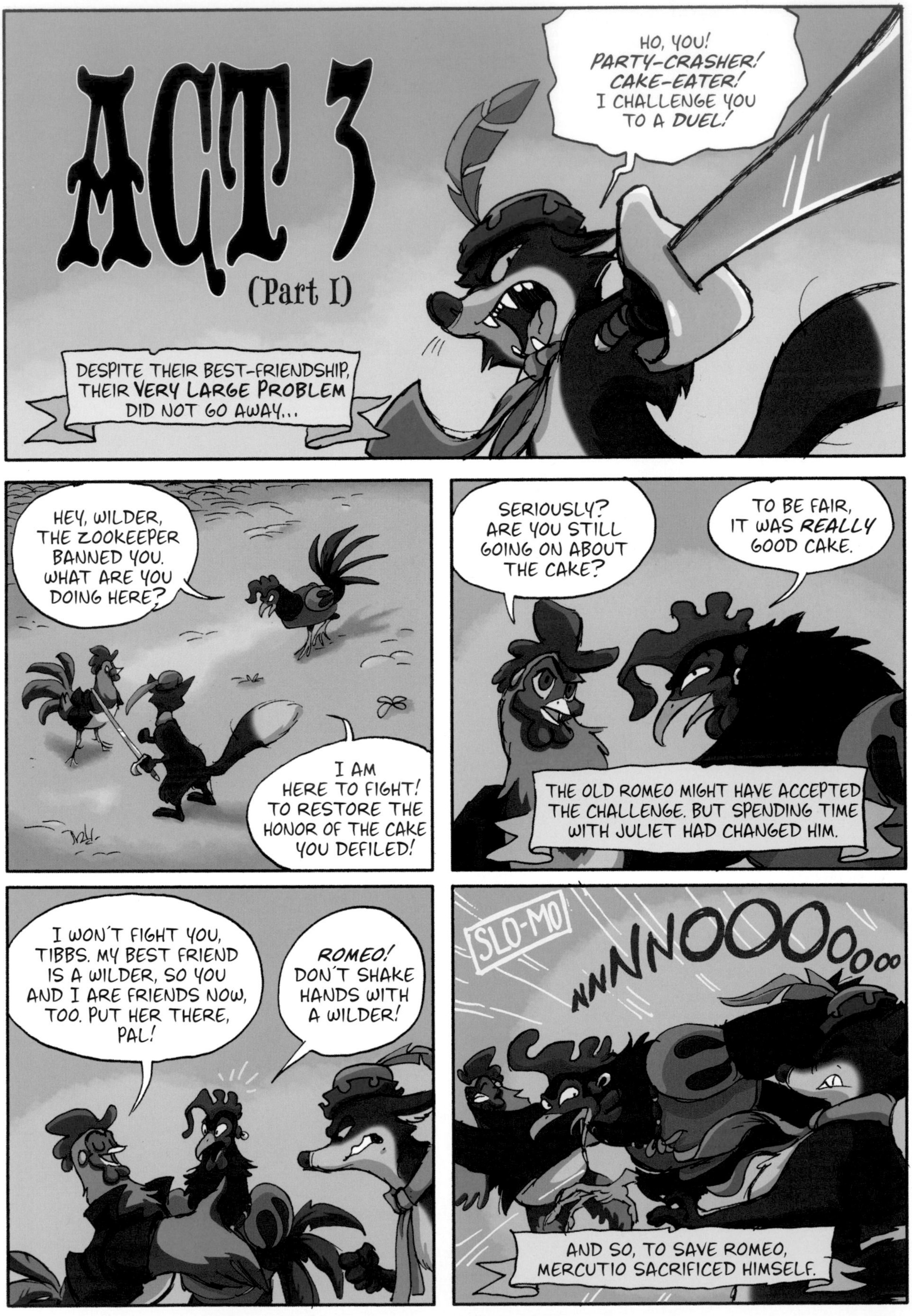
ACT 3
(Part I)
HO, YOU! PARTY-CRASHER! CAKE-EATER! I CHALLENGE YOU TO A DUEL!
DESPITE THEIR BEST-FRIENDSHIP, THEIR VERY LARGE PROBLEM DID NOT GO AWAY...
HEY, WILDER, THE ZOOKEEPER BANNED YOU. WHAT ARE YOU DOING HERE?
I AM HERE TO FIGHT! TO RESTORE THE HONOR OF THE CAKE YOU DEFILED!
SERIOUSLY? ARE YOU STILL GOING ON ABOUT THE CAKE?
TO BE FAIR, IT WAS REALLY GOOD CAKE.
THE OLD ROMEO MIGHT HAVE ACCEPTED THE CHALLENGE. BUT SPENDING TIME WITH JULIET HAD CHANGED HIM.
I WON'T FIGHT YOU, TIBBS. MY BEST FRIEND IS A WILDER, SO YOU AND I ARE FRIENDS NOW, TOO. PUT HER THERE, PAL!
ROMEO! DON'T SHAKE HANDS WITH A WILDER!
SLO-MO
NNNNOOOOOooo
AND SO, TO SAVE ROMEO, MERCUTIO SACRIFICED HIMSELF.

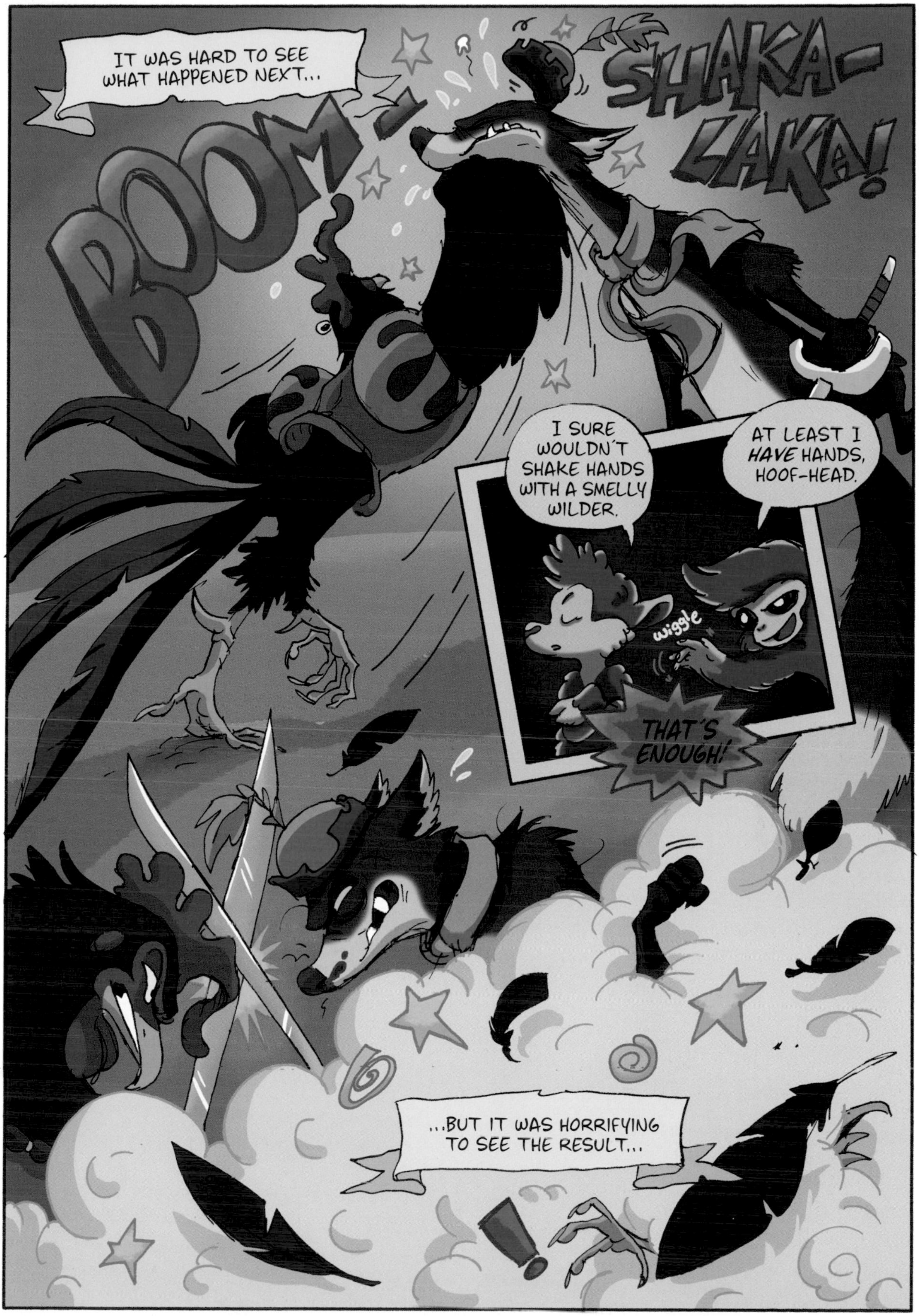

IT WAS HARD TO SEE WHAT HAPPENED NEXT...
BOOM!
SHAKA-LAKA!
I SURE WOULDN'T SHAKE HANDS WITH A SMELLY WILDER.
AT LEAST I *HAVE* HANDS, HOOF-HEAD.
wiggle
THAT'S ENOUGH!
...BUT IT WAS HORRIFYING TO SEE THE RESULT...

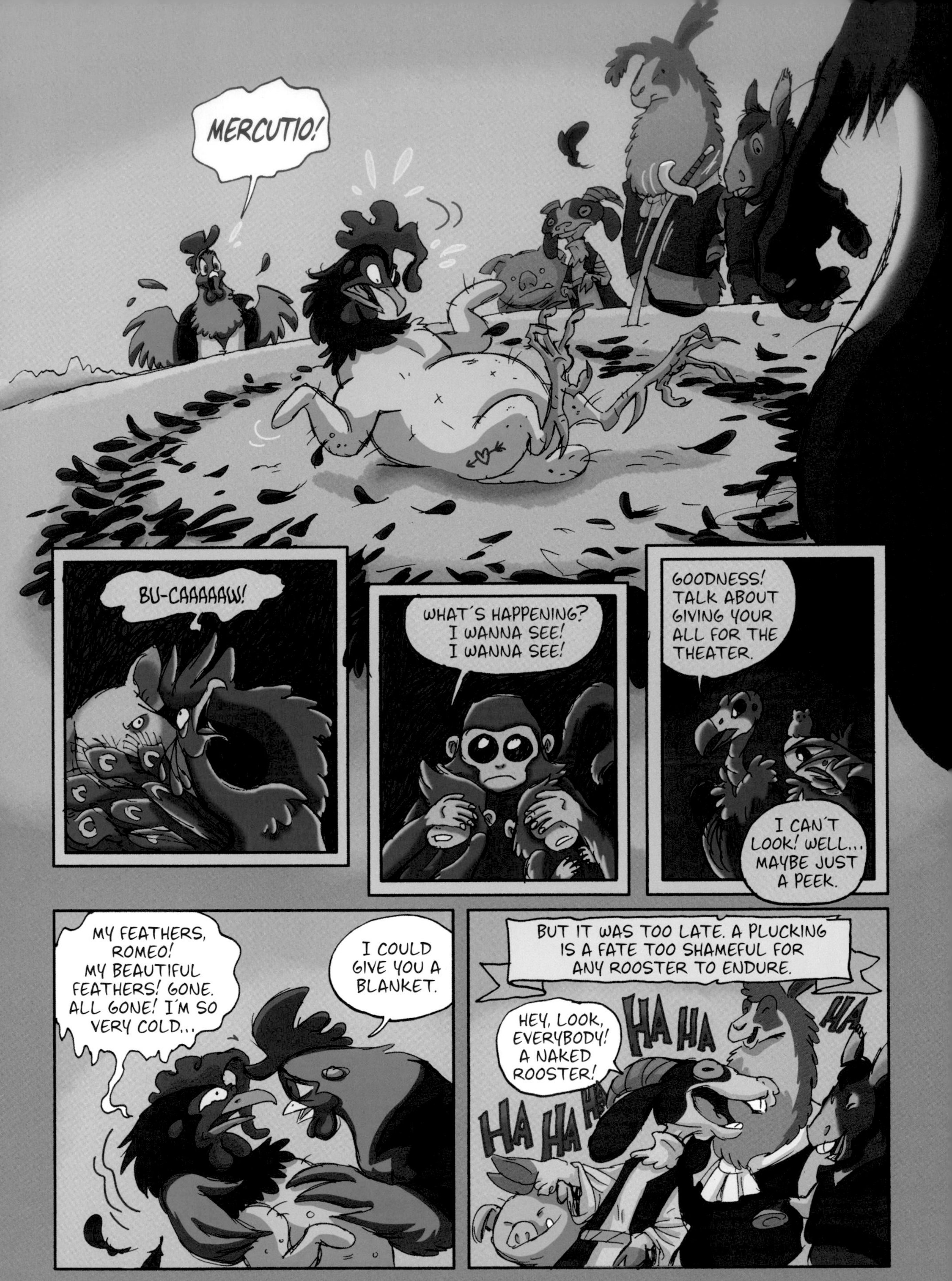

MERCUTIO!
BU-CAAAAAW!
WHAT´S HAPPENING? I WANNA SEE! I WANNA SEE!
GOODNESS! TALK ABOUT GIVING YOUR ALL FOR THE THEATER.
I CAN´T LOOK! WELL... MAYBE JUST A PEEK.
MY FEATHERS, ROMEO! MY BEAUTIFUL FEATHERS! GONE. ALL GONE! I´M SO VERY COLD...
I COULD GIVE YOU A BLANKET.
BUT IT WAS TOO LATE. A PLUCKING IS A FATE TOO SHAMEFUL FOR ANY ROOSTER TO ENDURE.
HEY, LOOK, EVERYBODY! A NAKED ROOSTER!
HA HA
HA
HA HA HA

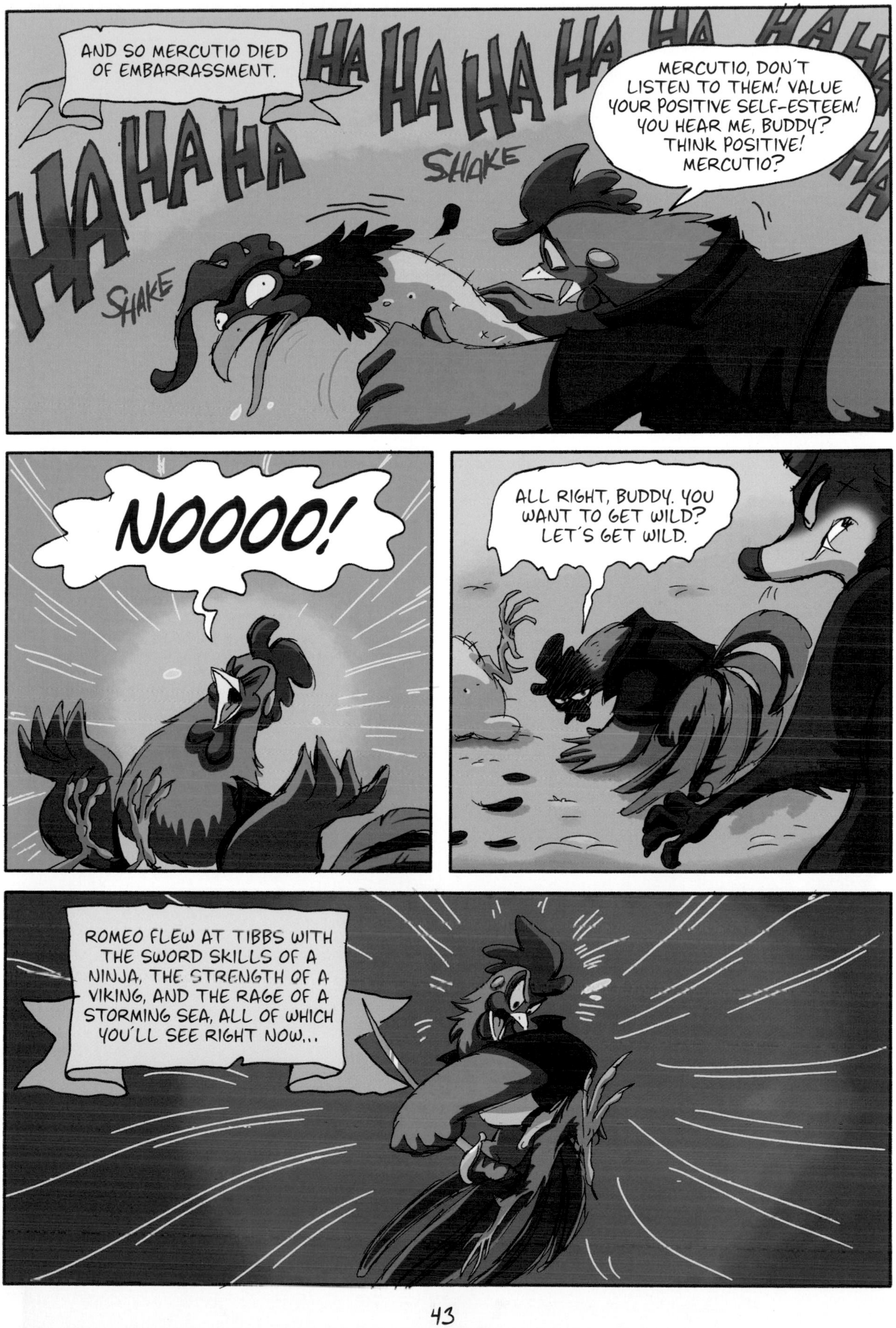

AND SO MERCUTIO DIED OF EMBARRASSMENT.
HA HA HA HA HA HA HA HA HA HA HA HA
MERCUTIO, DON´T LISTEN TO THEM! VALUE YOUR POSITIVE SELF-ESTEEM! YOU HEAR ME, BUDDY? THINK POSITIVE! MERCUTIO?
SHAKE
SHAKE
NOOOO!
ALL RIGHT, BUDDY. YOU WANT TO GET WILD? LET´S GET WILD.
ROMEO FLEW AT TIBBS WITH THE SWORD SKILLS OF A NINJA, THE STRENGTH OF A VIKING, AND THE RAGE OF A STORMING SEA, ALL OF WHICH YOU´LL SEE RIGHT NOW...

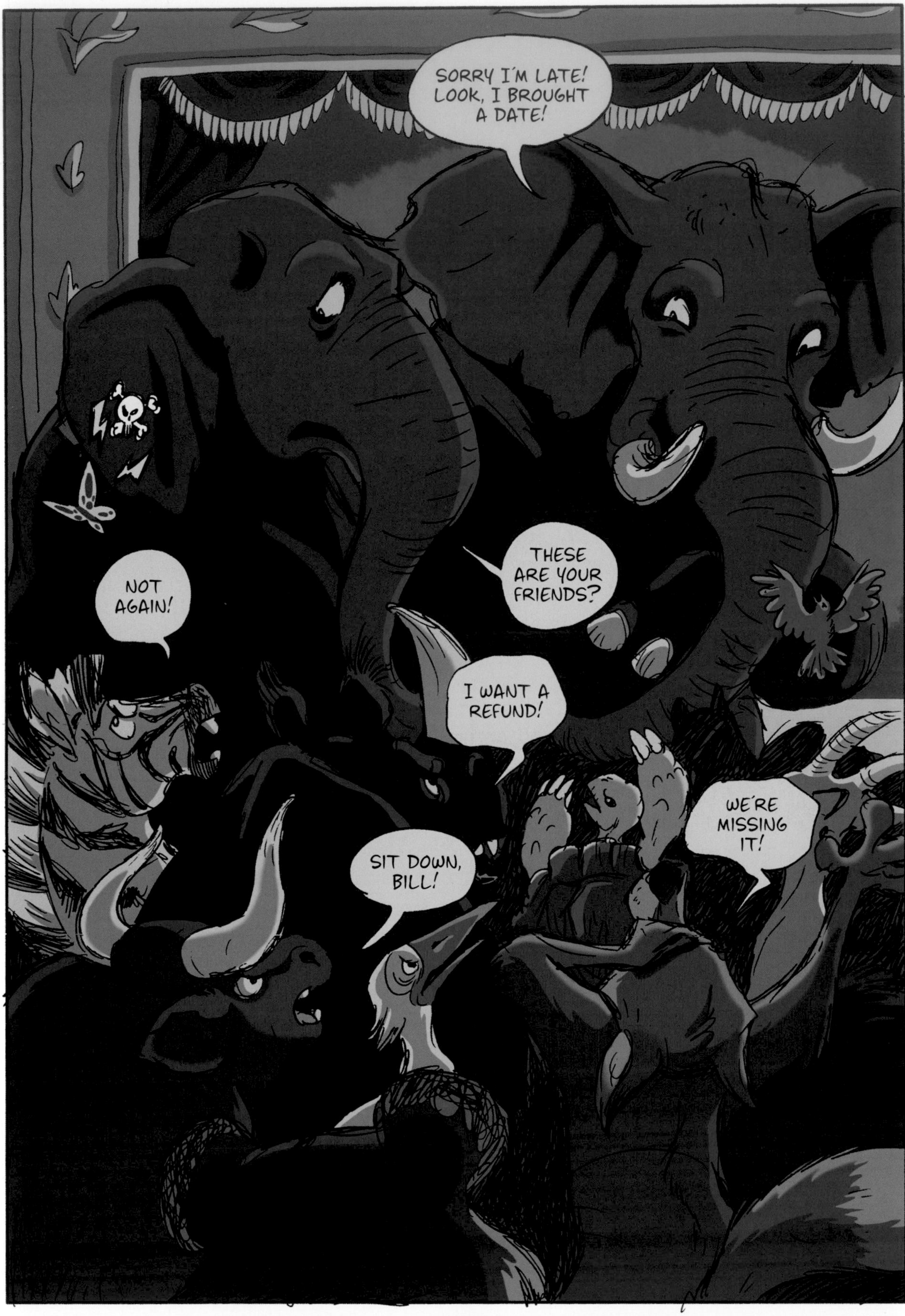
SORRY I'M LATE! LOOK, I BROUGHT A DATE!
NOT AGAIN!
THESE ARE YOUR FRIENDS?
I WANT A REFUND!
WE'RE MISSING IT!
SIT DOWN, BILL!

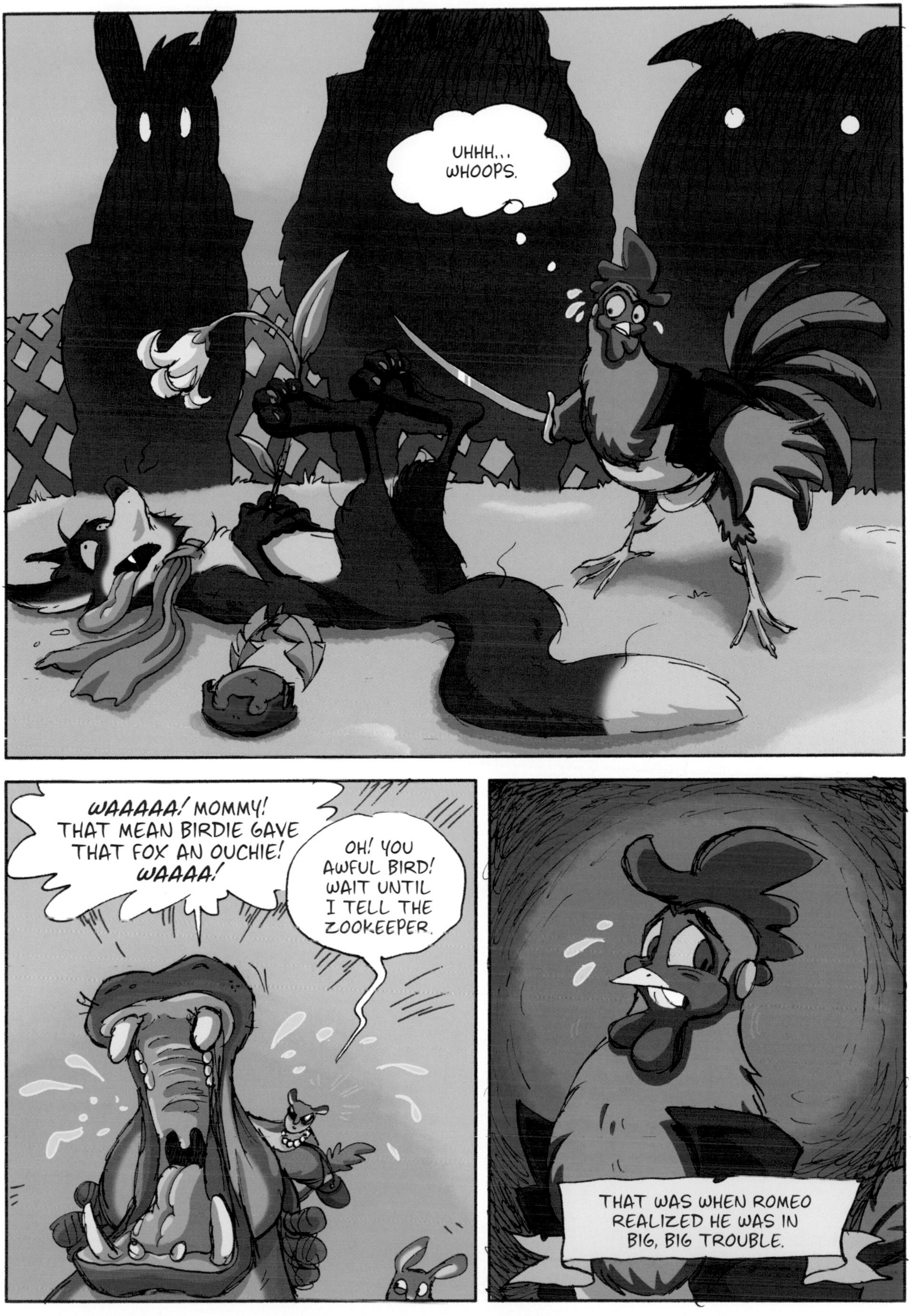
UHHH... WHOOPS.
WAAAAA! MOMMY! THAT MEAN BIRDIE GAVE THAT FOX AN OUCHIE! WAAAA!
OH! YOU AWFUL BIRD! WAIT UNTIL I TELL THE ZOOKEEPER.
THAT WAS WHEN ROMEO REALIZED HE WAS IN BIG, BIG TROUBLE.

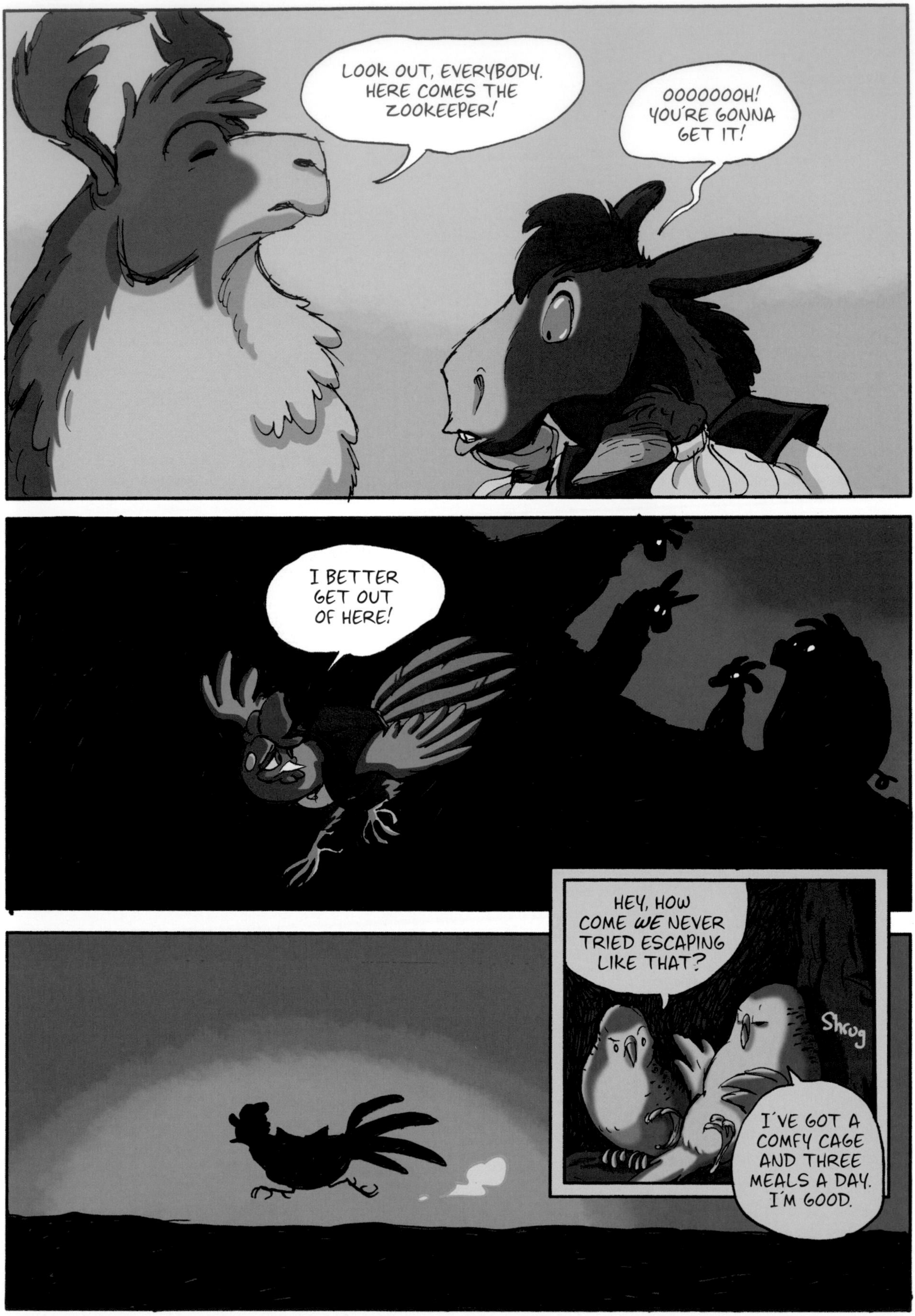
LOOK OUT, EVERYBODY. HERE COMES THE ZOOKEEPER!
OOOOOOOH! YOU'RE GONNA GET IT!
I BETTER GET OUT OF HERE!
HEY, HOW COME *WE* NEVER TRIED ESCAPING LIKE THAT?
Shrug
I'VE GOT A COMFY CAGE AND THREE MEALS A DAY. I'M GOOD.

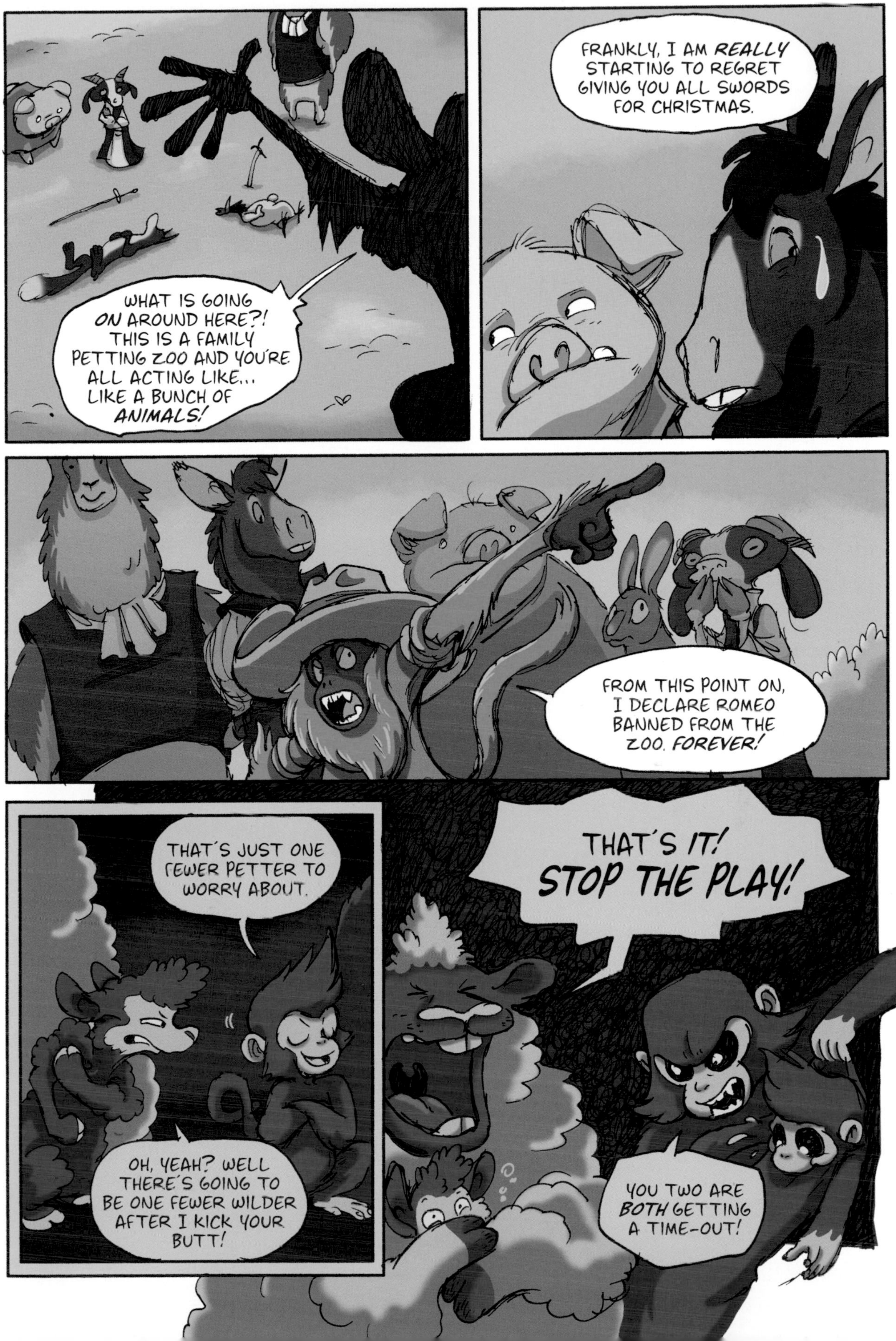
WHAT IS GOING ON AROUND HERE?! THIS IS A FAMILY PETTING ZOO AND YOU'RE ALL ACTING LIKE... LIKE A BUNCH OF ANIMALS!
FRANKLY, I AM REALLY STARTING TO REGRET GIVING YOU ALL SWORDS FOR CHRISTMAS.
FROM THIS POINT ON, I DECLARE ROMEO BANNED FROM THE ZOO. FOREVER!
THAT'S JUST ONE FEWER PETTER TO WORRY ABOUT.
OH, YEAH? WELL THERE'S GOING TO BE ONE FEWER WILDER AFTER I KICK YOUR BUTT!
THAT'S IT! STOP THE PLAY!
YOU TWO ARE BOTH GETTING A TIME-OUT!

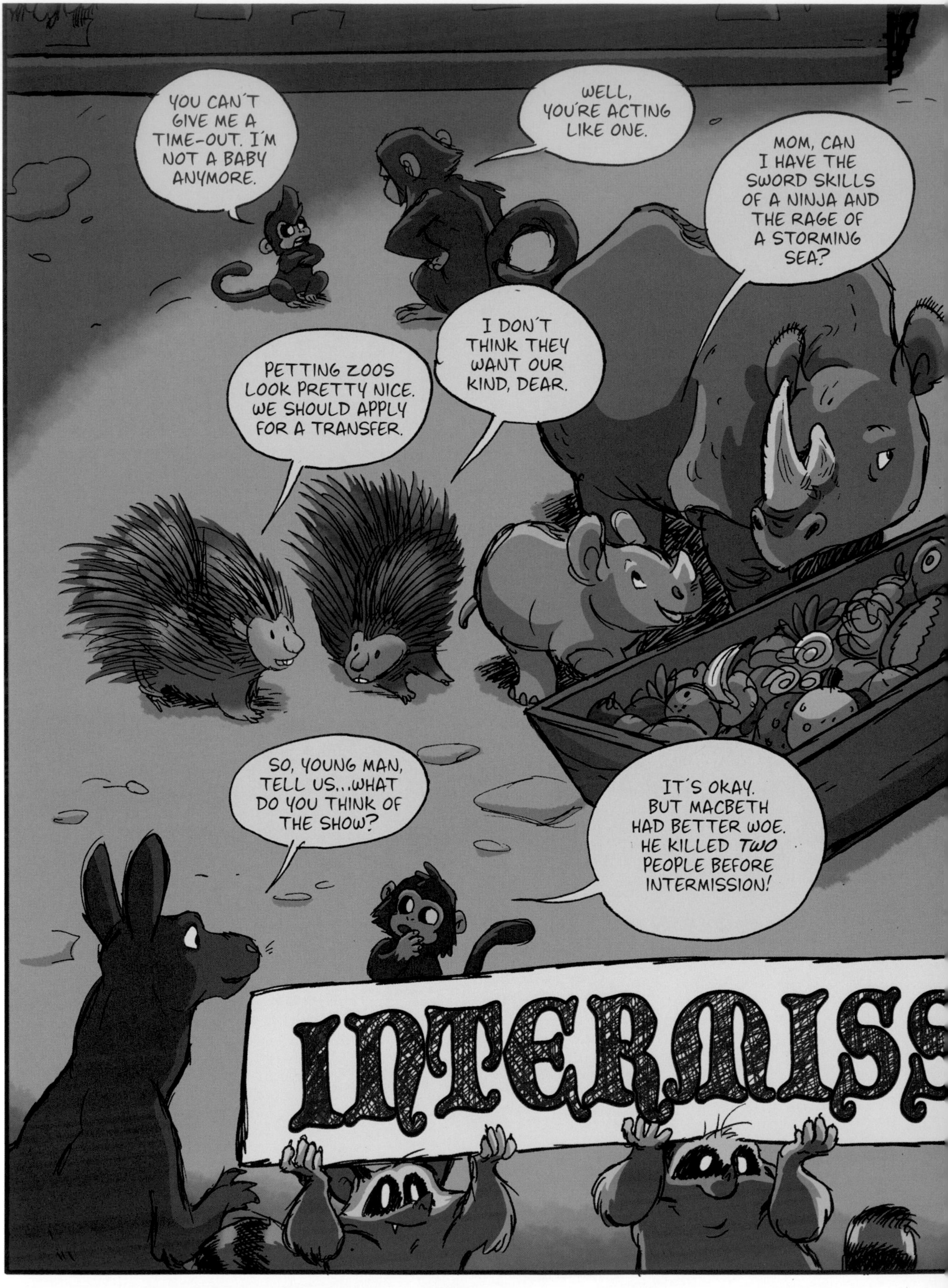

YOU CAN'T GIVE ME A TIME-OUT. I'M NOT A BABY ANYMORE.
WELL, YOU'RE ACTING LIKE ONE.
MOM, CAN I HAVE THE SWORD SKILLS OF A NINJA AND THE RAGE OF A STORMING SEA?
PETTING ZOOS LOOK PRETTY NICE. WE SHOULD APPLY FOR A TRANSFER.
I DON'T THINK THEY WANT OUR KIND, DEAR.
SO, YOUNG MAN, TELL US...WHAT DO YOU THINK OF THE SHOW?
IT'S OKAY. BUT MACBETH HAD BETTER WOE. HE KILLED TWO PEOPLE BEFORE INTERMISSION!
INTERMISS

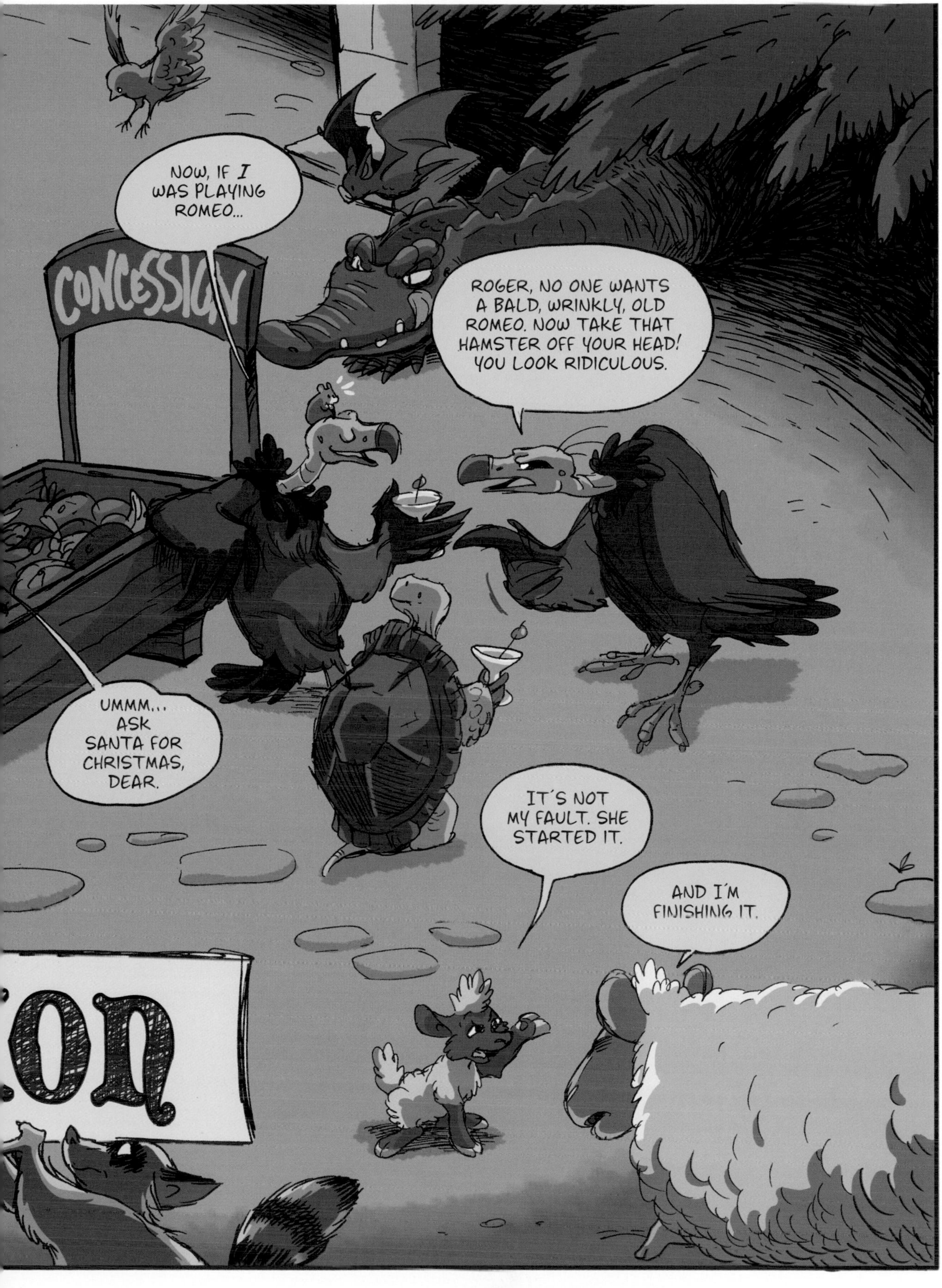
CONCESSION
NOW, IF I WAS PLAYING ROMEO...
ROGER, NO ONE WANTS A BALD, WRINKLY, OLD ROMEO. NOW TAKE THAT HAMSTER OFF YOUR HEAD! YOU LOOK RIDICULOUS.
UMMM... ASK SANTA FOR CHRISTMAS, DEAR.
IT'S NOT MY FAULT. SHE STARTED IT.
AND I'M FINISHING IT.
ON

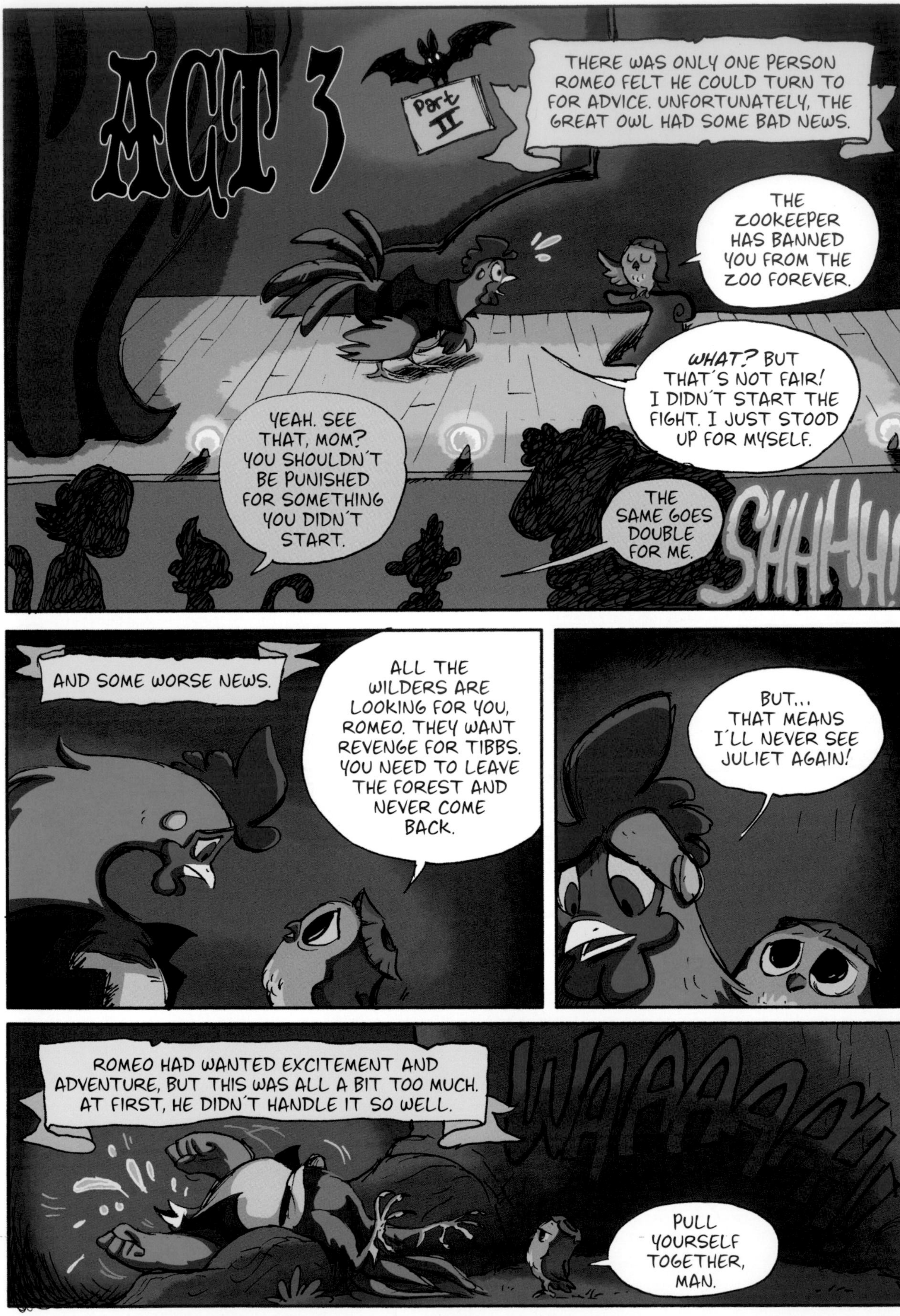
ACT 3
Part II
THERE WAS ONLY ONE PERSON ROMEO FELT HE COULD TURN TO FOR ADVICE. UNFORTUNATELY, THE GREAT OWL HAD SOME BAD NEWS.
THE ZOOKEEPER HAS BANNED YOU FROM THE ZOO FOREVER.
WHAT? BUT THAT´S NOT FAIR! I DIDN´T START THE FIGHT. I JUST STOOD UP FOR MYSELF.
YEAH. SEE THAT, MOM? YOU SHOULDN´T BE PUNISHED FOR SOMETHING YOU DIDN´T START.
THE SAME GOES DOUBLE FOR ME.
SHHHH!
AND SOME WORSE NEWS.
ALL THE WILDERS ARE LOOKING FOR YOU, ROMEO. THEY WANT REVENGE FOR TIBBS. YOU NEED TO LEAVE THE FOREST AND NEVER COME BACK.
BUT... THAT MEANS I´LL NEVER SEE JULIET AGAIN!
ROMEO HAD WANTED EXCITEMENT AND ADVENTURE, BUT THIS WAS ALL A BIT TOO MUCH. AT FIRST, HE DIDN´T HANDLE IT SO WELL.
WAAAAAH!
PULL YOURSELF TOGETHER, MAN.

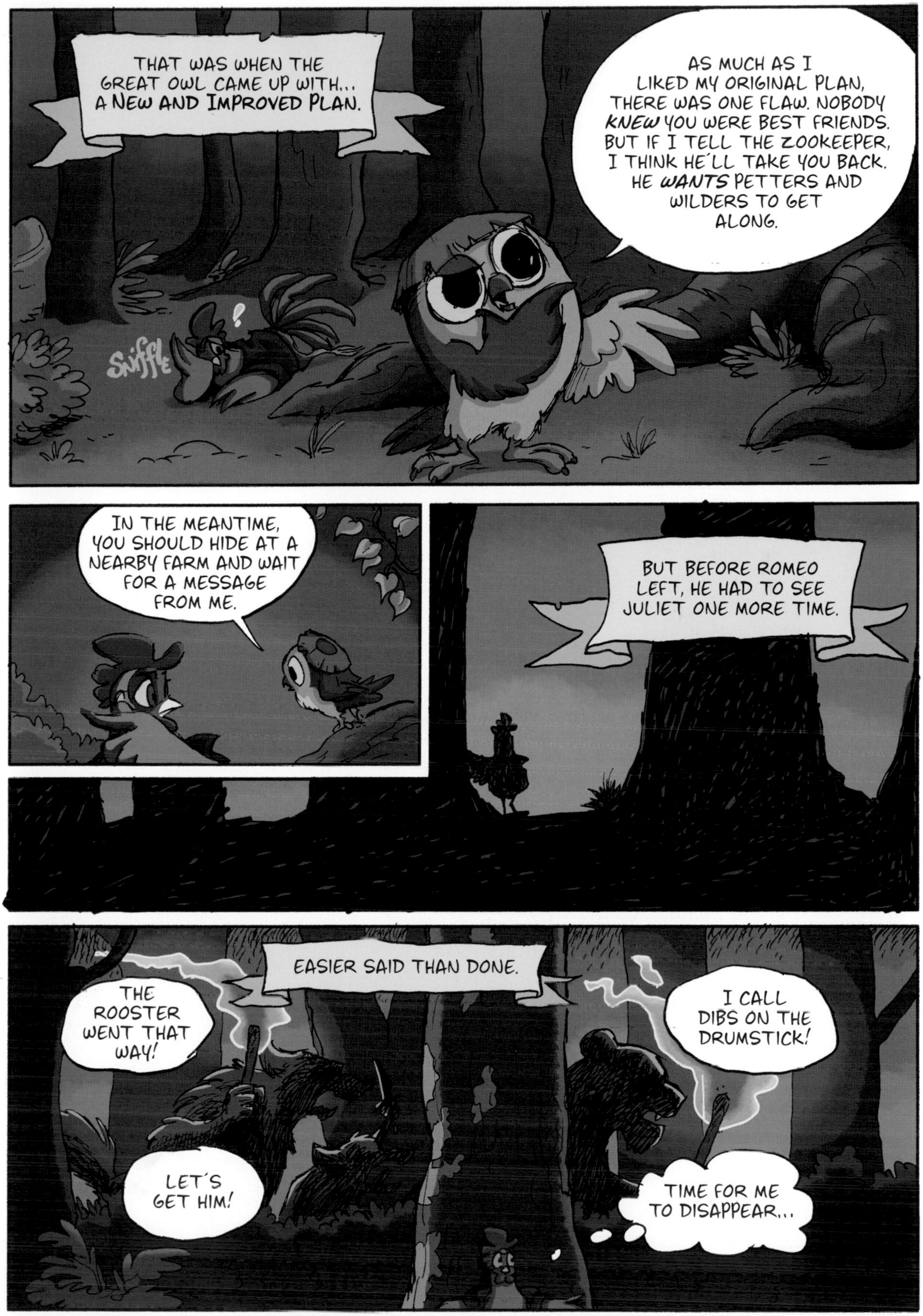
THAT WAS WHEN THE GREAT OWL CAME UP WITH... A NEW AND IMPROVED PLAN.
AS MUCH AS I LIKED MY ORIGINAL PLAN, THERE WAS ONE FLAW. NOBODY KNEW YOU WERE BEST FRIENDS. BUT IF I TELL THE ZOOKEEPER, I THINK HE'LL TAKE YOU BACK. HE WANTS PETTERS AND WILDERS TO GET ALONG.
!
SNIFFLE
IN THE MEANTIME, YOU SHOULD HIDE AT A NEARBY FARM AND WAIT FOR A MESSAGE FROM ME.
BUT BEFORE ROMEO LEFT, HE HAD TO SEE JULIET ONE MORE TIME.
EASIER SAID THAN DONE.
THE ROOSTER WENT THAT WAY!
I CALL DIBS ON THE DRUMSTICK!
LET'S GET HIM!
TIME FOR ME TO DISAPPEAR...

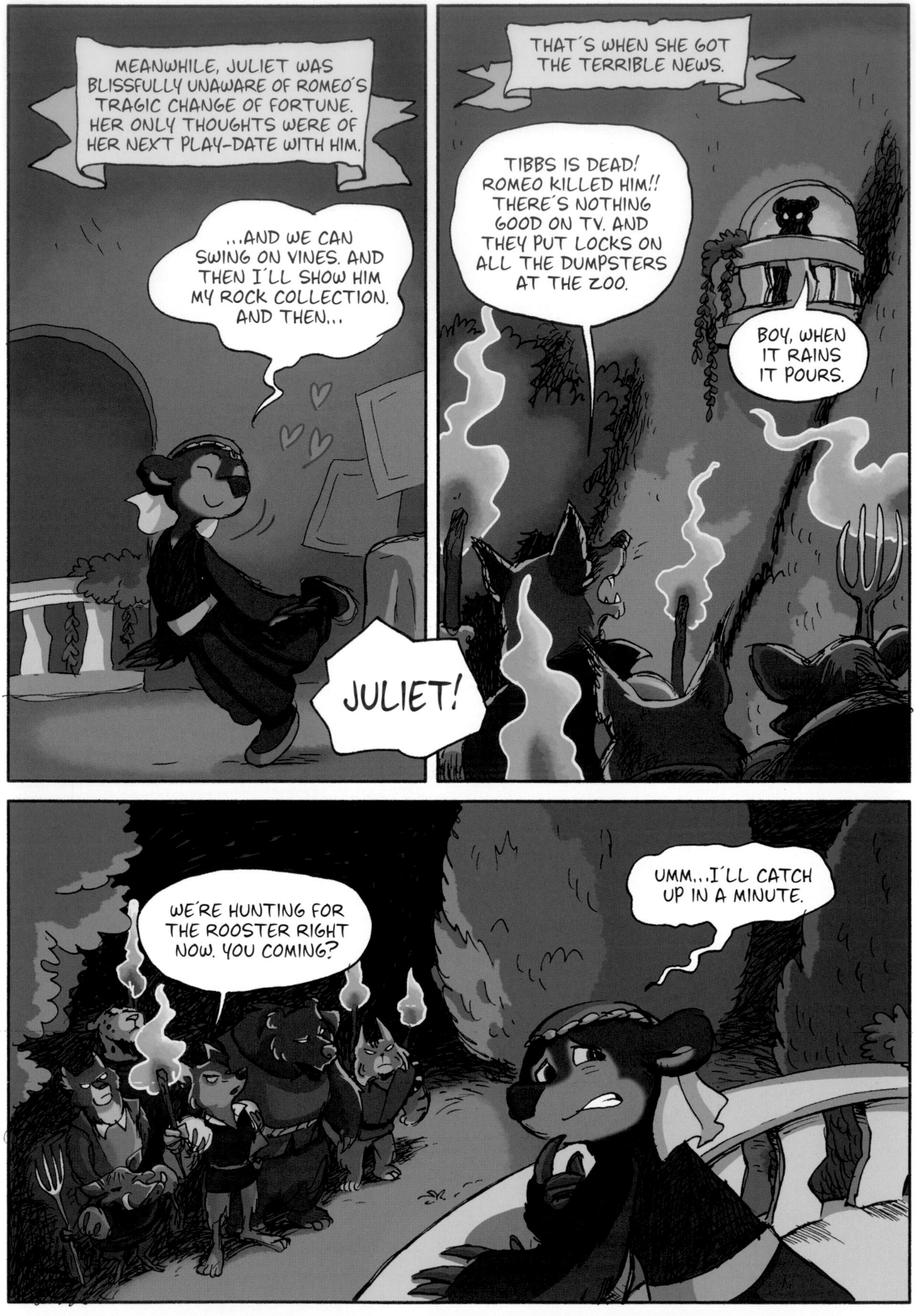
MEANWHILE, JULIET WAS BLISSFULLY UNAWARE OF ROMEO'S TRAGIC CHANGE OF FORTUNE. HER ONLY THOUGHTS WERE OF HER NEXT PLAY-DATE WITH HIM.
...AND WE CAN SWING ON VINES. AND THEN I'LL SHOW HIM MY ROCK COLLECTION. AND THEN...
JULIET!
THAT'S WHEN SHE GOT THE TERRIBLE NEWS.
TIBBS IS DEAD! ROMEO KILLED HIM!! THERE'S NOTHING GOOD ON TV. AND THEY PUT LOCKS ON ALL THE DUMPSTERS AT THE ZOO.
BOY, WHEN IT RAINS IT POURS.
WE'RE HUNTING FOR THE ROOSTER RIGHT NOW. YOU COMING?
UMM...I'LL CATCH UP IN A MINUTE.

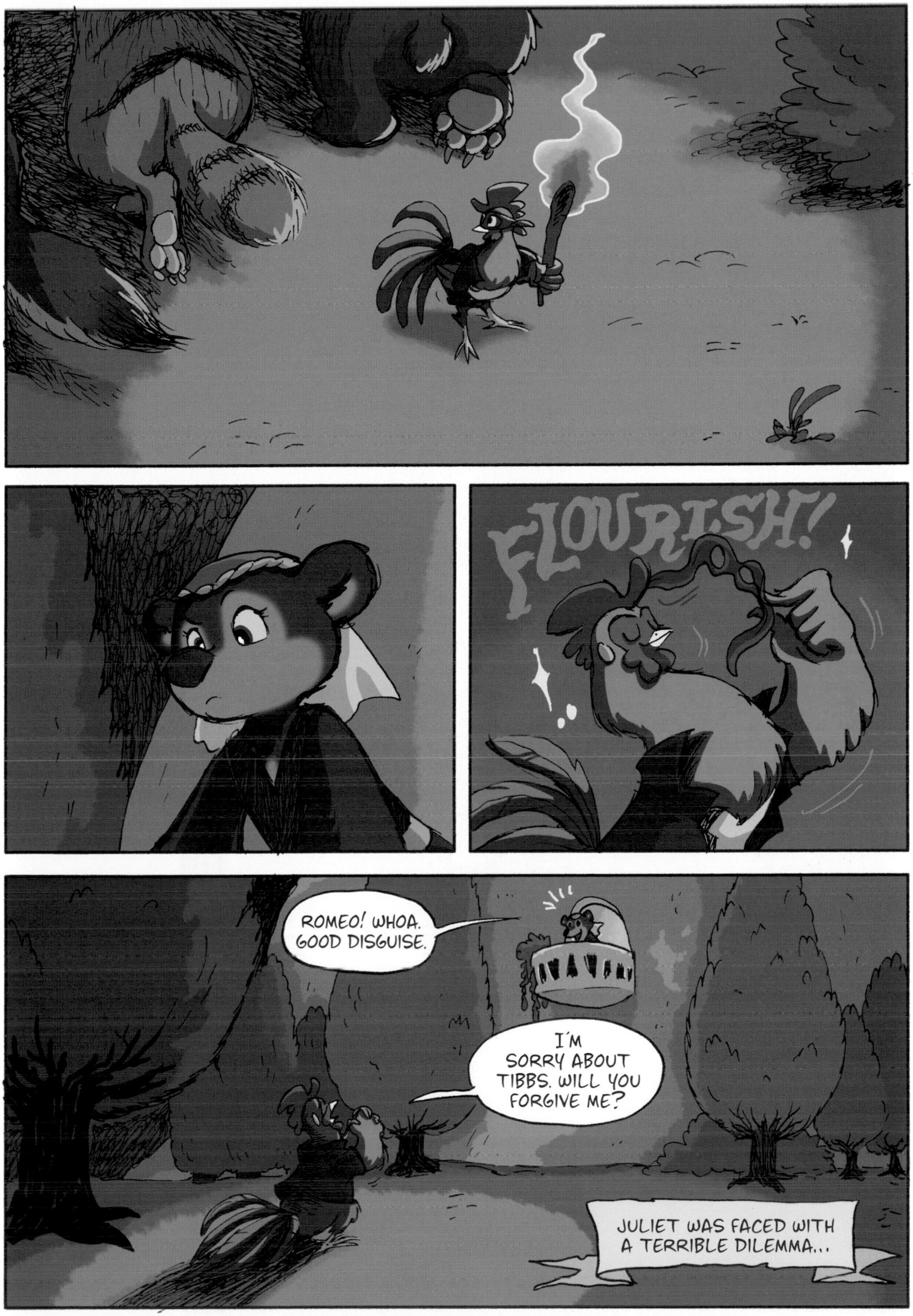
FLOURISH!
ROMEO! WHOA. GOOD DISGUISE.
I'M SORRY ABOUT TIBBS. WILL YOU FORGIVE ME?
JULIET WAS FACED WITH A TERRIBLE DILEMMA...

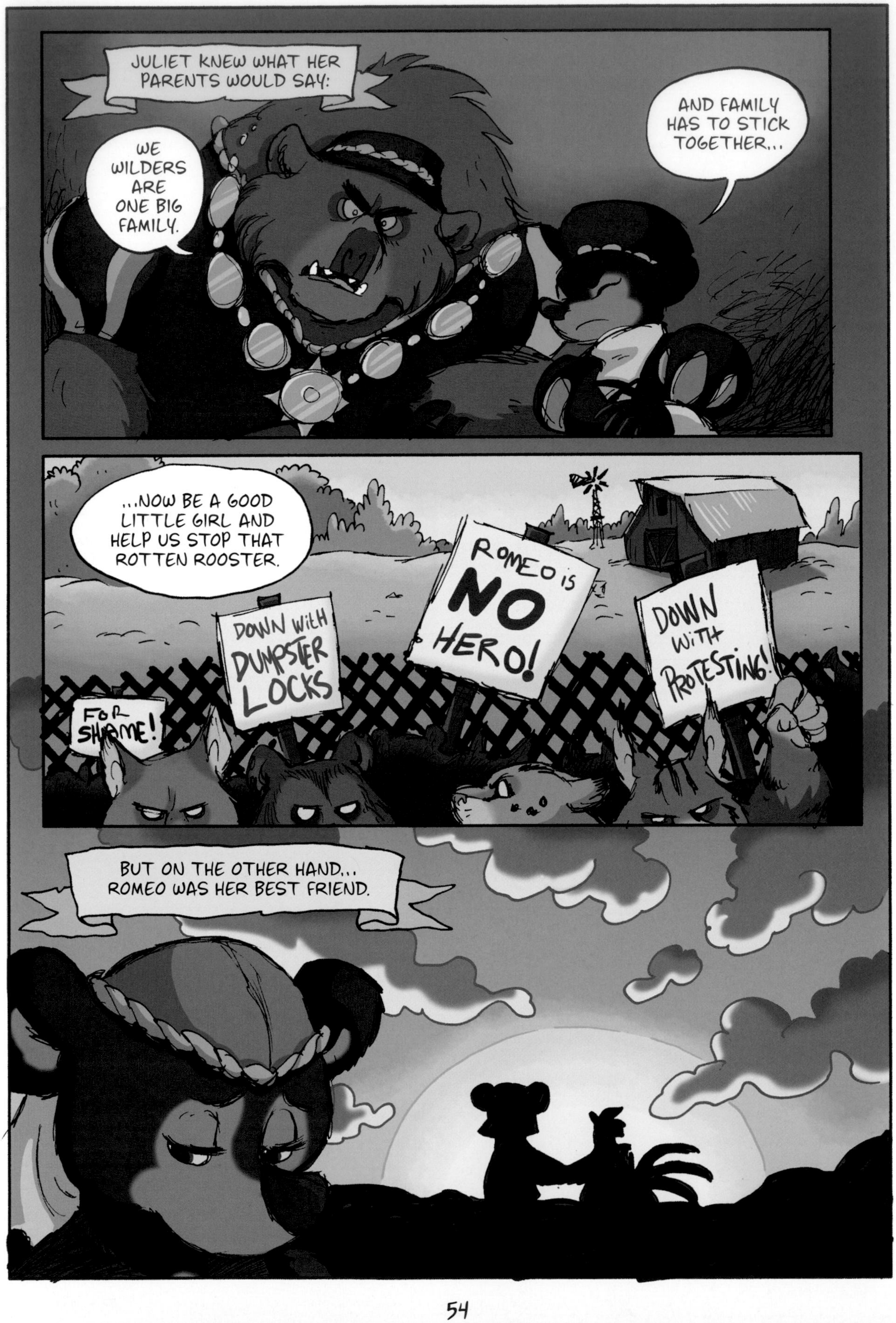
JULIET KNEW WHAT HER PARENTS WOULD SAY:
WE WILDERS ARE ONE BIG FAMILY.
AND FAMILY HAS TO STICK TOGETHER...
...NOW BE A GOOD LITTLE GIRL AND HELP US STOP THAT ROTTEN ROOSTER.
ROMEO IS NO HERO!
DOWN WITH DUMPSTER LOCKS
DOWN WITH PROTESTING!
FOR SHAME!
BUT ON THE OTHER HAND... ROMEO WAS HER BEST FRIEND.

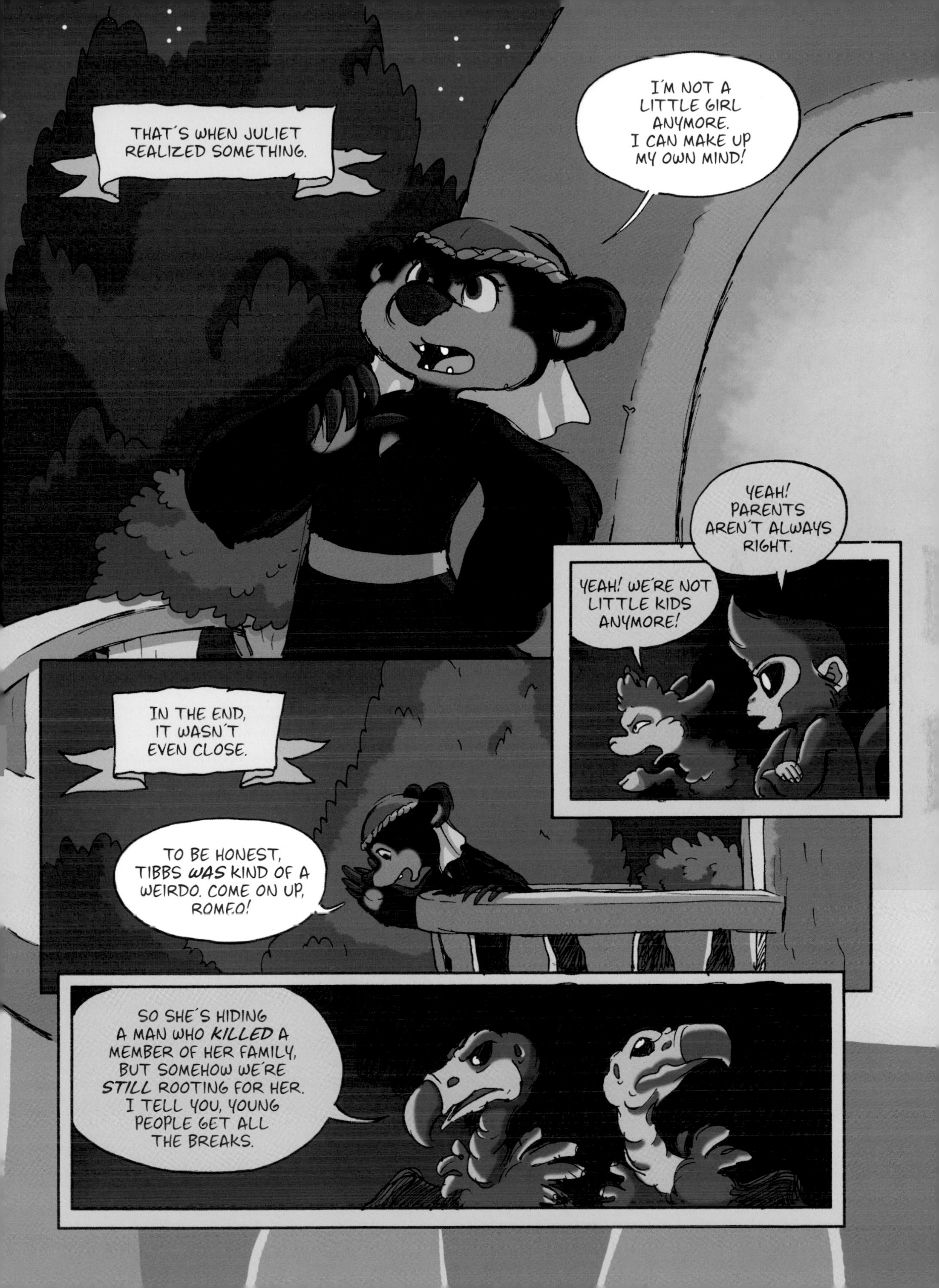

THAT'S WHEN JULIET REALIZED SOMETHING.
I'M NOT A LITTLE GIRL ANYMORE. I CAN MAKE UP MY OWN MIND!
YEAH! PARENTS AREN'T ALWAYS RIGHT.
YEAH! WE'RE NOT LITTLE KIDS ANYMORE!
IN THE END, IT WASN'T EVEN CLOSE.
TO BE HONEST, TIBBS *WAS* KIND OF A WEIRDO. COME ON UP, ROMEO!
SO SHE'S HIDING A MAN WHO *KILLED* A MEMBER OF HER FAMILY, BUT SOMEHOW WE'RE *STILL* ROOTING FOR HER. I TELL YOU, YOUNG PEOPLE GET ALL THE BREAKS.

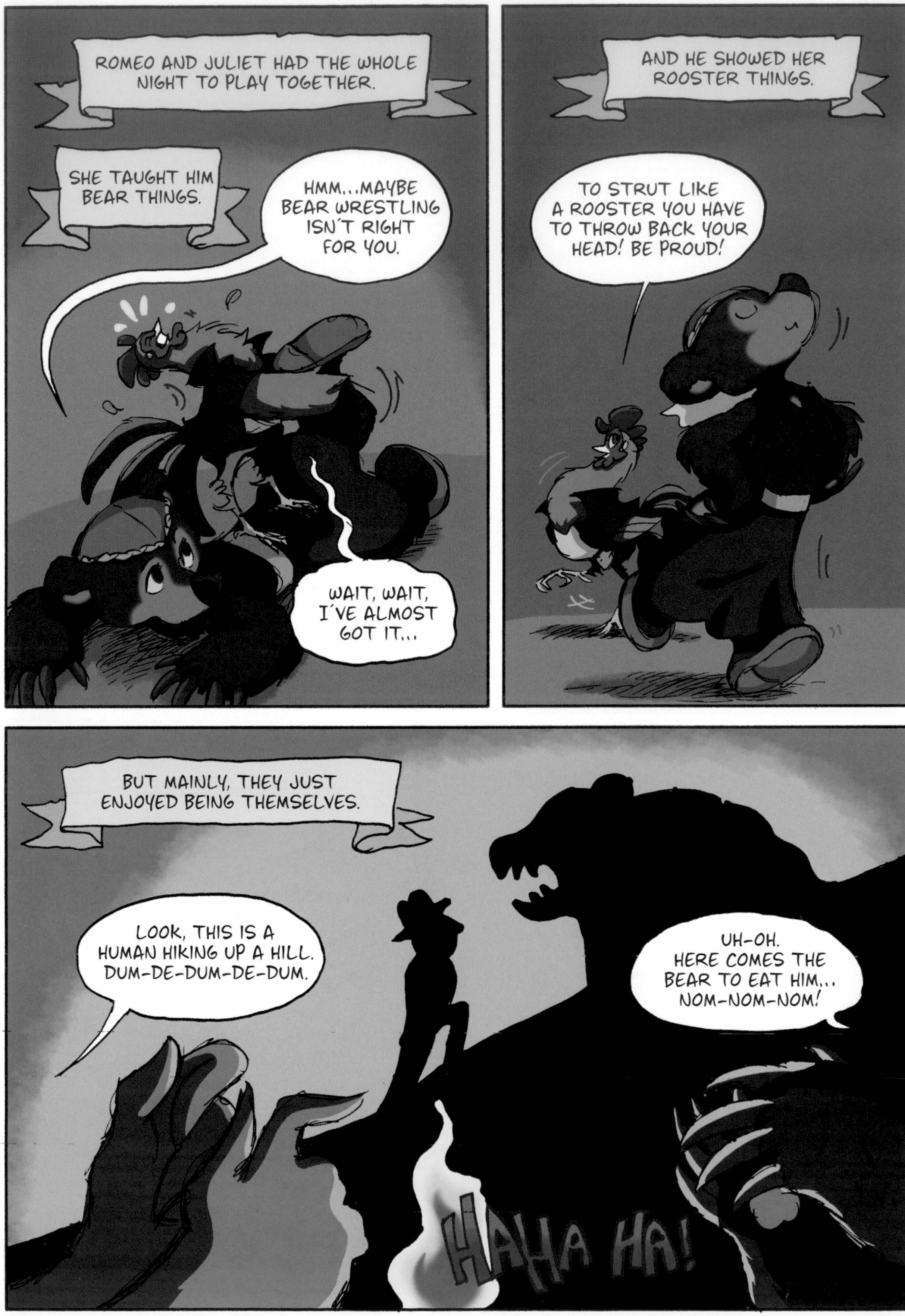
ROMEO AND JULIET HAD THE WHOLE NIGHT TO PLAY TOGETHER.
SHE TAUGHT HIM BEAR THINGS.
HMM...MAYBE BEAR WRESTLING ISN'T RIGHT FOR YOU.
WAIT, WAIT, I'VE ALMOST GOT IT...
AND HE SHOWED HER ROOSTER THINGS.
TO STRUT LIKE A ROOSTER YOU HAVE TO THROW BACK YOUR HEAD! BE PROUD!
BUT MAINLY, THEY JUST ENJOYED BEING THEMSELVES.
LOOK, THIS IS A HUMAN HIKING UP A HILL. DUM-DE-DUM-DE-DUM.
UH-OH. HERE COMES THE BEAR TO EAT HIM... NOM-NOM-NOM!
HAHA HA!

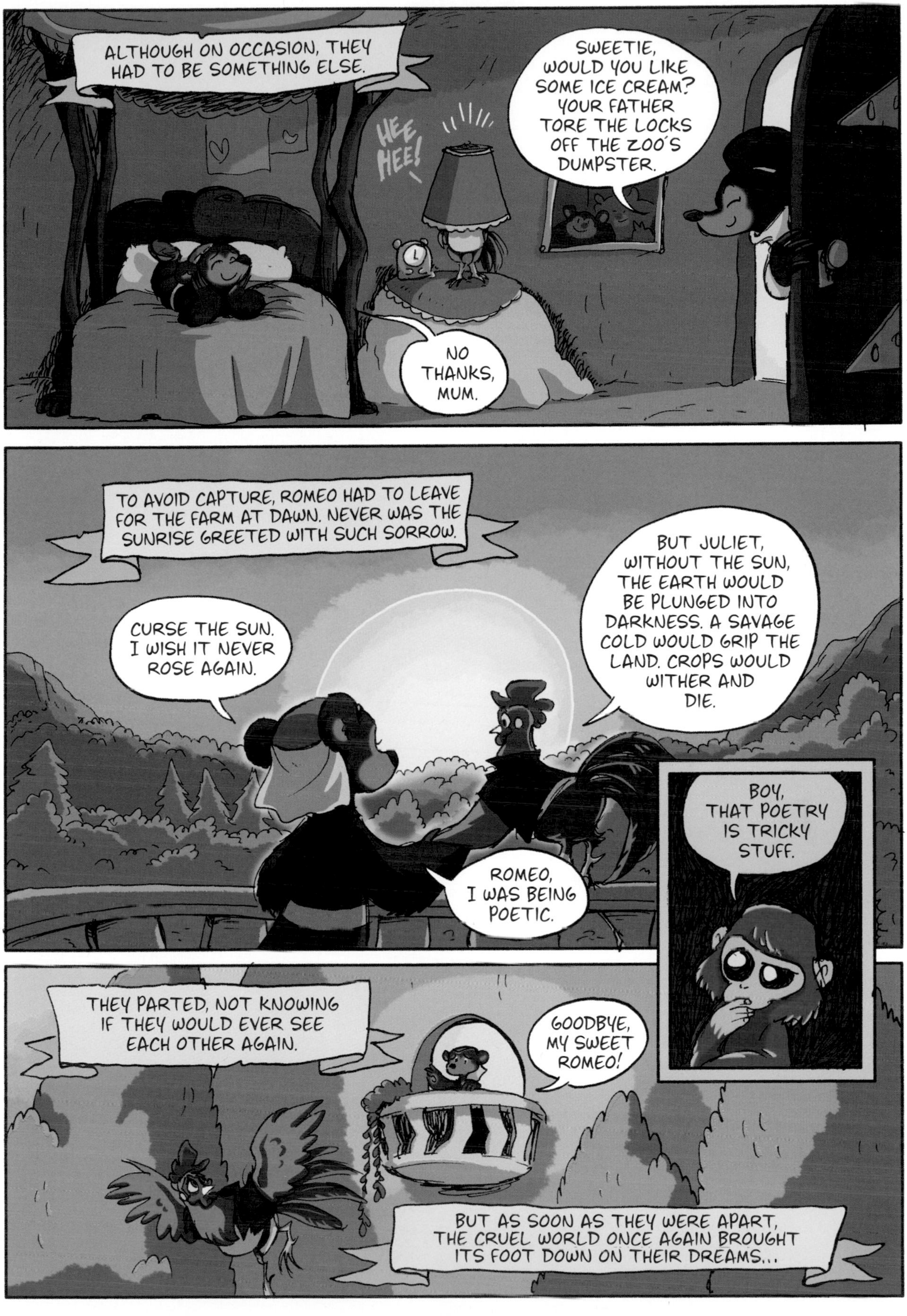

ALTHOUGH ON OCCASION, THEY HAD TO BE SOMETHING ELSE.
HEE HEE!
SWEETIE, WOULD YOU LIKE SOME ICE CREAM? YOUR FATHER TORE THE LOCKS OFF THE ZOO'S DUMPSTER.
NO THANKS, MUM.
TO AVOID CAPTURE, ROMEO HAD TO LEAVE FOR THE FARM AT DAWN. NEVER WAS THE SUNRISE GREETED WITH SUCH SORROW.
CURSE THE SUN. I WISH IT NEVER ROSE AGAIN.
BUT JULIET, WITHOUT THE SUN, THE EARTH WOULD BE PLUNGED INTO DARKNESS. A SAVAGE COLD WOULD GRIP THE LAND. CROPS WOULD WITHER AND DIE.
ROMEO, I WAS BEING POETIC.
BOY, THAT POETRY IS TRICKY STUFF.
THEY PARTED, NOT KNOWING IF THEY WOULD EVER SEE EACH OTHER AGAIN.
GOODBYE, MY SWEET ROMEO!
BUT AS SOON AS THEY WERE APART, THE CRUEL WORLD ONCE AGAIN BROUGHT ITS FOOT DOWN ON THEIR DREAMS...

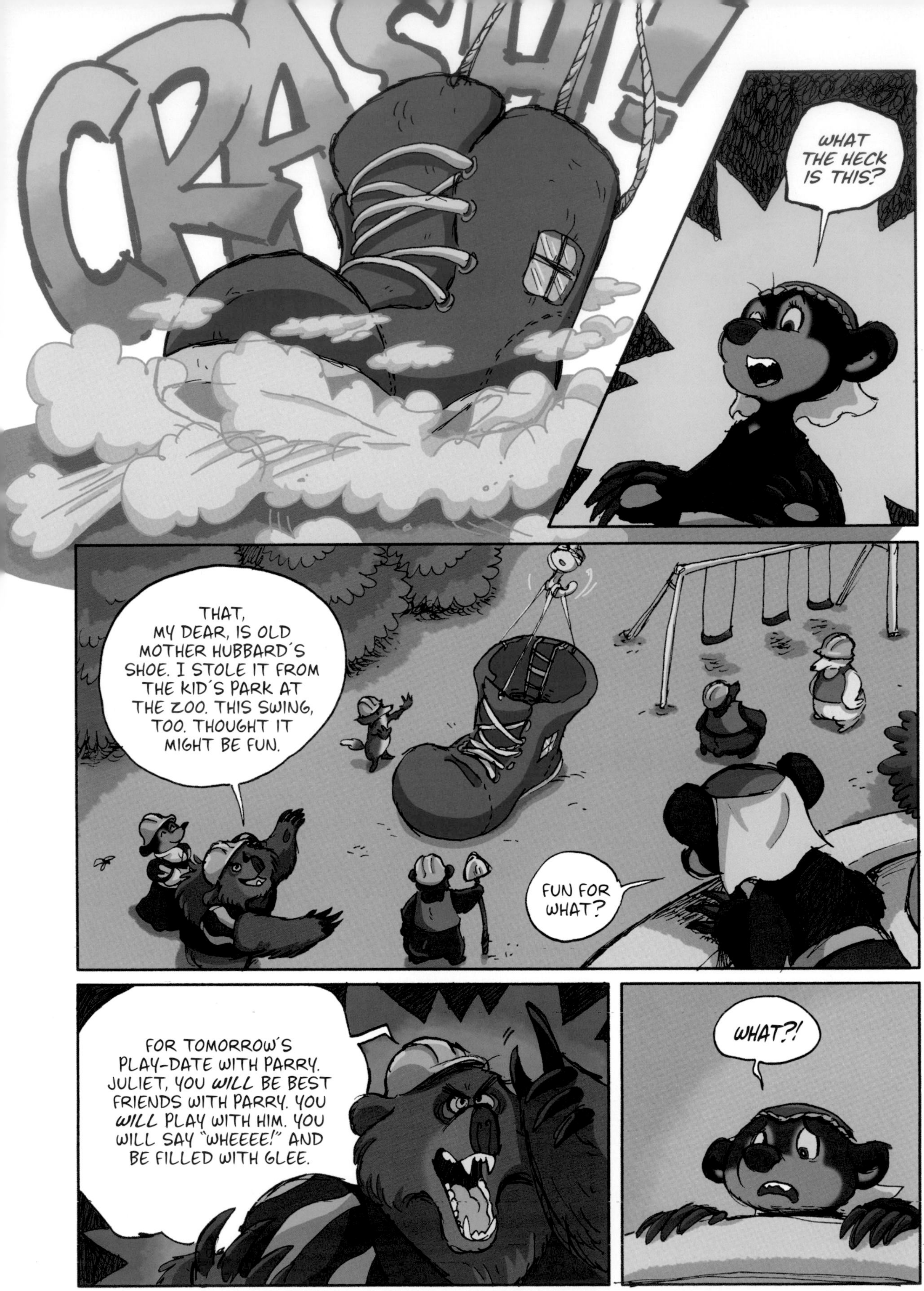
CRASH!
WHAT THE HECK IS THIS?
THAT, MY DEAR, IS OLD MOTHER HUBBARD´S SHOE. I STOLE IT FROM THE KID´S PARK AT THE ZOO. THIS SWING, TOO. THOUGHT IT MIGHT BE FUN.
FUN FOR WHAT?
FOR TOMORROW´S PLAY-DATE WITH PARRY. JULIET, YOU *WILL* BE BEST FRIENDS WITH PARRY. YOU *WILL* PLAY WITH HIM. YOU WILL SAY "WHEEEE!" AND BE FILLED WITH GLEE.
WHAT?!

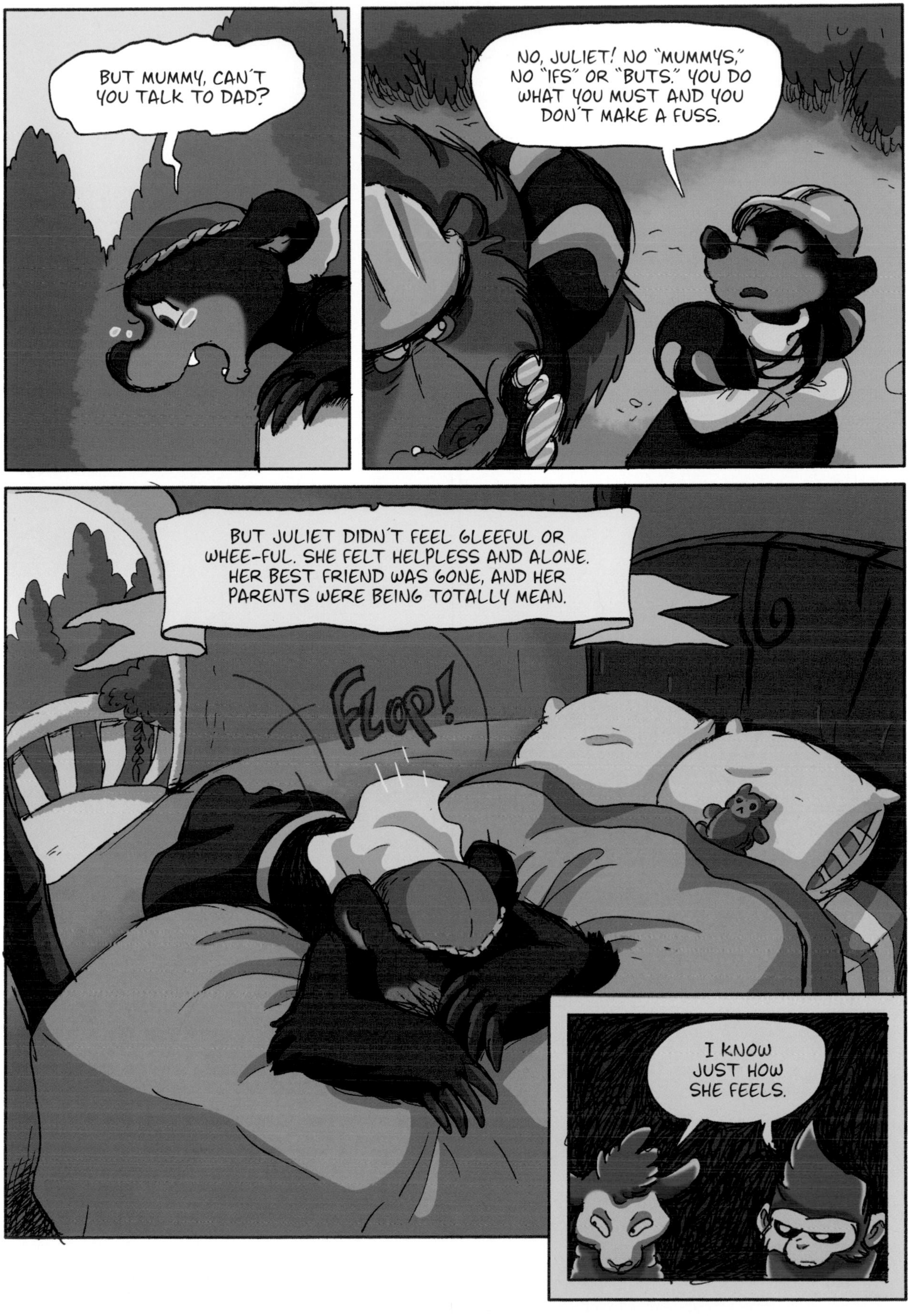
BUT MUMMY, CAN'T YOU TALK TO DAD?
NO, JULIET! NO "MUMMYS," NO "IFS" OR "BUTS." YOU DO WHAT YOU MUST AND YOU DON'T MAKE A FUSS.
BUT JULIET DIDN'T FEEL GLEEFUL OR WHEE-FUL. SHE FELT HELPLESS AND ALONE. HER BEST FRIEND WAS GONE, AND HER PARENTS WERE BEING TOTALLY MEAN.
FLOP!
I KNOW JUST HOW SHE FEELS.

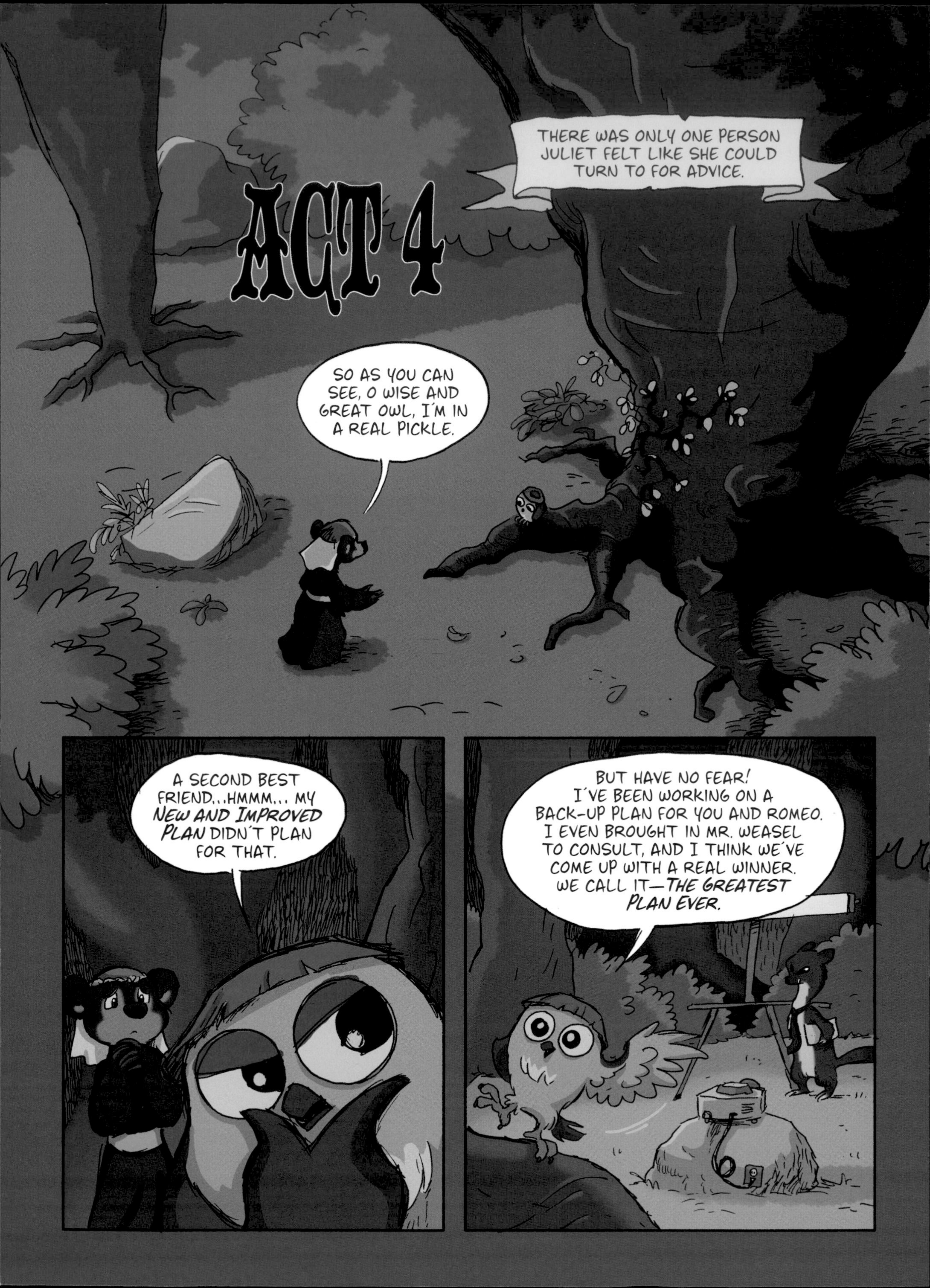
THERE WAS ONLY ONE PERSON JULIET FELT LIKE SHE COULD TURN TO FOR ADVICE.
ACT 4
SO AS YOU CAN SEE, O WISE AND GREAT OWL, I'M IN A REAL PICKLE.
A SECOND BEST FRIEND...HMMM... MY *NEW AND IMPROVED PLAN* DIDN'T PLAN FOR THAT.
BUT HAVE NO FEAR! I'VE BEEN WORKING ON A BACK-UP PLAN FOR YOU AND ROMEO. I EVEN BROUGHT IN MR. WEASEL TO CONSULT, AND I THINK WE'VE COME UP WITH A REAL WINNER. WE CALL IT—*THE GREATEST PLAN EVER.*

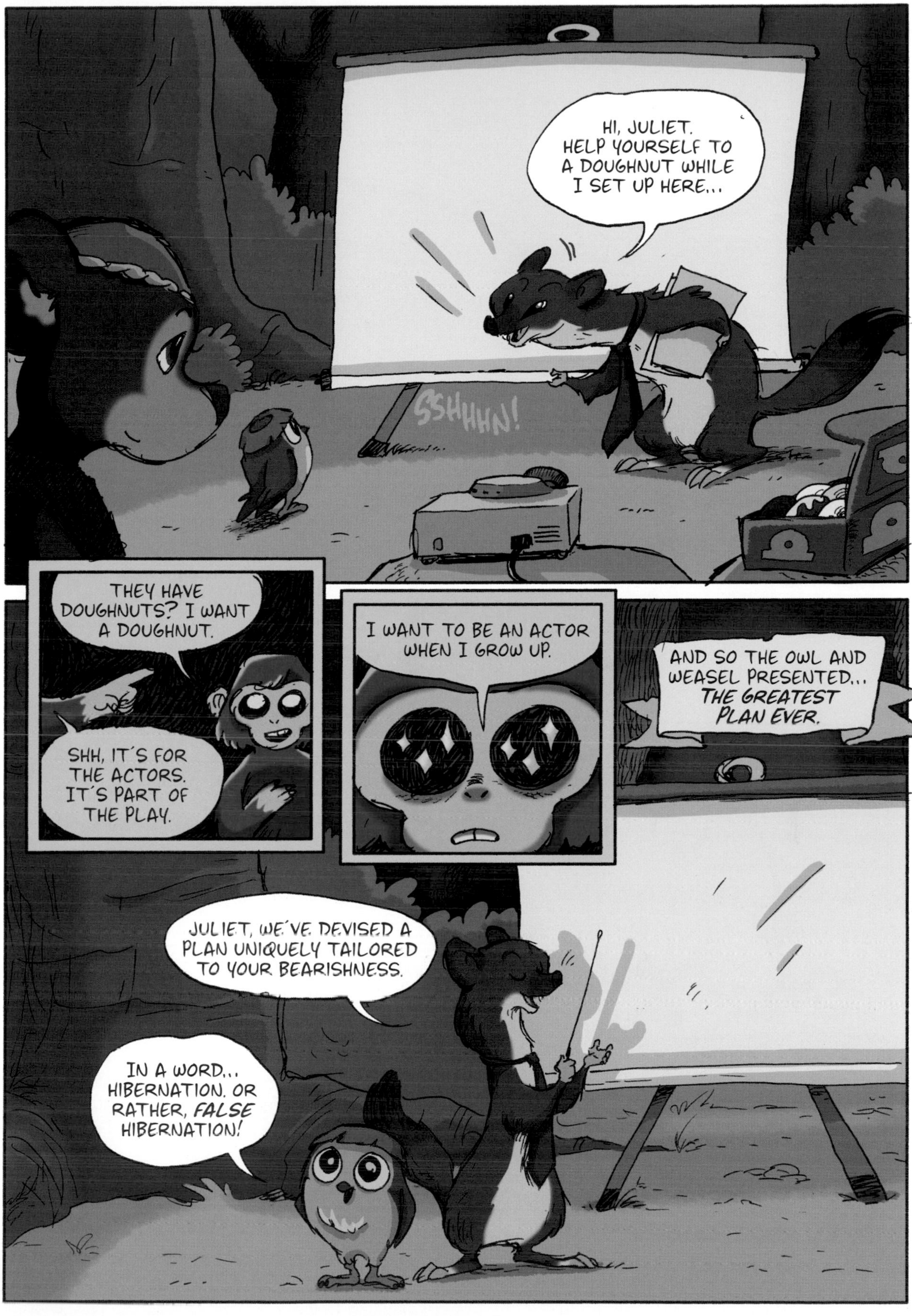

HI, JULIET. HELP YOURSELF TO A DOUGHNUT WHILE I SET UP HERE...
SSHHHN!
THEY HAVE DOUGHNUTS? I WANT A DOUGHNUT.
SHH, IT´S FOR THE ACTORS. IT´S PART OF THE PLAY.
I WANT TO BE AN ACTOR WHEN I GROW UP.
AND SO THE OWL AND WEASEL PRESENTED... *THE GREATEST PLAN EVER.*
JULIET, WE´VE DEVISED A PLAN UNIQUELY TAILORED TO YOUR BEARISHNESS.
IN A WORD... HIBERNATION. OR RATHER, *FALSE* HIBERNATION!

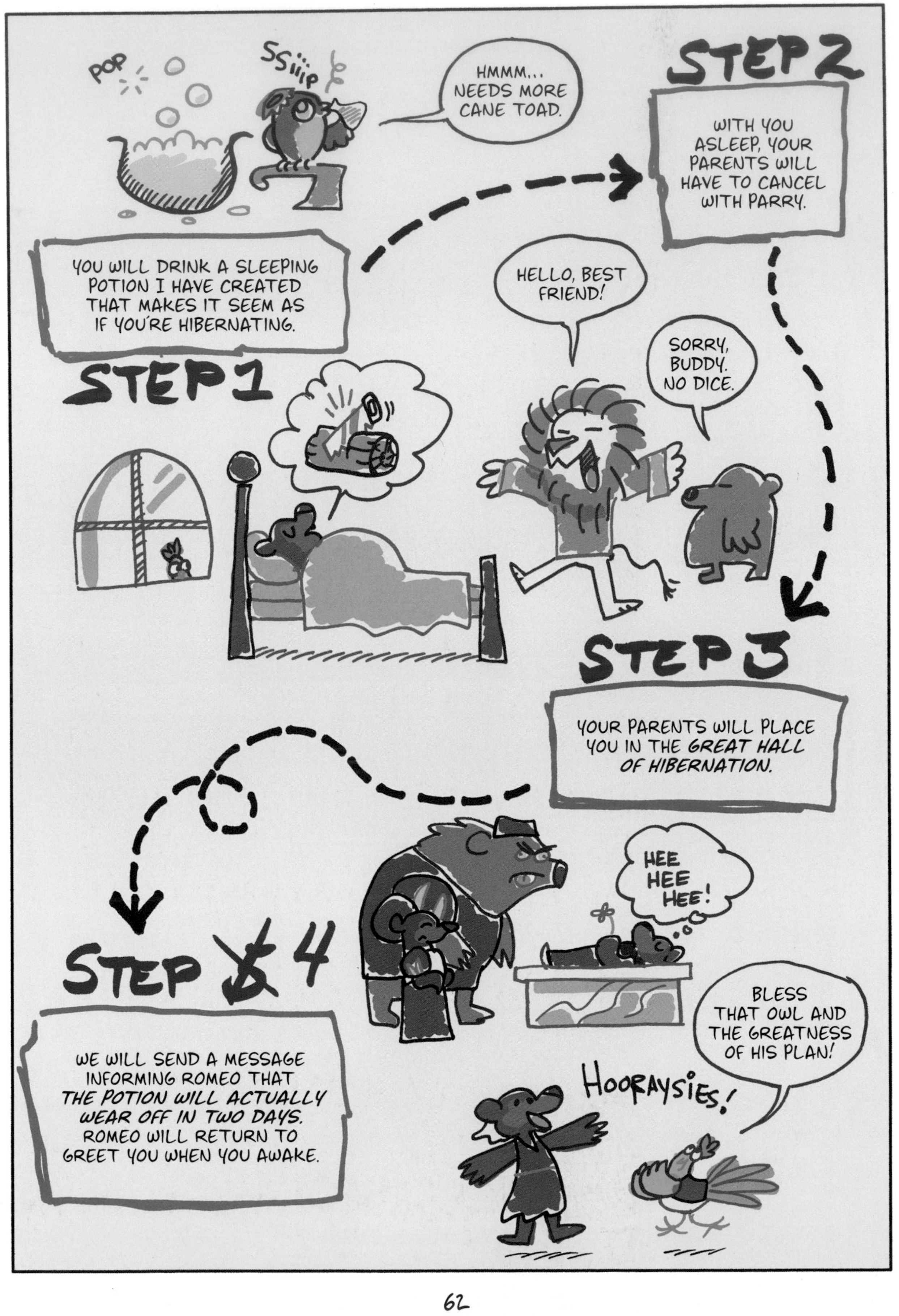
POP
SSiiip
HMMM... NEEDS MORE CANE TOAD.
YOU WILL DRINK A SLEEPING POTION I HAVE CREATED THAT MAKES IT SEEM AS IF YOU'RE HIBERNATING.
STEP 1
STEP 2
WITH YOU ASLEEP, YOUR PARENTS WILL HAVE TO CANCEL WITH PARRY.
HELLO, BEST FRIEND!
SORRY, BUDDY. NO DICE.
STEP 3
YOUR PARENTS WILL PLACE YOU IN THE *GREAT HALL OF HIBERNATION.*
HEE HEE HEE!
STEP 5 4
WE WILL SEND A MESSAGE INFORMING ROMEO THAT *THE POTION WILL ACTUALLY WEAR OFF IN TWO DAYS.* ROMEO WILL RETURN TO GREET YOU WHEN YOU AWAKE.
BLESS THAT OWL AND THE GREATNESS OF HIS PLAN!
HOORAYSIES!

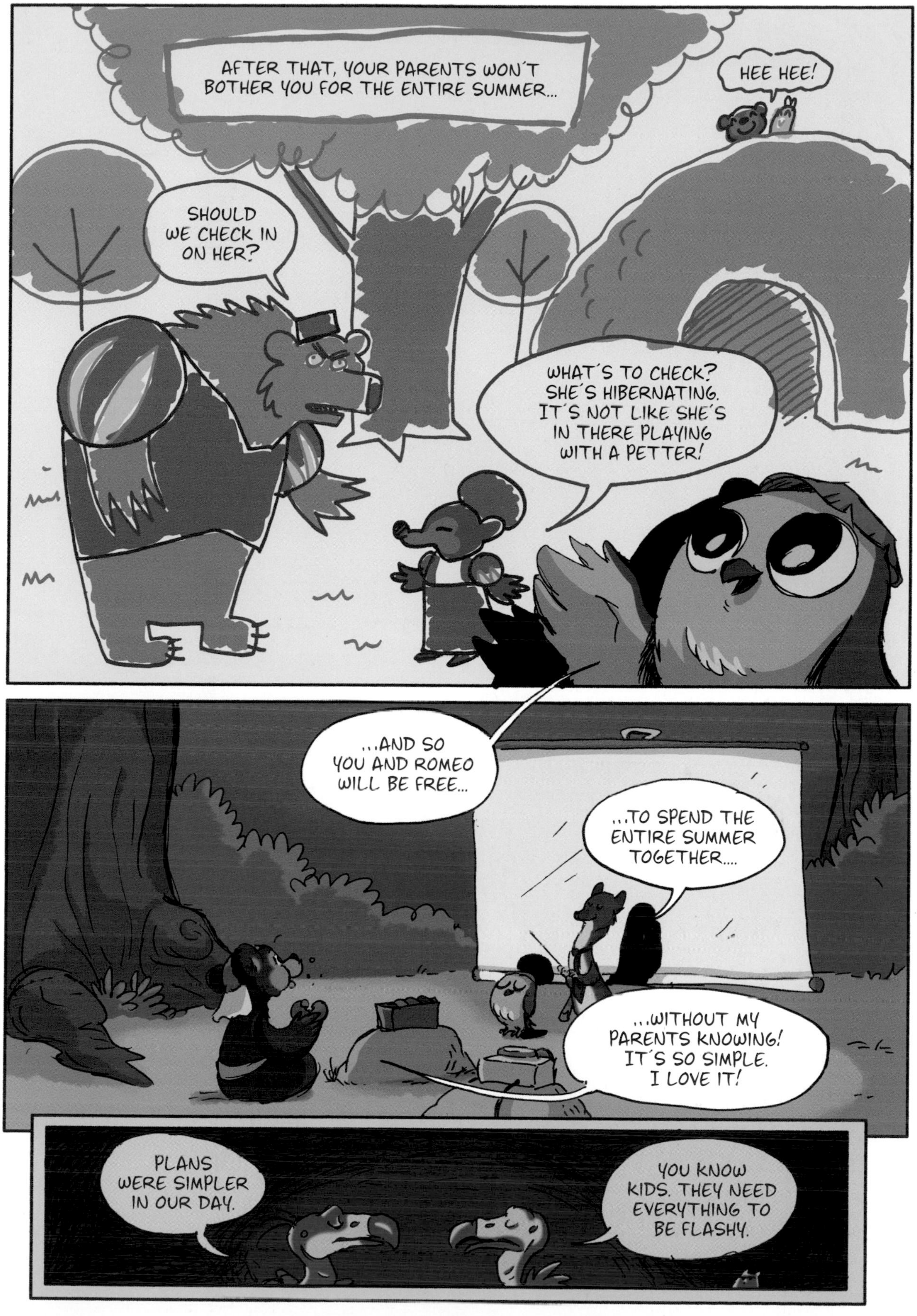
AFTER THAT, YOUR PARENTS WON'T BOTHER YOU FOR THE ENTIRE SUMMER...
HEE HEE!
SHOULD WE CHECK IN ON HER?
WHAT'S TO CHECK? SHE'S HIBERNATING. IT'S NOT LIKE SHE'S IN THERE PLAYING WITH A PETTER!
...AND SO YOU AND ROMEO WILL BE FREE...
...TO SPEND THE ENTIRE SUMMER TOGETHER....
...WITHOUT MY PARENTS KNOWING! IT'S SO SIMPLE. I LOVE IT!
PLANS WERE SIMPLER IN OUR DAY.
YOU KNOW KIDS. THEY NEED EVERYTHING TO BE FLASHY.

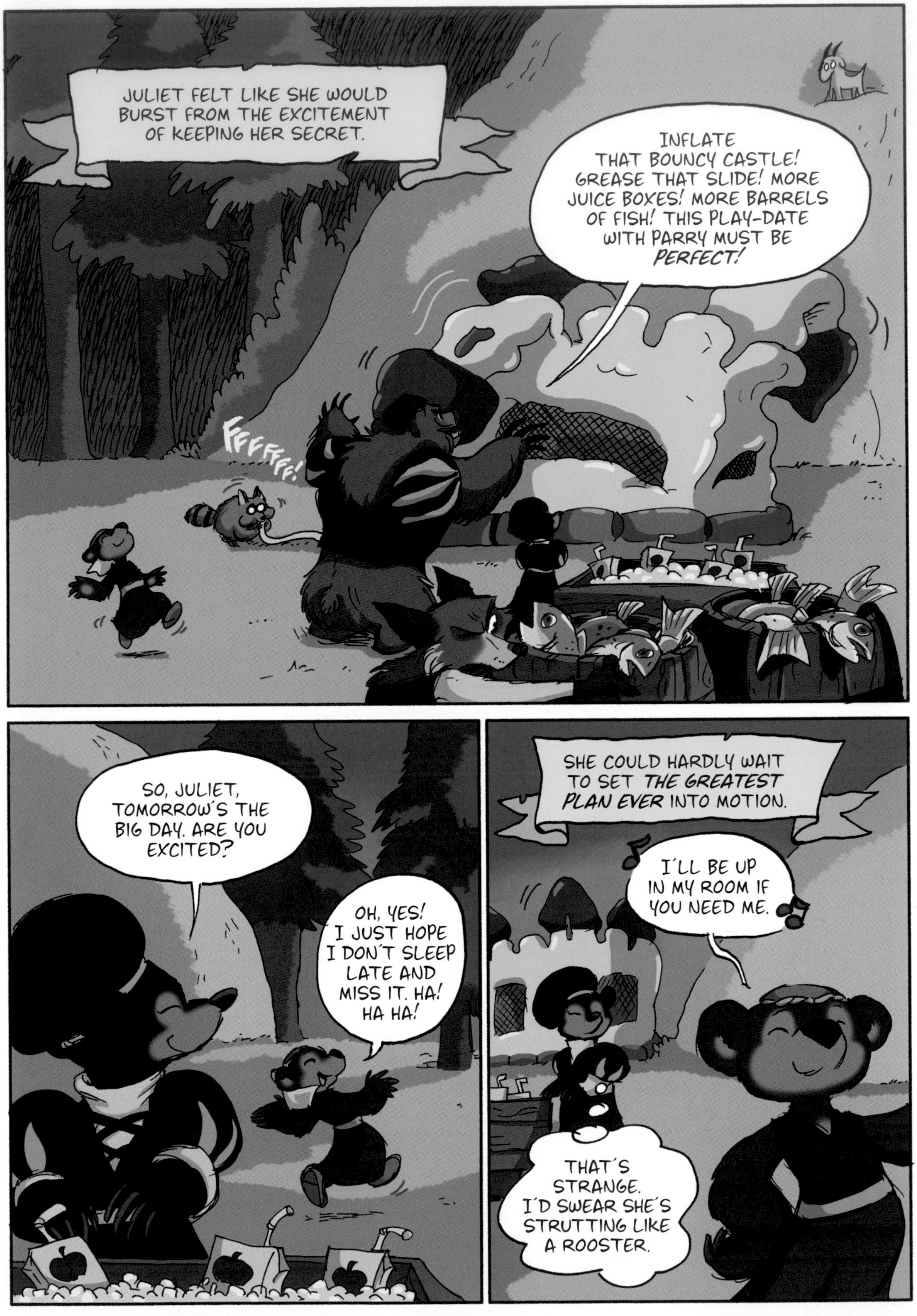
JULIET FELT LIKE SHE WOULD BURST FROM THE EXCITEMENT OF KEEPING HER SECRET.
INFLATE THAT BOUNCY CASTLE! GREASE THAT SLIDE! MORE JUICE BOXES! MORE BARRELS OF FISH! THIS PLAY-DATE WITH PARRY MUST BE *PERFECT!*
FFFFFFF!
SO, JULIET, TOMORROW'S THE BIG DAY. ARE YOU EXCITED?
OH, YES! I JUST HOPE I DON'T SLEEP LATE AND MISS IT. HA! HA HA!
SHE COULD HARDLY WAIT TO SET ***THE GREATEST PLAN EVER*** INTO MOTION.
I'LL BE UP IN MY ROOM IF YOU NEED ME.
THAT'S STRANGE. I'D SWEAR SHE'S STRUTTING LIKE A ROOSTER.

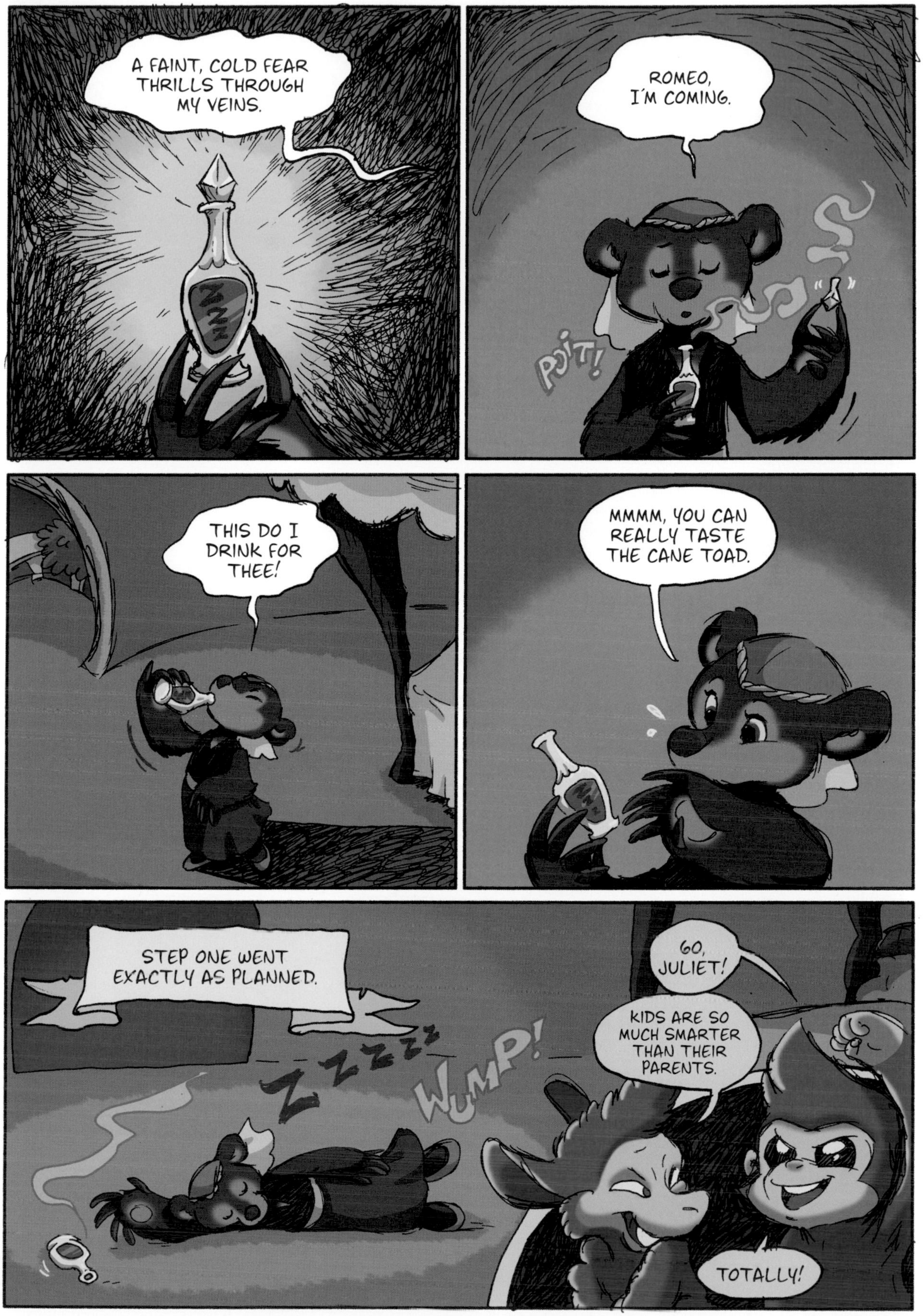
A FAINT, COLD FEAR THRILLS THROUGH MY VEINS.
ROMEO, I'M COMING.
POIT!
THIS DO I DRINK FOR THEE!
MMMM, YOU CAN REALLY TASTE THE CANE TOAD.
STEP ONE WENT EXACTLY AS PLANNED.
ZZZZZ
WUMP!
GO, JULIET!
KIDS ARE SO MUCH SMARTER THAN THEIR PARENTS.
TOTALLY!

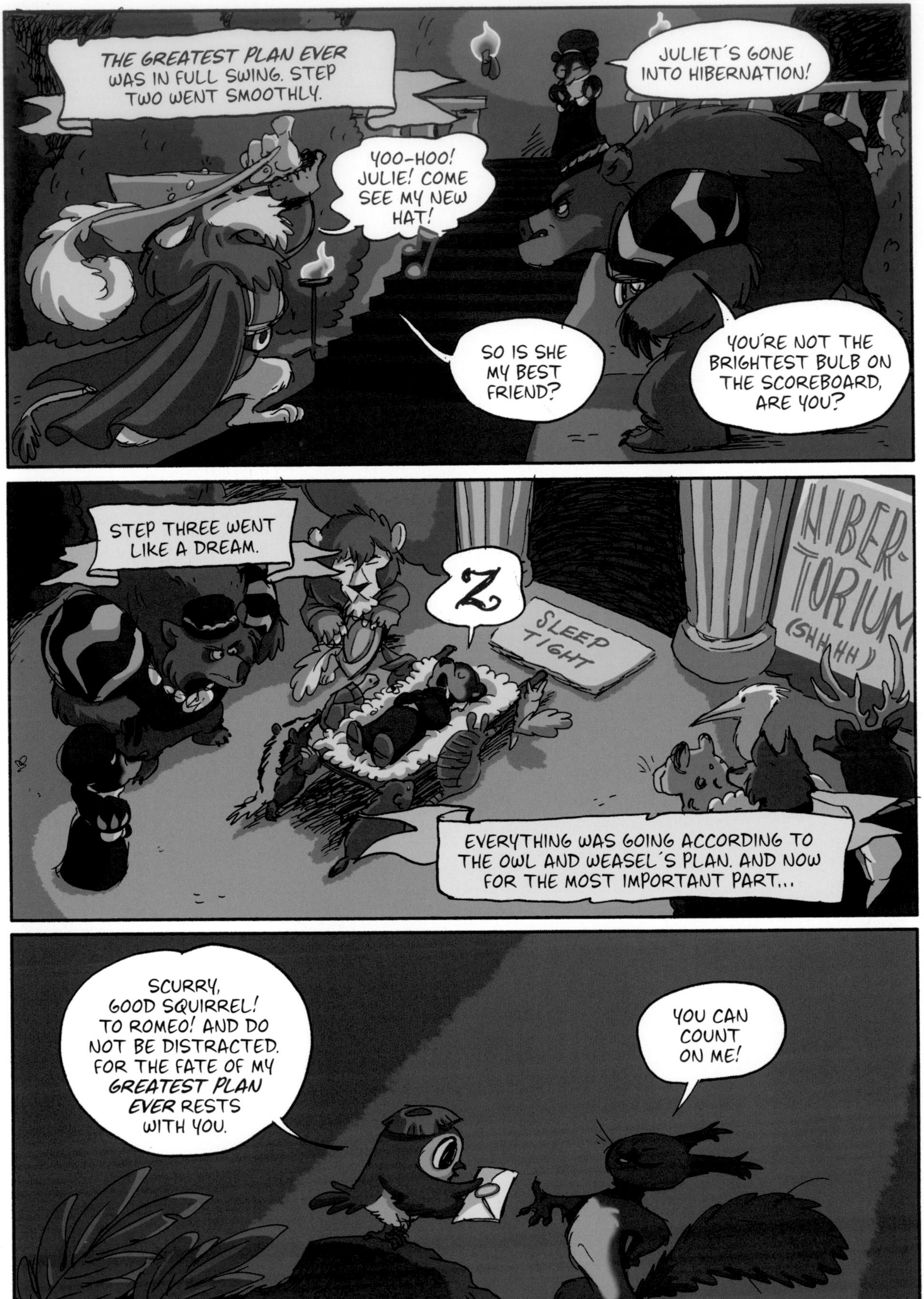
THE GREATEST PLAN EVER WAS IN FULL SWING. STEP TWO WENT SMOOTHLY.
JULIET'S GONE INTO HIBERNATION!
YOO-HOO! JULIE! COME SEE MY NEW HAT!
SO IS SHE MY BEST FRIEND?
YOU'RE NOT THE BRIGHTEST BULB ON THE SCOREBOARD, ARE YOU?
STEP THREE WENT LIKE A DREAM.
Z
SLEEP TIGHT
HIBER-TORIUM (SHHHHH)
EVERYTHING WAS GOING ACCORDING TO THE OWL AND WEASEL'S PLAN. AND NOW FOR THE MOST IMPORTANT PART...
SCURRY, GOOD SQUIRREL! TO ROMEO! AND DO NOT BE DISTRACTED. FOR THE FATE OF MY GREATEST PLAN EVER RESTS WITH YOU.
YOU CAN COUNT ON ME!

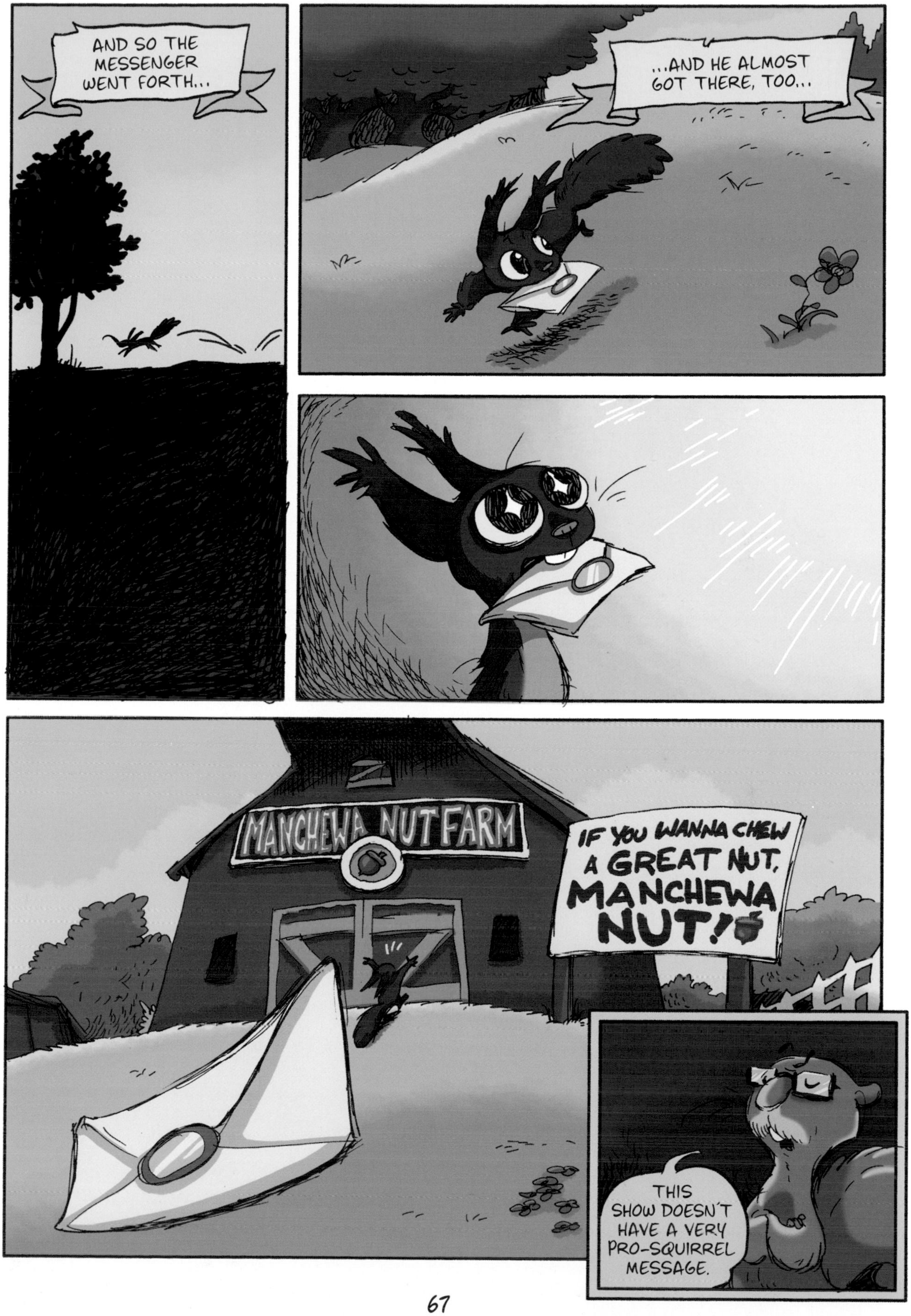
AND SO THE MESSENGER WENT FORTH...
...AND HE ALMOST GOT THERE, TOO...
MANCHEWA NUT FARM
IF YOU WANNA CHEW A GREAT NUT, MANCHEWA NUT!
THIS SHOW DOESN'T HAVE A VERY PRO-SQUIRREL MESSAGE.

ACT 5

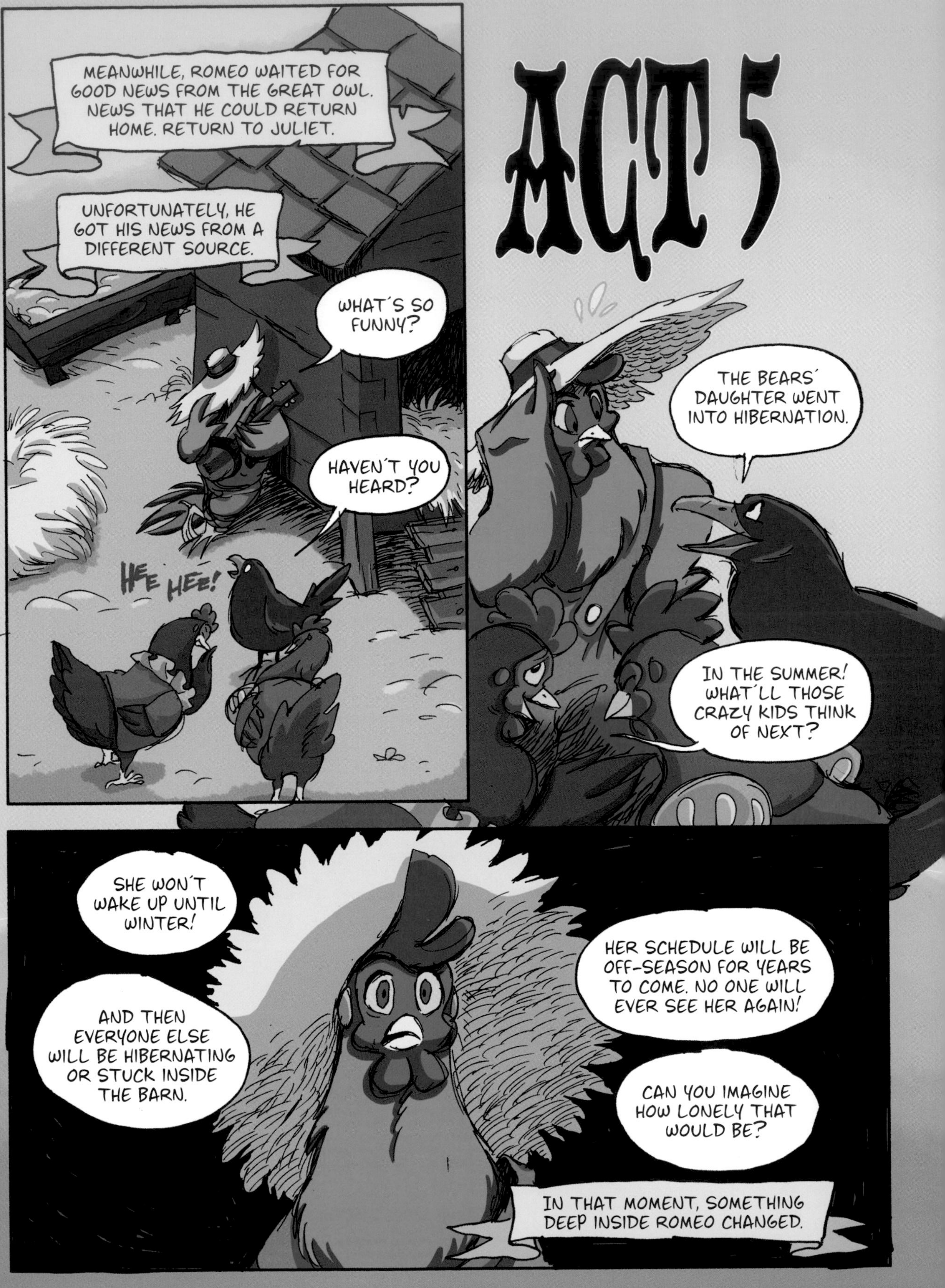
MEANWHILE, ROMEO WAITED FOR GOOD NEWS FROM THE GREAT OWL. NEWS THAT HE COULD RETURN HOME. RETURN TO JULIET.
UNFORTUNATELY, HE GOT HIS NEWS FROM A DIFFERENT SOURCE.
WHAT'S SO FUNNY?
HAVEN'T YOU HEARD?
HEE HEE!
THE BEARS' DAUGHTER WENT INTO HIBERNATION.
IN THE SUMMER! WHAT'LL THOSE CRAZY KIDS THINK OF NEXT?
SHE WON'T WAKE UP UNTIL WINTER!
AND THEN EVERYONE ELSE WILL BE HIBERNATING OR STUCK INSIDE THE BARN.
HER SCHEDULE WILL BE OFF-SEASON FOR YEARS TO COME. NO ONE WILL EVER SEE HER AGAIN!
CAN YOU IMAGINE HOW LONELY THAT WOULD BE?
IN THAT MOMENT, SOMETHING DEEP INSIDE ROMEO CHANGED.

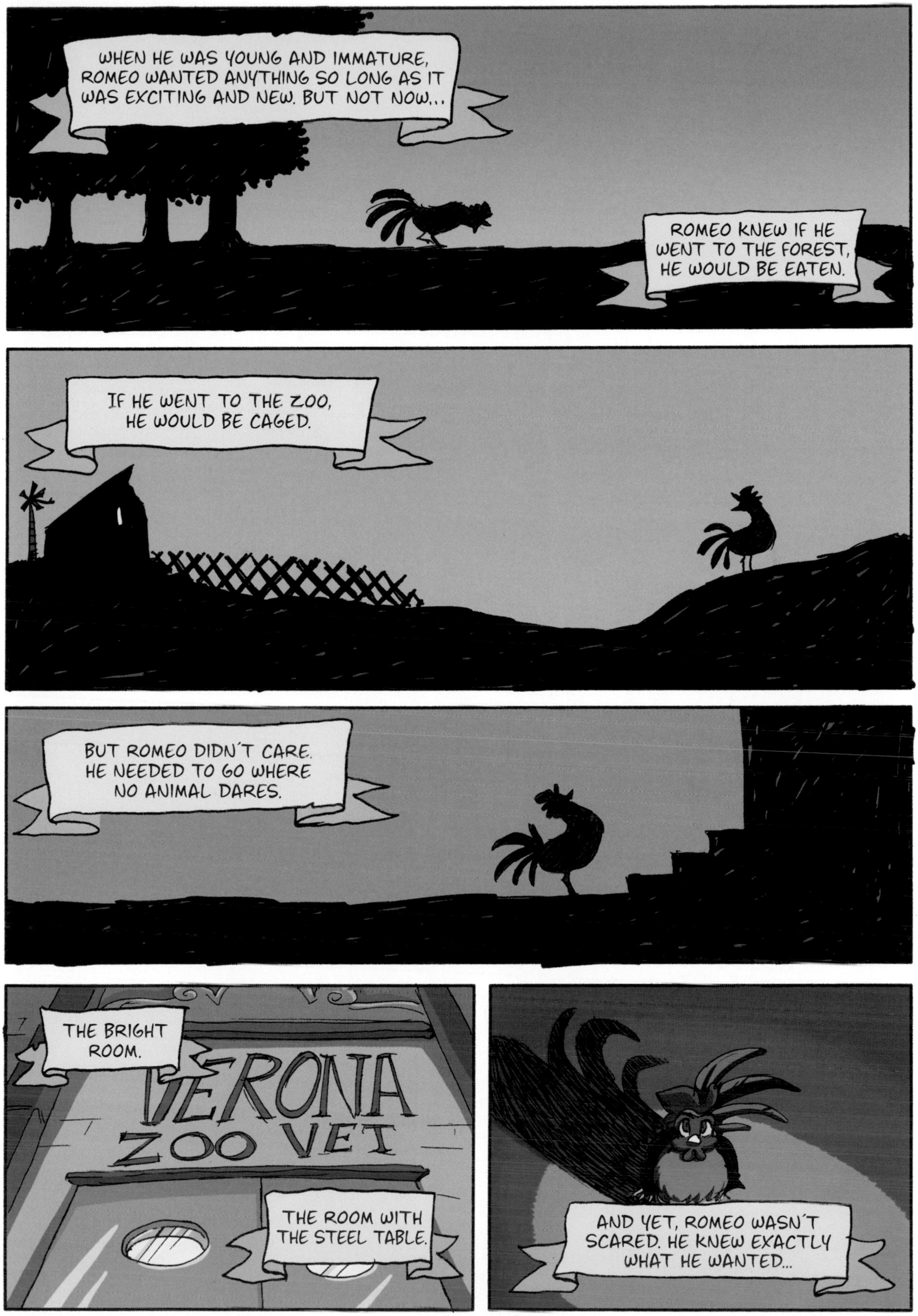
WHEN HE WAS YOUNG AND IMMATURE, ROMEO WANTED ANYTHING SO LONG AS IT WAS EXCITING AND NEW. BUT NOT NOW...
ROMEO KNEW IF HE WENT TO THE FOREST, HE WOULD BE EATEN.
IF HE WENT TO THE ZOO, HE WOULD BE CAGED.
BUT ROMEO DIDN´T CARE. HE NEEDED TO GO WHERE NO ANIMAL DARES.
THE BRIGHT ROOM.
VERONA ZOO VET
THE ROOM WITH THE STEEL TABLE.
AND YET, ROMEO WASN´T SCARED. HE KNEW EXACTLY WHAT HE WANTED...

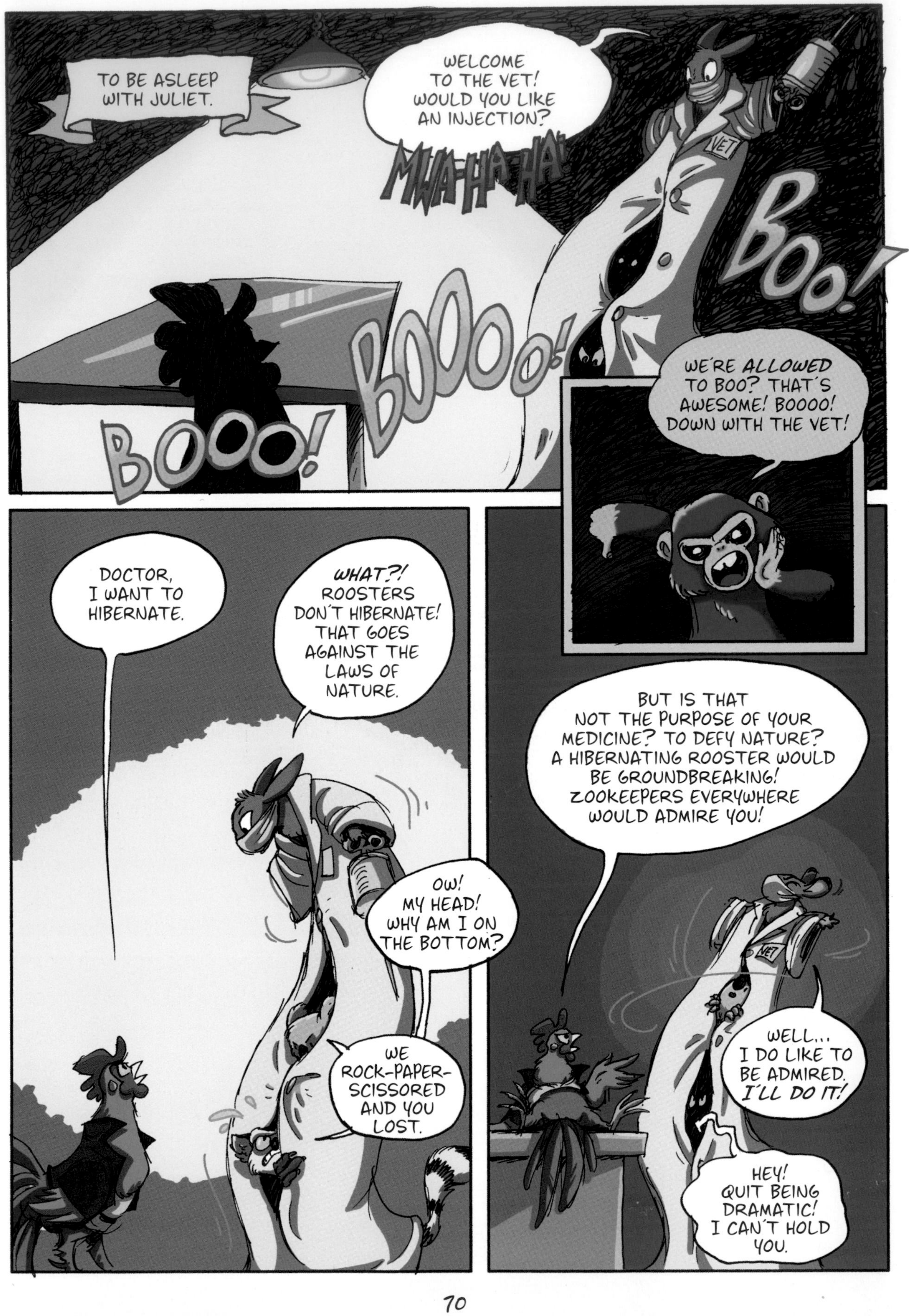
TO BE ASLEEP WITH JULIET.
WELCOME TO THE VET! WOULD YOU LIKE AN INJECTION?
MWA-HA-HA!
BOO!
BOOOOO!
BOOO!
WE'RE *ALLOWED* TO BOO? THAT'S AWESOME! BOOOO! DOWN WITH THE VET!
DOCTOR, I WANT TO HIBERNATE.
WHAT?! ROOSTERS DON'T HIBERNATE! THAT GOES AGAINST THE LAWS OF NATURE.
OW! MY HEAD! WHY AM I ON THE BOTTOM?
WE ROCK-PAPER-SCISSORED AND YOU LOST.
BUT IS THAT NOT THE PURPOSE OF YOUR MEDICINE? TO DEFY NATURE? A HIBERNATING ROOSTER WOULD BE GROUNDBREAKING! ZOOKEEPERS EVERYWHERE WOULD ADMIRE YOU!
WELL... I DO LIKE TO BE ADMIRED. *I'LL DO IT!*
HEY! QUIT BEING DRAMATIC! I CAN'T HOLD YOU.

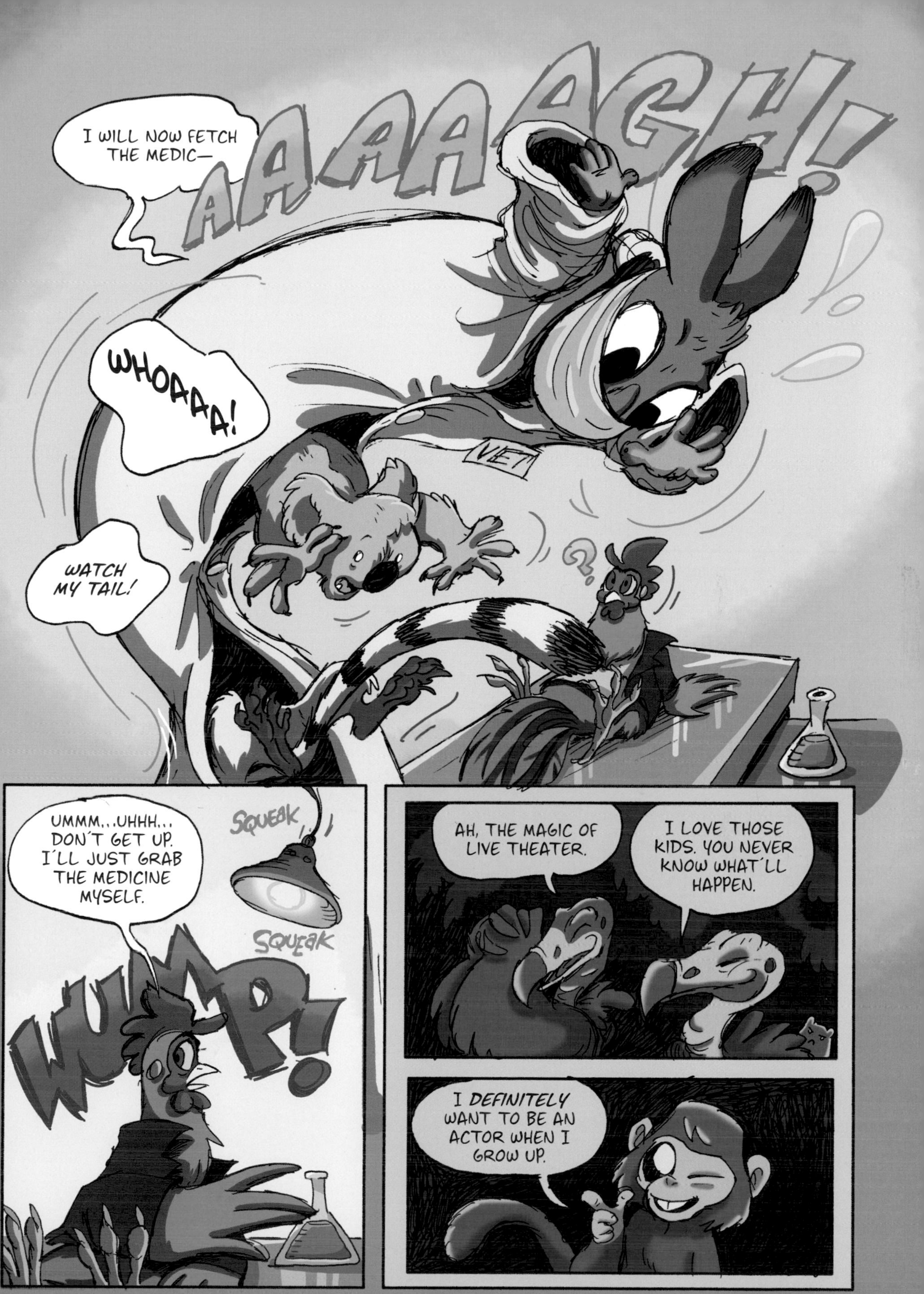
I WILL NOW FETCH THE MEDIC—
AAAAAGH!
WHOAAAA!
VET
WATCH MY TAIL!
UMMM...UHHH... DON'T GET UP. I'LL JUST GRAB THE MEDICINE MYSELF.
SQUEAK
SQUEAK
WUMP!
AH, THE MAGIC OF LIVE THEATER.
I LOVE THOSE KIDS. YOU NEVER KNOW WHAT'LL HAPPEN.
I *DEFINITELY* WANT TO BE AN ACTOR WHEN I GROW UP.

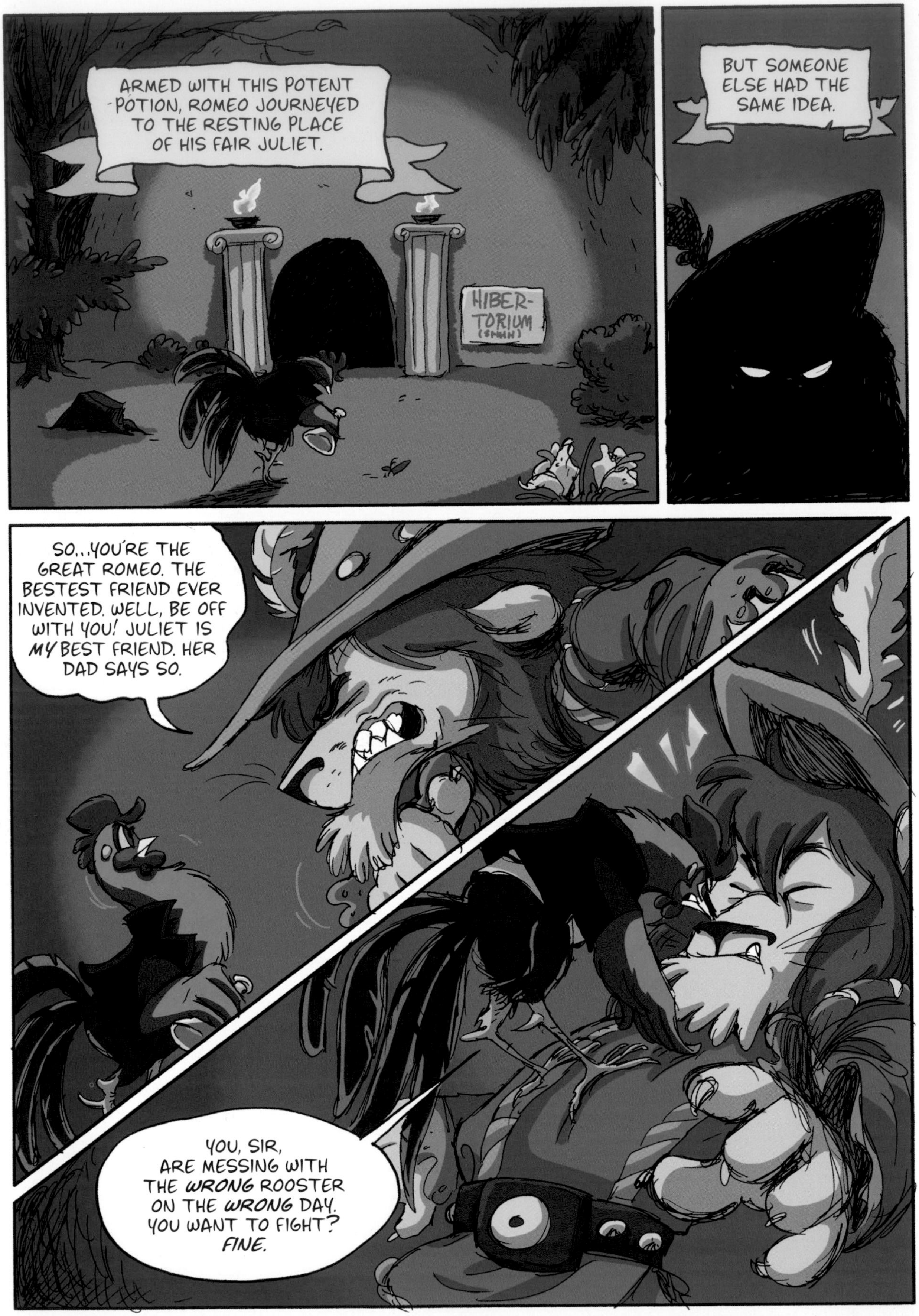

ARMED WITH THIS POTENT POTION, ROMEO JOURNEYED TO THE RESTING PLACE OF HIS FAIR JULIET.
HIBER-TORIUM
BUT SOMEONE ELSE HAD THE SAME IDEA.
SO...YOU'RE THE GREAT ROMEO. THE BESTEST FRIEND EVER INVENTED. WELL, BE OFF WITH YOU! JULIET IS *MY* BEST FRIEND. HER DAD SAYS SO.
YOU, SIR, ARE MESSING WITH THE *WRONG* ROOSTER ON THE *WRONG* DAY. YOU WANT TO FIGHT? *FINE.*

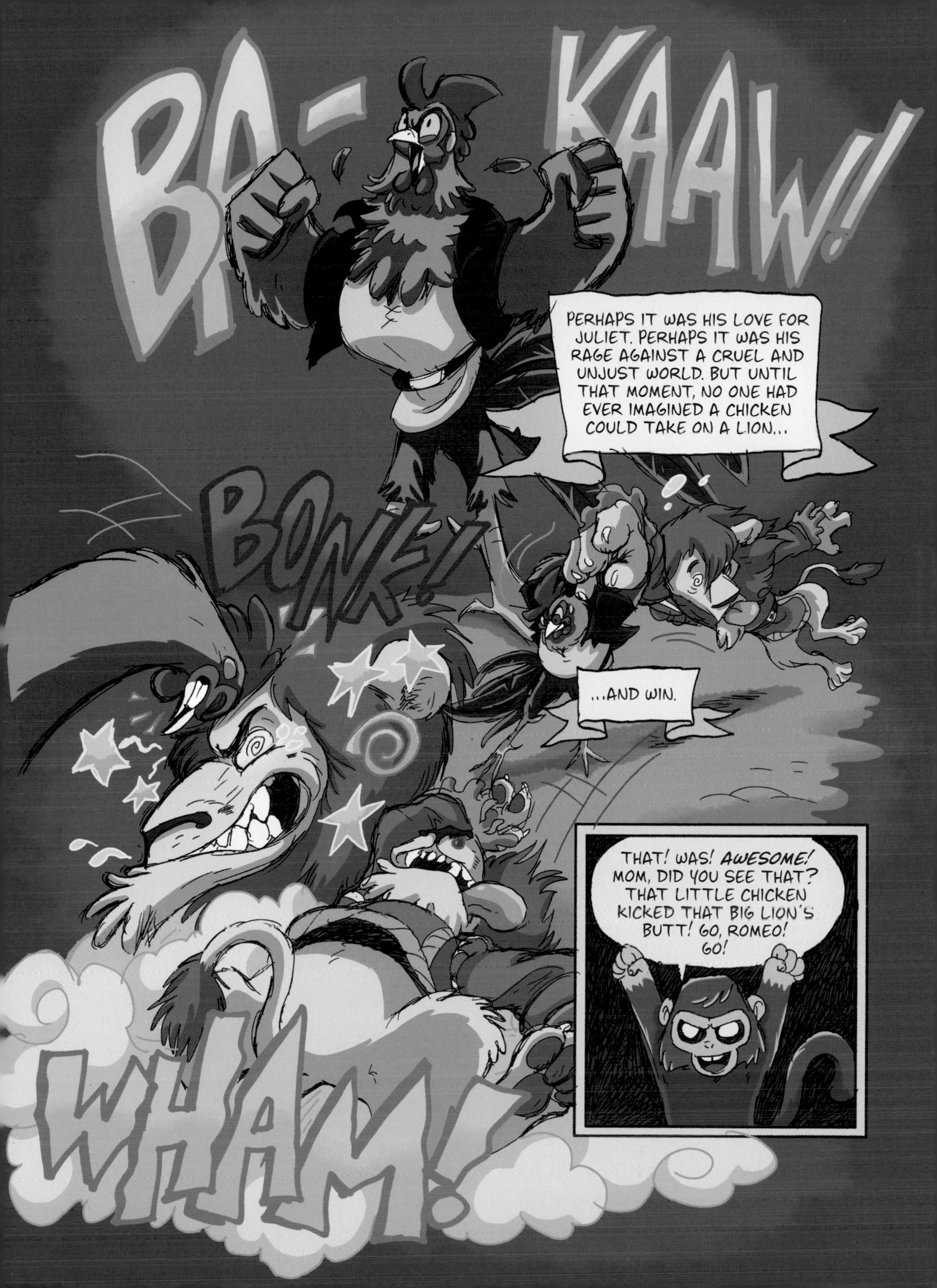
BA-KAAW!
PERHAPS IT WAS HIS LOVE FOR JULIET. PERHAPS IT WAS HIS RAGE AGAINST A CRUEL AND UNJUST WORLD. BUT UNTIL THAT MOMENT, NO ONE HAD EVER IMAGINED A CHICKEN COULD TAKE ON A LION...
BONK!
...AND WIN.
WHAM!
THAT! WAS! *AWESOME!* MOM, DID YOU SEE THAT? THAT LITTLE CHICKEN KICKED THAT BIG LION'S BUTT! GO, ROMEO! GO!

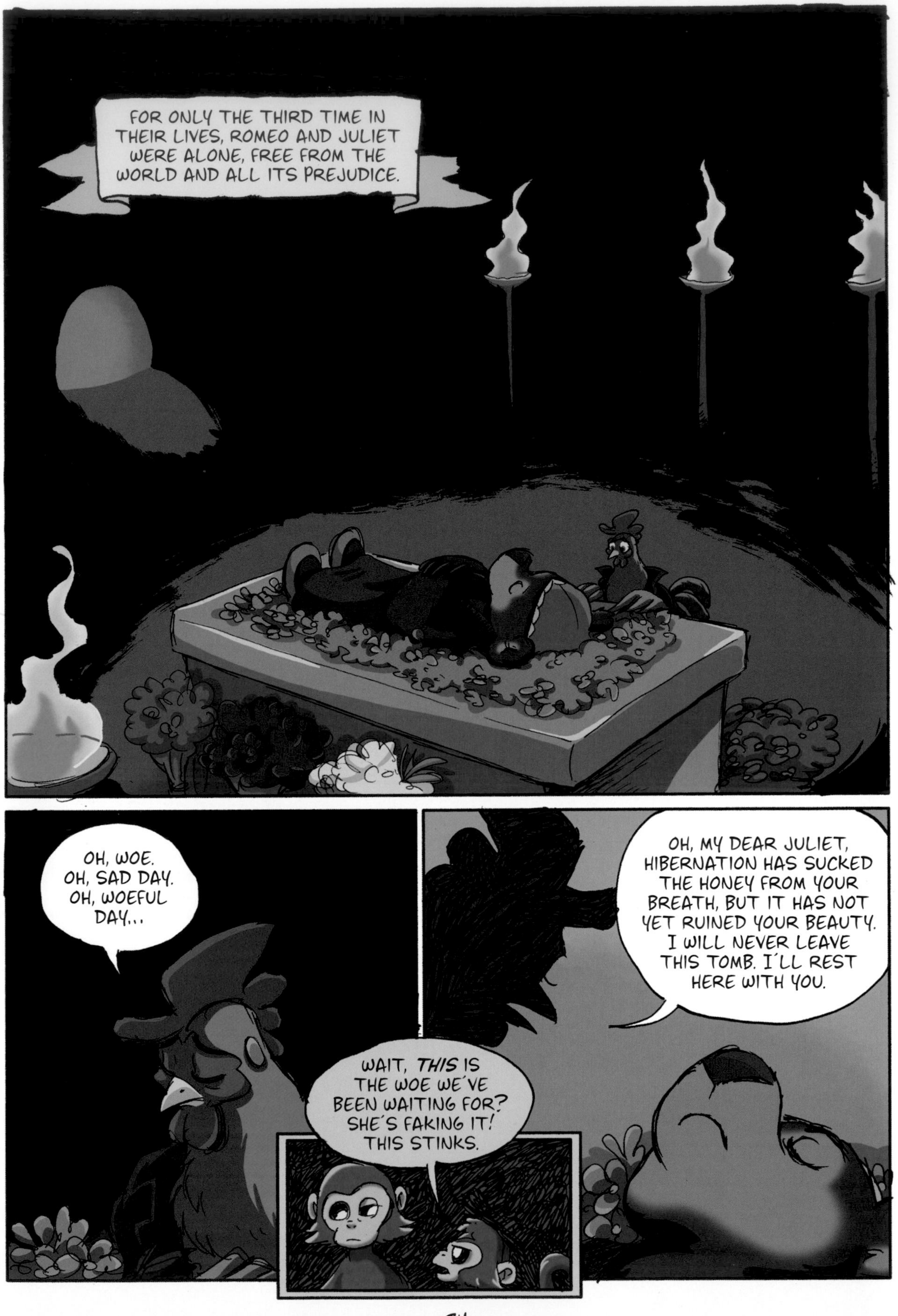
FOR ONLY THE THIRD TIME IN THEIR LIVES, ROMEO AND JULIET WERE ALONE, FREE FROM THE WORLD AND ALL ITS PREJUDICE.
OH, WOE. OH, SAD DAY. OH, WOEFUL DAY...
OH, MY DEAR JULIET, HIBERNATION HAS SUCKED THE HONEY FROM YOUR BREATH, BUT IT HAS NOT YET RUINED YOUR BEAUTY. I WILL NEVER LEAVE THIS TOMB. I´LL REST HERE WITH YOU.
WAIT, *THIS* IS THE WOE WE´VE BEEN WAITING FOR? SHE´S FAKING IT! THIS STINKS.

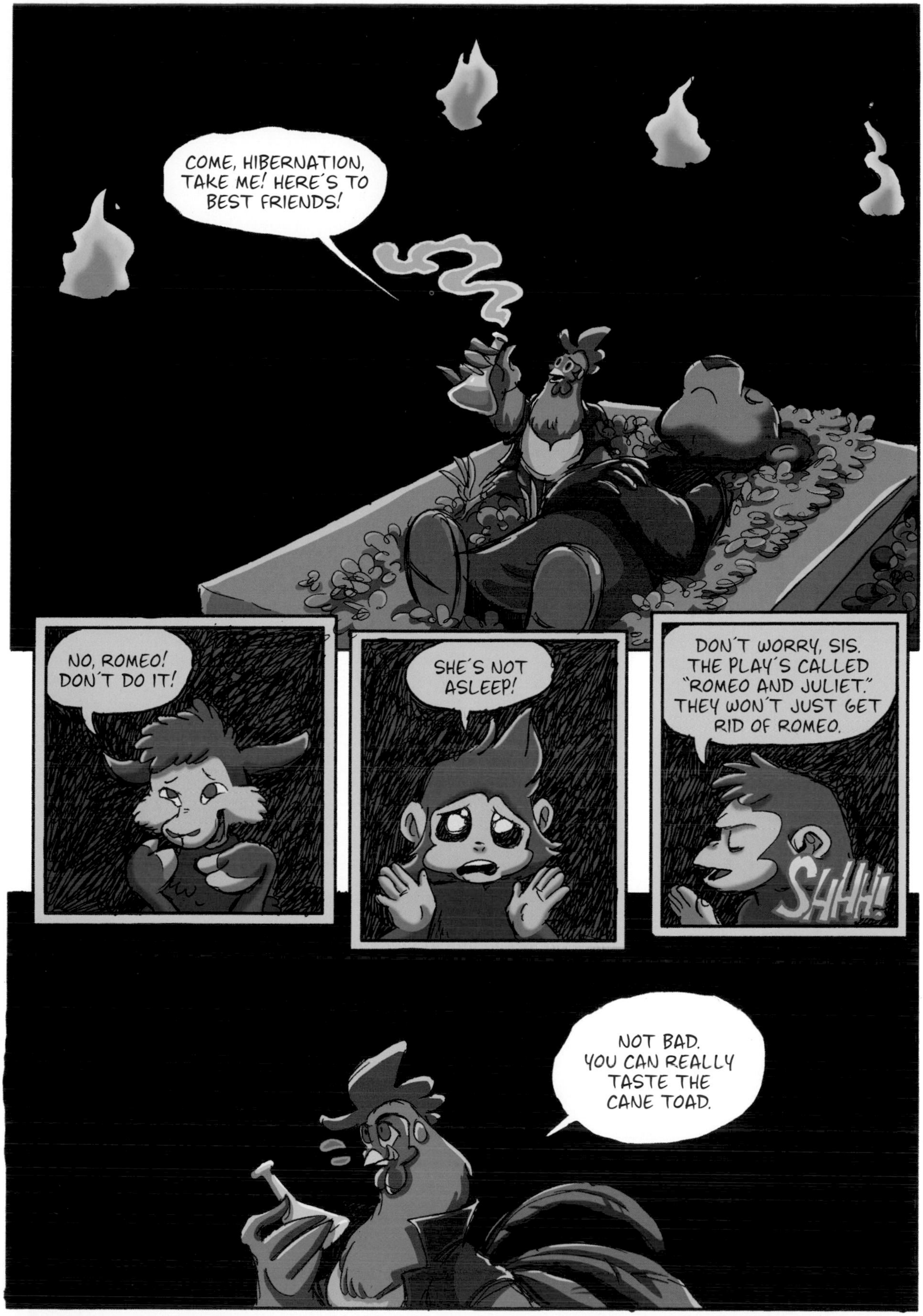
COME, HIBERNATION, TAKE ME! HERE´S TO BEST FRIENDS!
NO, ROMEO! DON´T DO IT!
SHE´S NOT ASLEEP!
DON´T WORRY, SIS. THE PLAY´S CALLED "ROMEO AND JULIET." THEY WON´T JUST GET RID OF ROMEO.
SHHH!
NOT BAD. YOU CAN REALLY TASTE THE CANE TOAD.

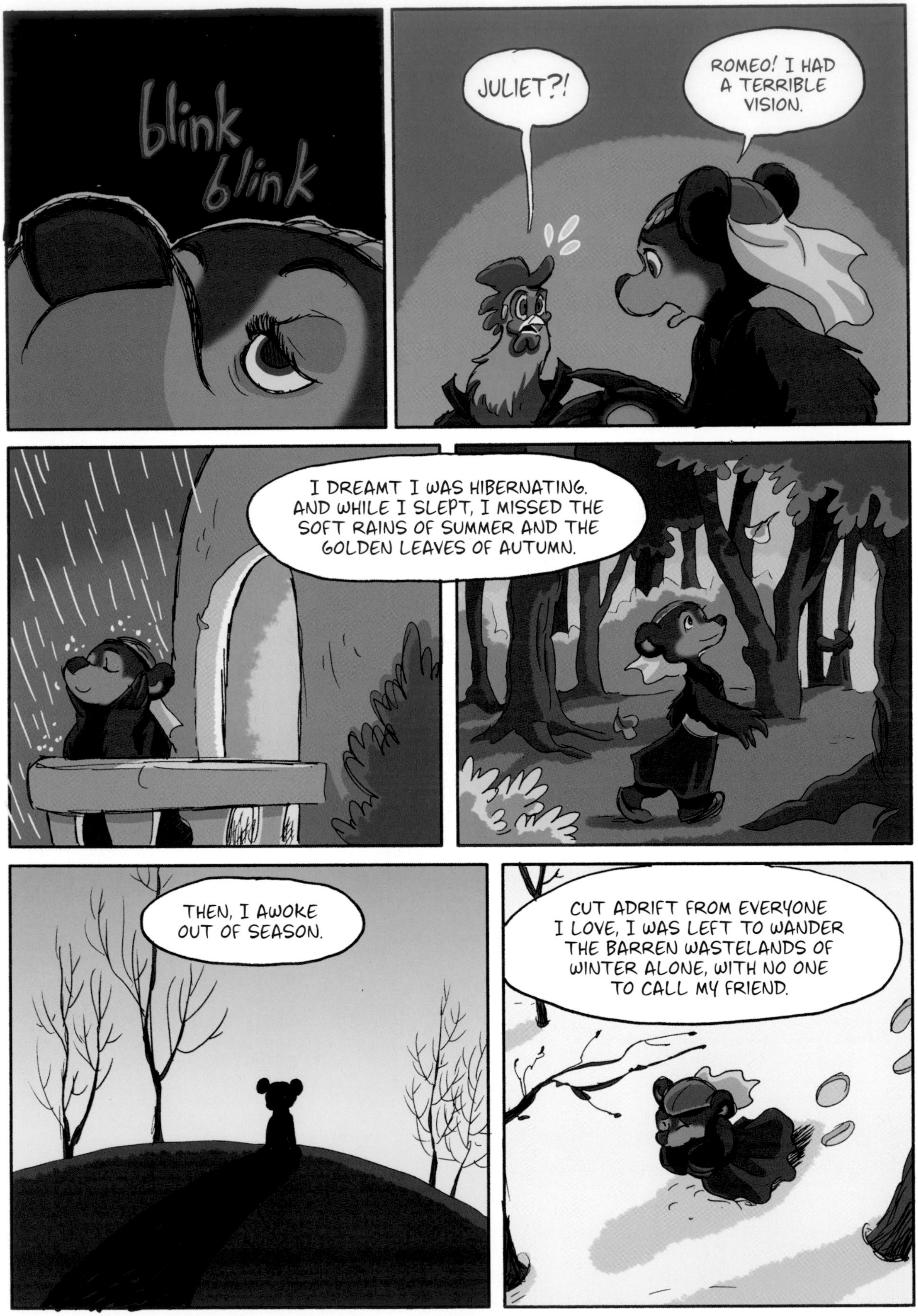
blink
blink
JULIET?!
ROMEO! I HAD A TERRIBLE VISION.
I DREAMT I WAS HIBERNATING. AND WHILE I SLEPT, I MISSED THE SOFT RAINS OF SUMMER AND THE GOLDEN LEAVES OF AUTUMN.
THEN, I AWOKE OUT OF SEASON.
CUT ADRIFT FROM EVERYONE I LOVE, I WAS LEFT TO WANDER THE BARREN WASTELANDS OF WINTER ALONE, WITH NO ONE TO CALL MY FRIEND.

RIIIGHT. SO...YOU'RE *NOT* HIBERNATING?

OF COURSE NOT! IT WAS ALL PART OF THE PLAN.

UHH... WHOOPS.

ROOS'TER HIBERNATION JUICE Z Zz

I'M GOING TO KILL THAT STUPID OWL.

WELL, SEE YOU AROUND SOME TIME.

NO! STAY AWAKE, ROMEO! WE HAVE SO MANY THINGS TO DO! MY DAD GOT ME A SWINGSET. A BOUNCY CASTLE. AND I LEARNED HOW TO DO A CAT'S CRADLE WITH A YO-YO!

THAT SOUNDS FUN, EXCEPT FOR THE YO-YO THING. I NEVER SAW THE ATTRACTION. THE STRING ALWAYS GETS TANGLED AND...AND...

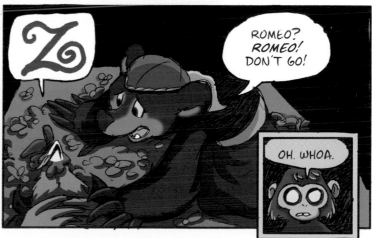

ROMEO? *ROMEO!* DON'T GO!

OH. WHOA.

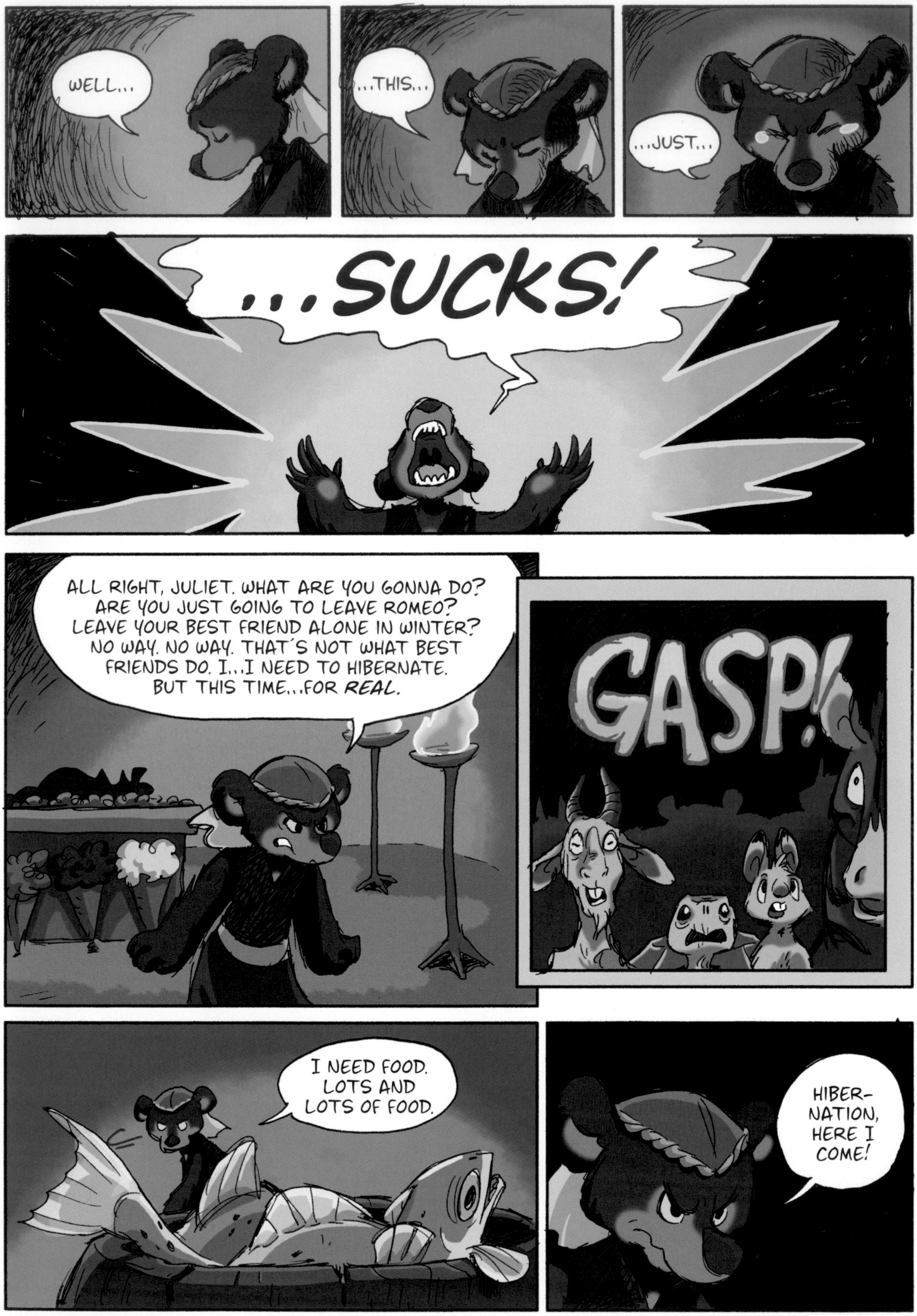
WELL...
...THIS...
...JUST...
...SUCKS!
ALL RIGHT, JULIET. WHAT ARE YOU GONNA DO? ARE YOU JUST GOING TO LEAVE ROMEO? LEAVE YOUR BEST FRIEND ALONE IN WINTER? NO WAY. NO WAY. THAT´S NOT WHAT BEST FRIENDS DO. I...I NEED TO HIBERNATE. BUT THIS TIME...FOR *REAL.*
GASP!
I NEED FOOD. LOTS AND LOTS OF FOOD.
HIBER-NATION, HERE I COME!

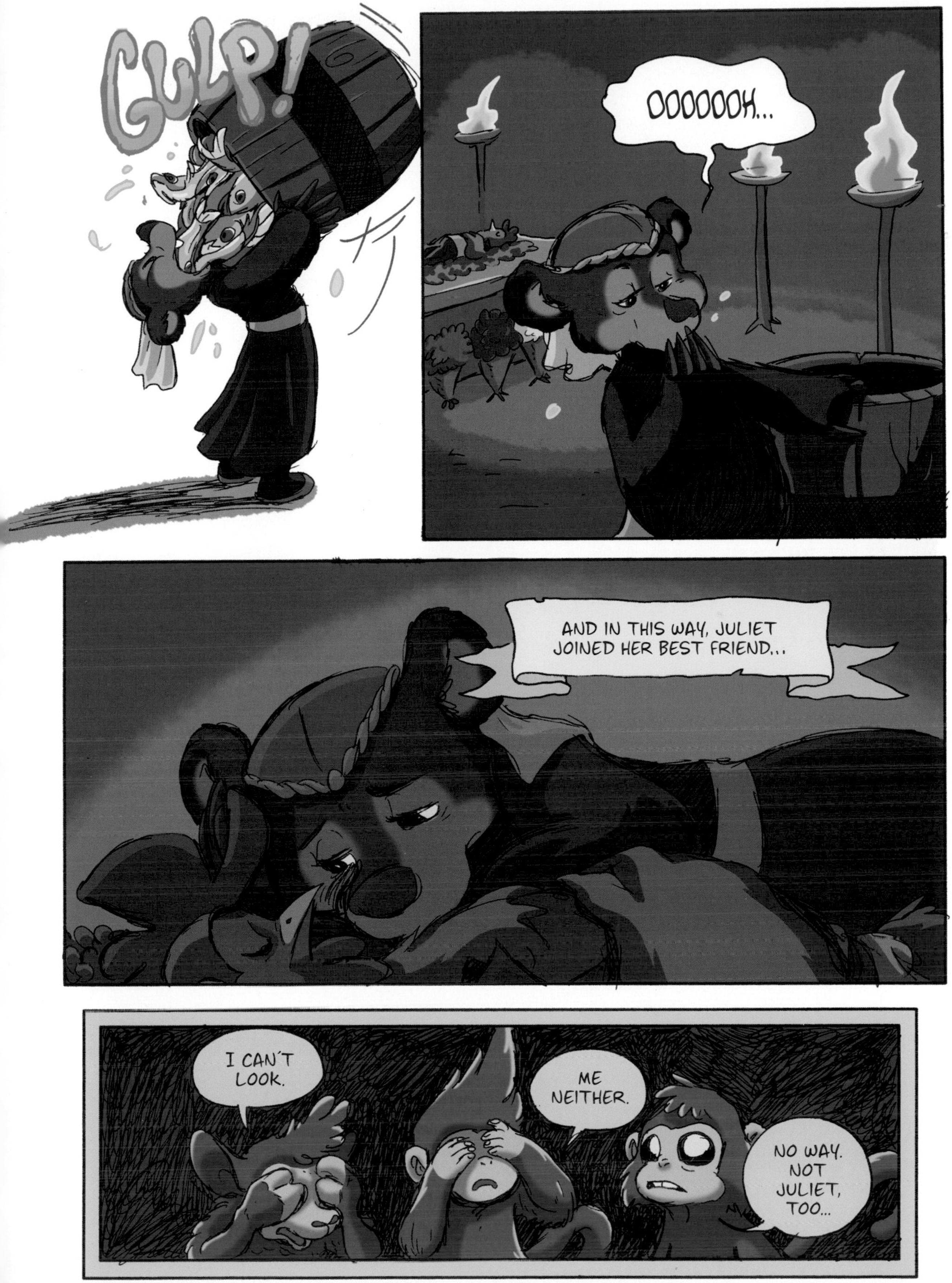
GULP!
OOOOOOH...
AND IN THIS WAY, JULIET JOINED HER BEST FRIEND...
I CAN'T LOOK.
ME NEITHER.
NO WAY. NOT JULIET, TOO...

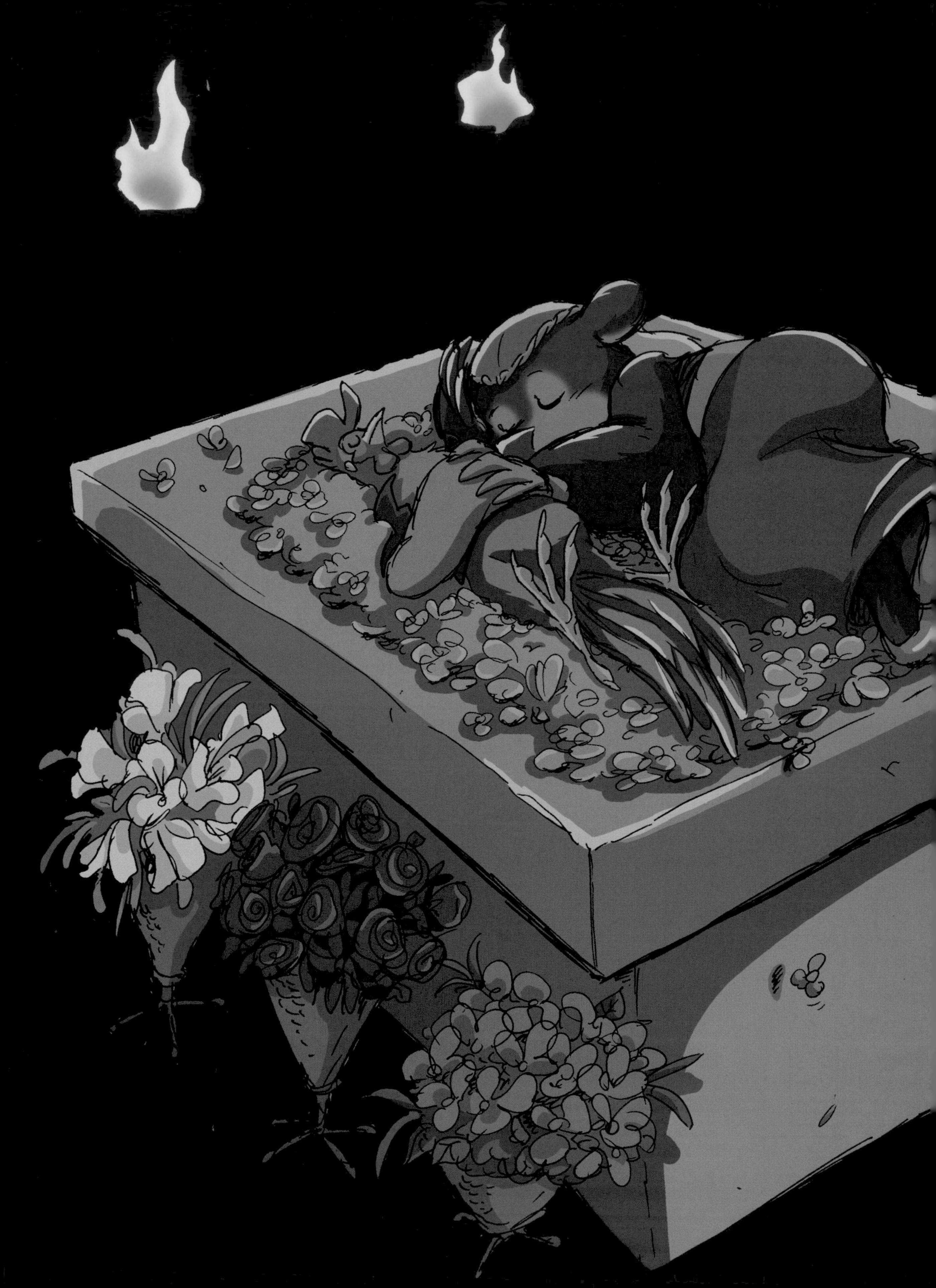

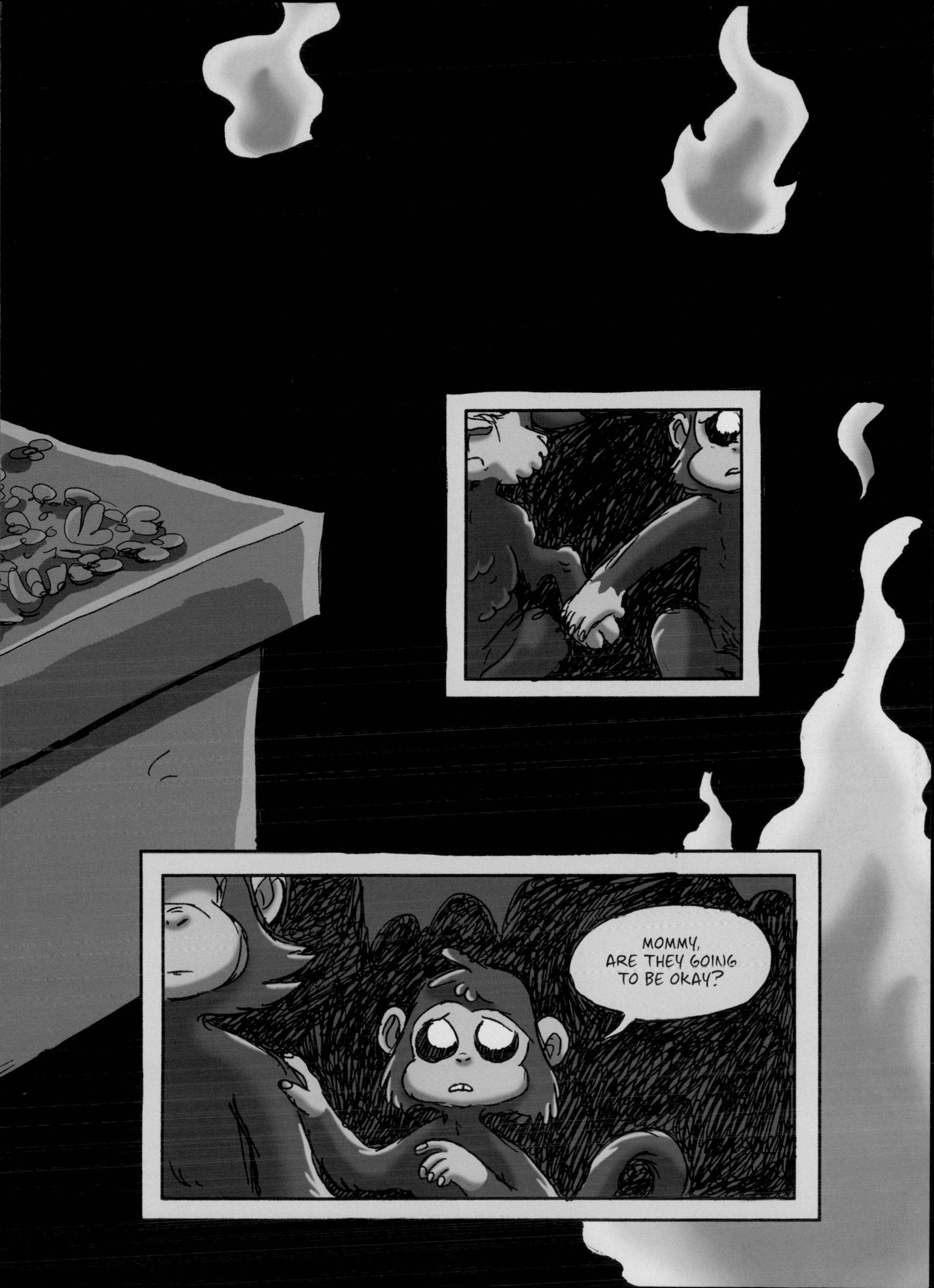
MOMMY, ARE THEY GOING TO BE OKAY?

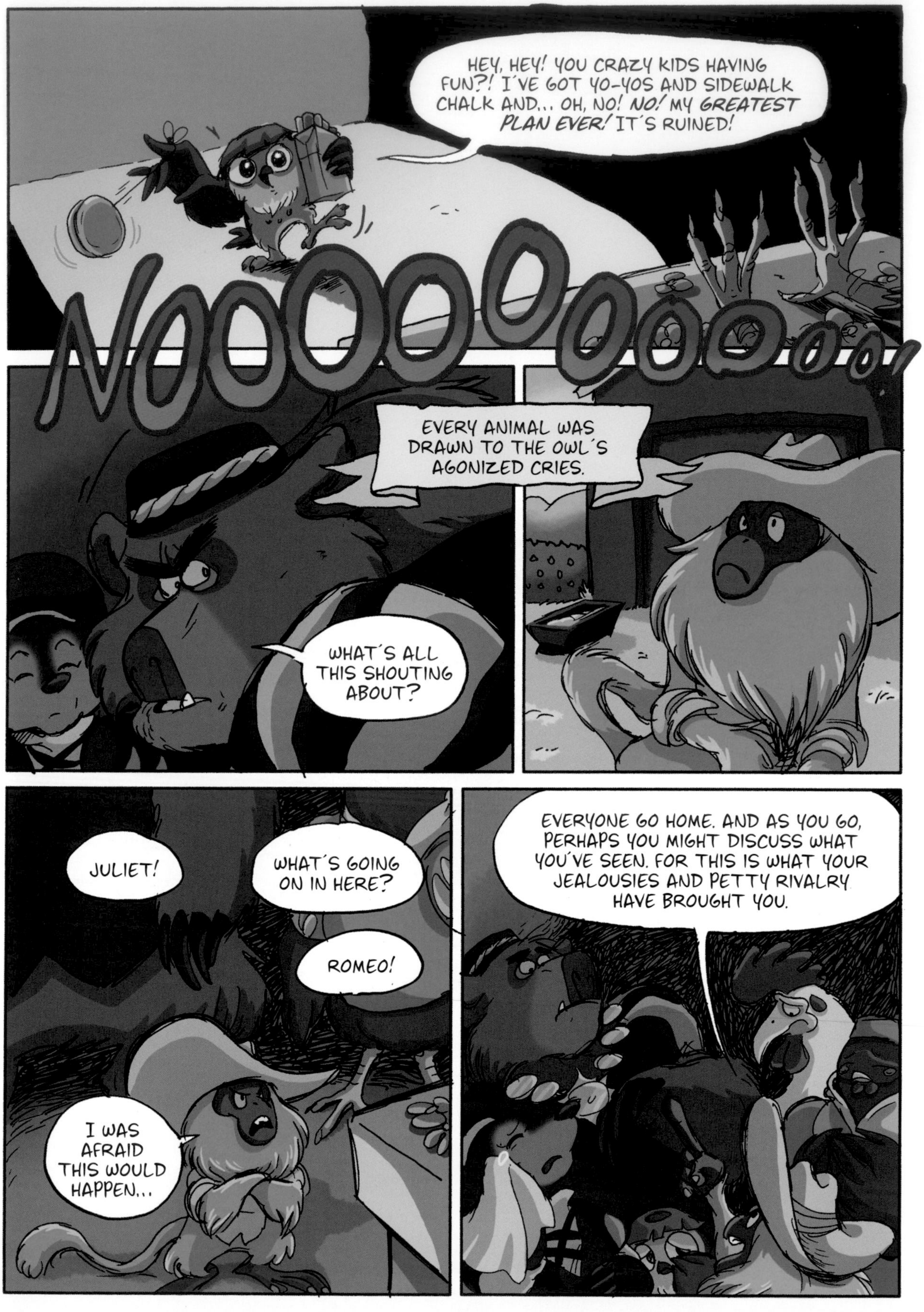

HEY, HEY! YOU CRAZY KIDS HAVING FUN?! I'VE GOT YO-YOS AND SIDEWALK CHALK AND... OH, NO! *NO!* MY *GREATEST PLAN EVER!* IT'S RUINED!
NOOOOOOOOOOO...
EVERY ANIMAL WAS DRAWN TO THE OWL'S AGONIZED CRIES.
WHAT'S ALL THIS SHOUTING ABOUT?
JULIET!
WHAT'S GOING ON IN HERE?
ROMEO!
I WAS AFRAID THIS WOULD HAPPEN...
EVERYONE GO HOME. AND AS YOU GO, PERHAPS YOU MIGHT DISCUSS WHAT YOU'VE SEEN. FOR THIS IS WHAT YOUR JEALOUSIES AND PETTY RIVALRY HAVE BROUGHT YOU.

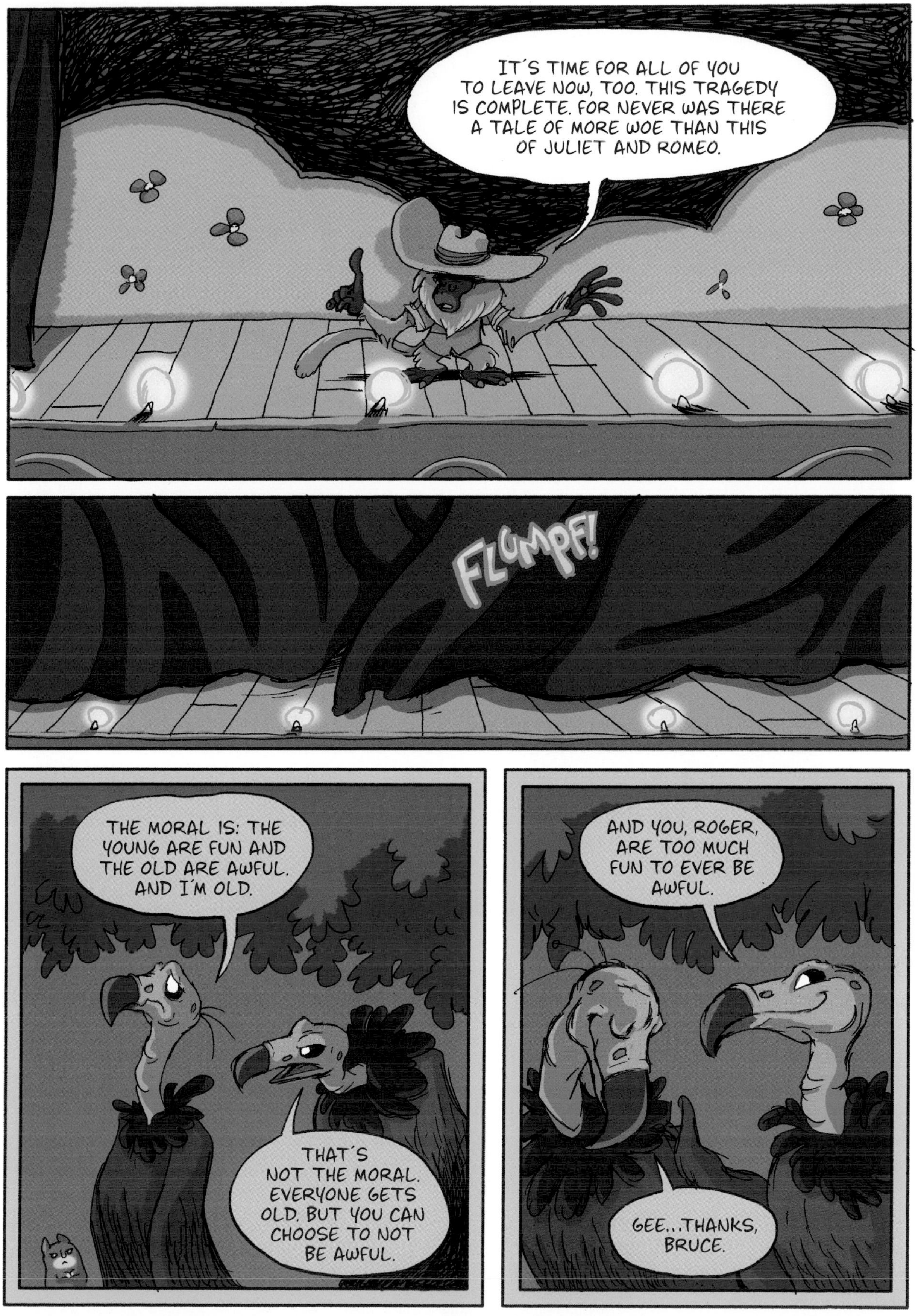
IT´S TIME FOR ALL OF YOU TO LEAVE NOW, TOO. THIS TRAGEDY IS COMPLETE. FOR NEVER WAS THERE A TALE OF MORE WOE THAN THIS OF JULIET AND ROMEO.
FLUMPF!
THE MORAL IS: THE YOUNG ARE FUN AND THE OLD ARE AWFUL. AND I´M OLD.
THAT´S NOT THE MORAL. EVERYONE GETS OLD. BUT YOU CAN CHOOSE TO NOT BE AWFUL.
AND YOU, ROGER, ARE TOO MUCH FUN TO EVER BE AWFUL.
GEE...THANKS, BRUCE.

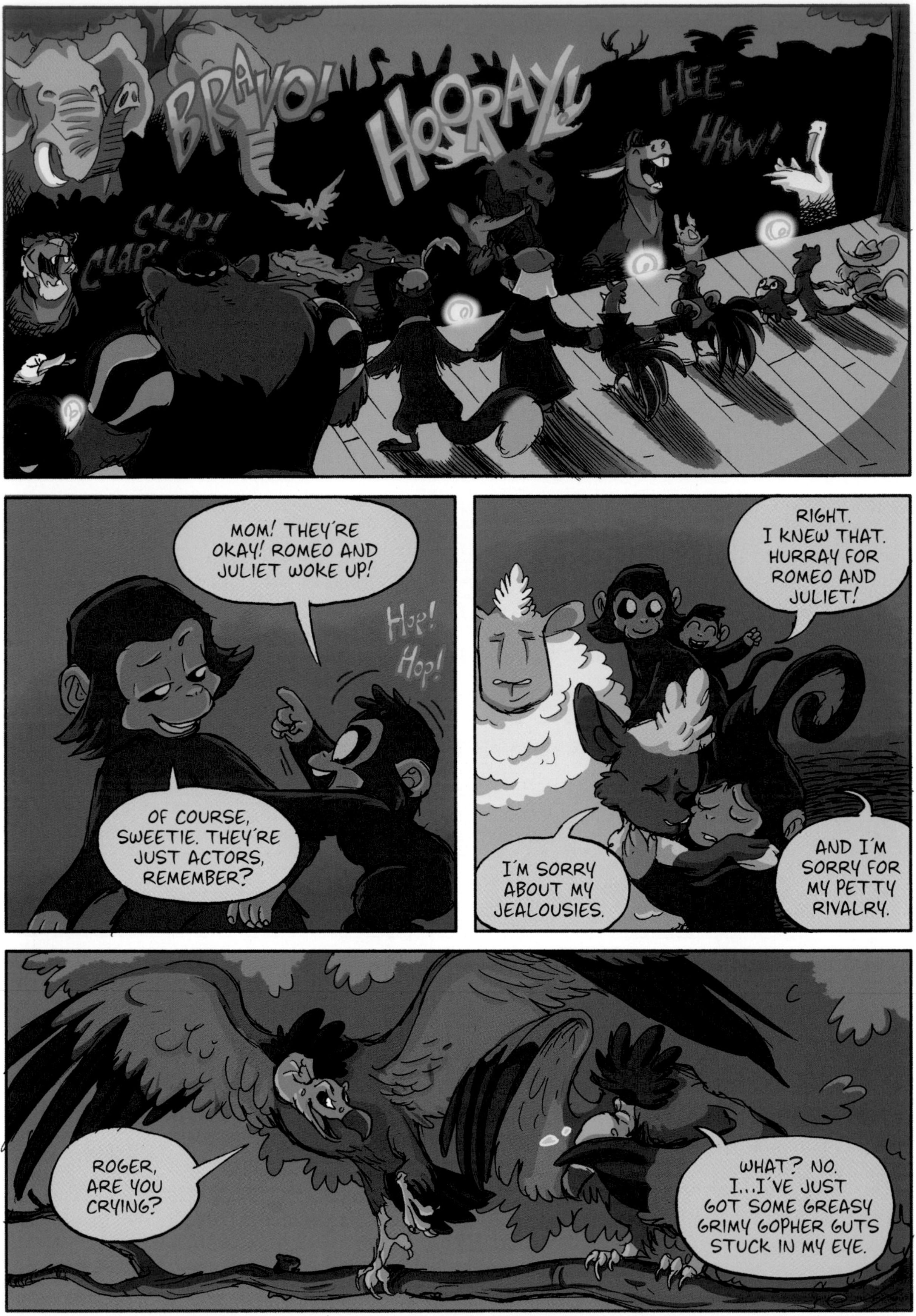
BRAVO!
HOORAY!
HEE-HAW!
CLAP! CLAP!
MOM! THEY'RE OKAY! ROMEO AND JULIET WOKE UP!
Hop! Hop!
OF COURSE, SWEETIE. THEY'RE JUST ACTORS, REMEMBER?
RIGHT. I KNEW THAT. HURRAY FOR ROMEO AND JULIET!
I'M SORRY ABOUT MY JEALOUSIES.
AND I'M SORRY FOR MY PETTY RIVALRY.
ROGER, ARE YOU CRYING?
WHAT? NO. I...I'VE JUST GOT SOME GREASY GRIMY GOPHER GUTS STUCK IN MY EYE.

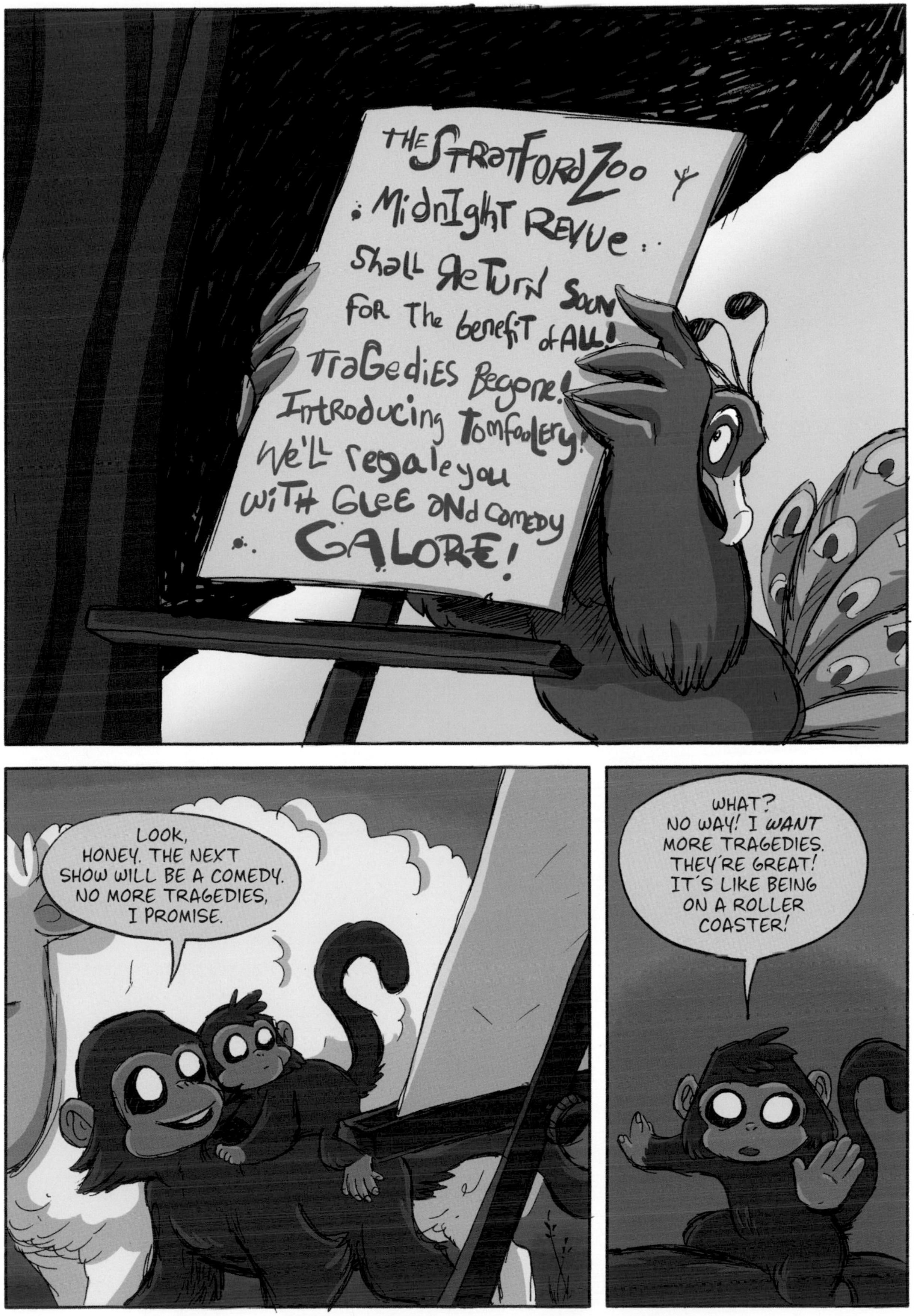
THE STRATFORD ZOO
MIDNIGHT REVUE
SHALL RETURN SOON
FOR THE BENEFIT OF ALL!
TRAGEDIES BEGONE!
INTRODUCING TOMFOOLERY!
WE'LL REGALE YOU
WITH GLEE AND COMEDY
GALORE!
LOOK, HONEY. THE NEXT SHOW WILL BE A COMEDY. NO MORE TRAGEDIES, I PROMISE.
WHAT? NO WAY! I *WANT* MORE TRAGEDIES. THEY'RE GREAT! IT'S LIKE BEING ON A ROLLER COASTER!

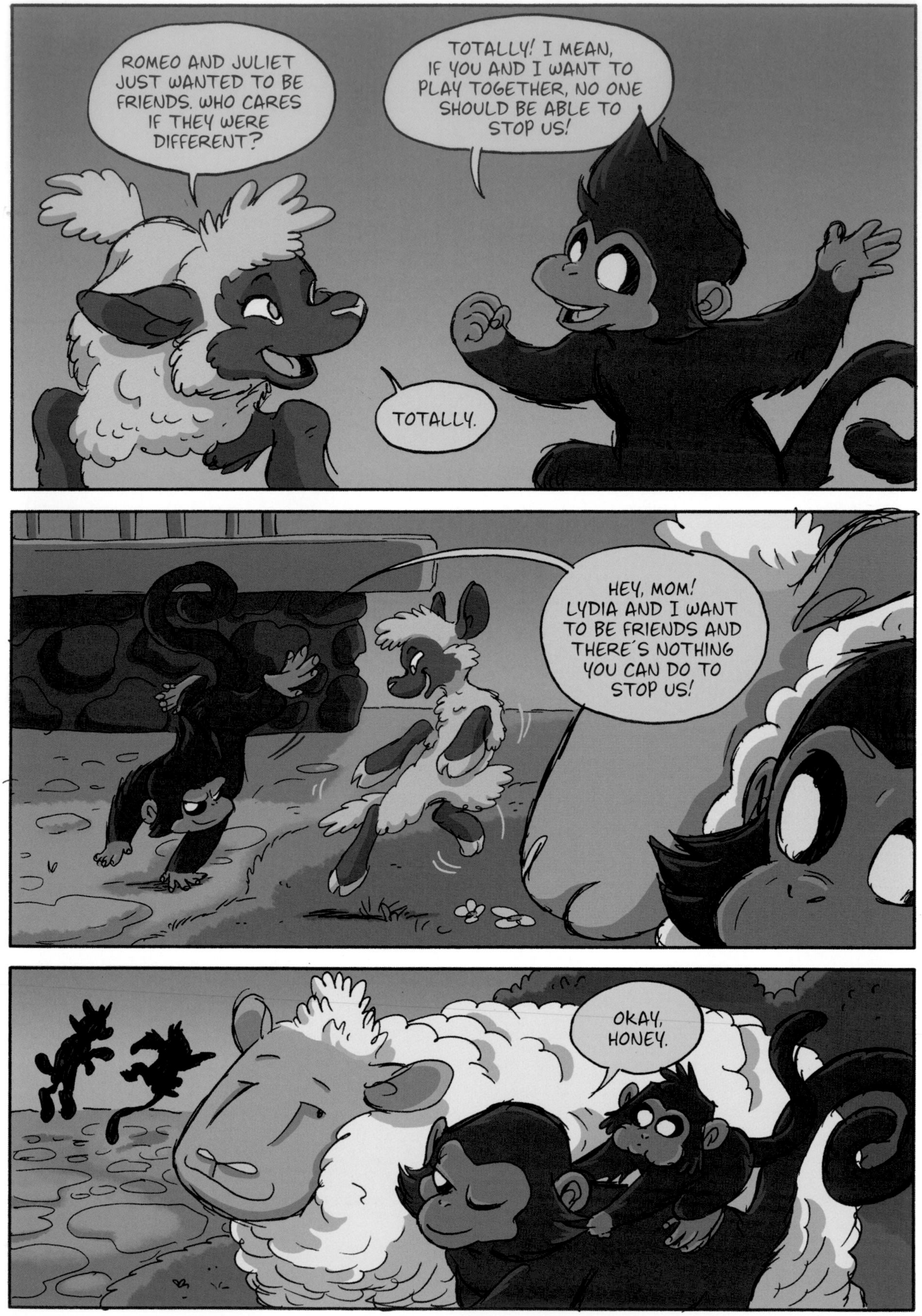
ROMEO AND JULIET JUST WANTED TO BE FRIENDS. WHO CARES IF THEY WERE DIFFERENT?
TOTALLY! I MEAN, IF YOU AND I WANT TO PLAY TOGETHER, NO ONE SHOULD BE ABLE TO STOP US!
TOTALLY.
HEY, MOM! LYDIA AND I WANT TO BE FRIENDS AND THERE'S NOTHING YOU CAN DO TO STOP US!
OKAY, HONEY.

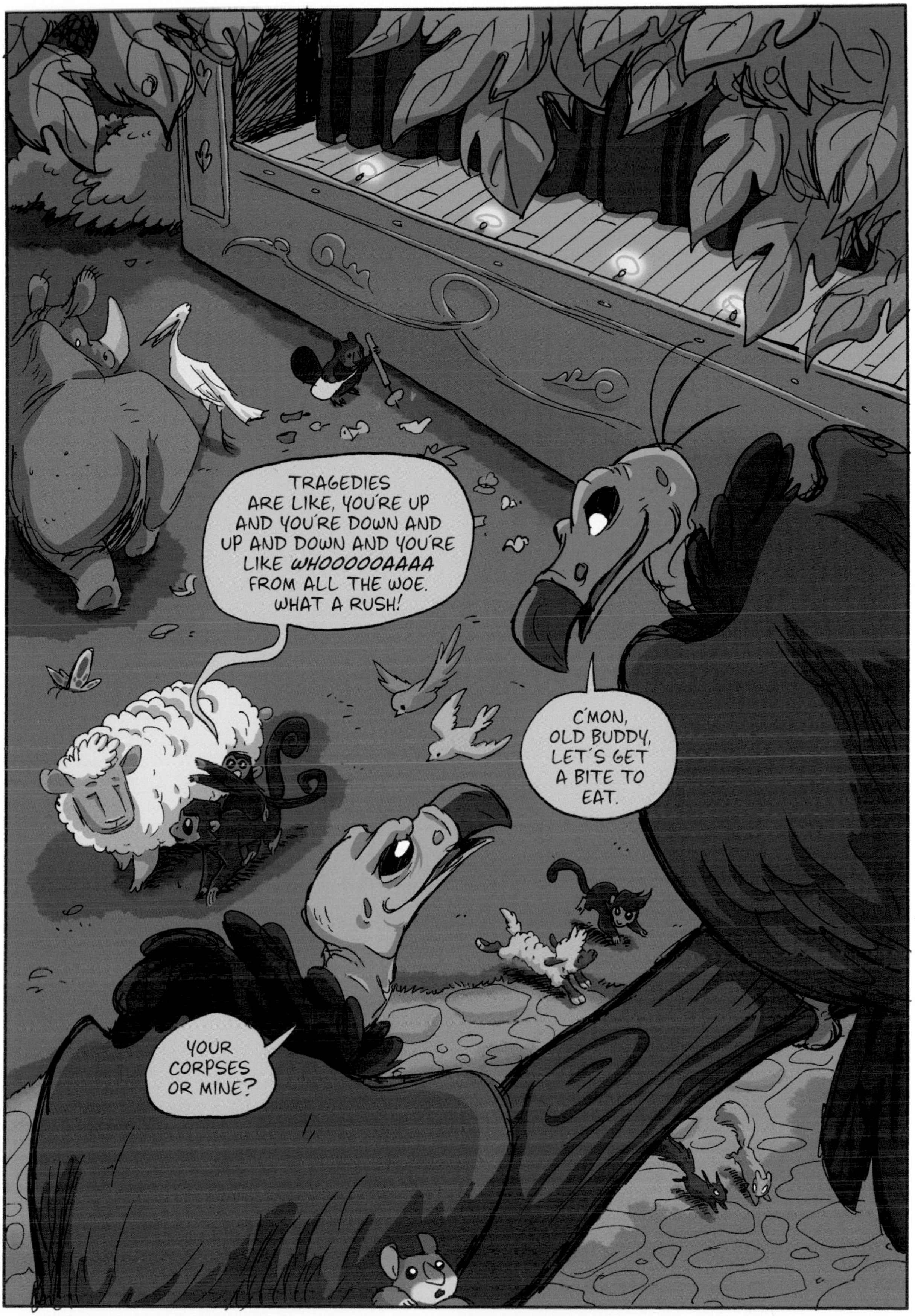
TRAGEDIES ARE LIKE, YOU'RE UP AND YOU'RE DOWN AND UP AND DOWN AND YOU'RE LIKE *WHOOOOOAAAA* FROM ALL THE WOE. WHAT A RUSH!
C'MON, OLD BUDDY, LET'S GET A BITE TO EAT.
YOUR CORPSES OR MINE?

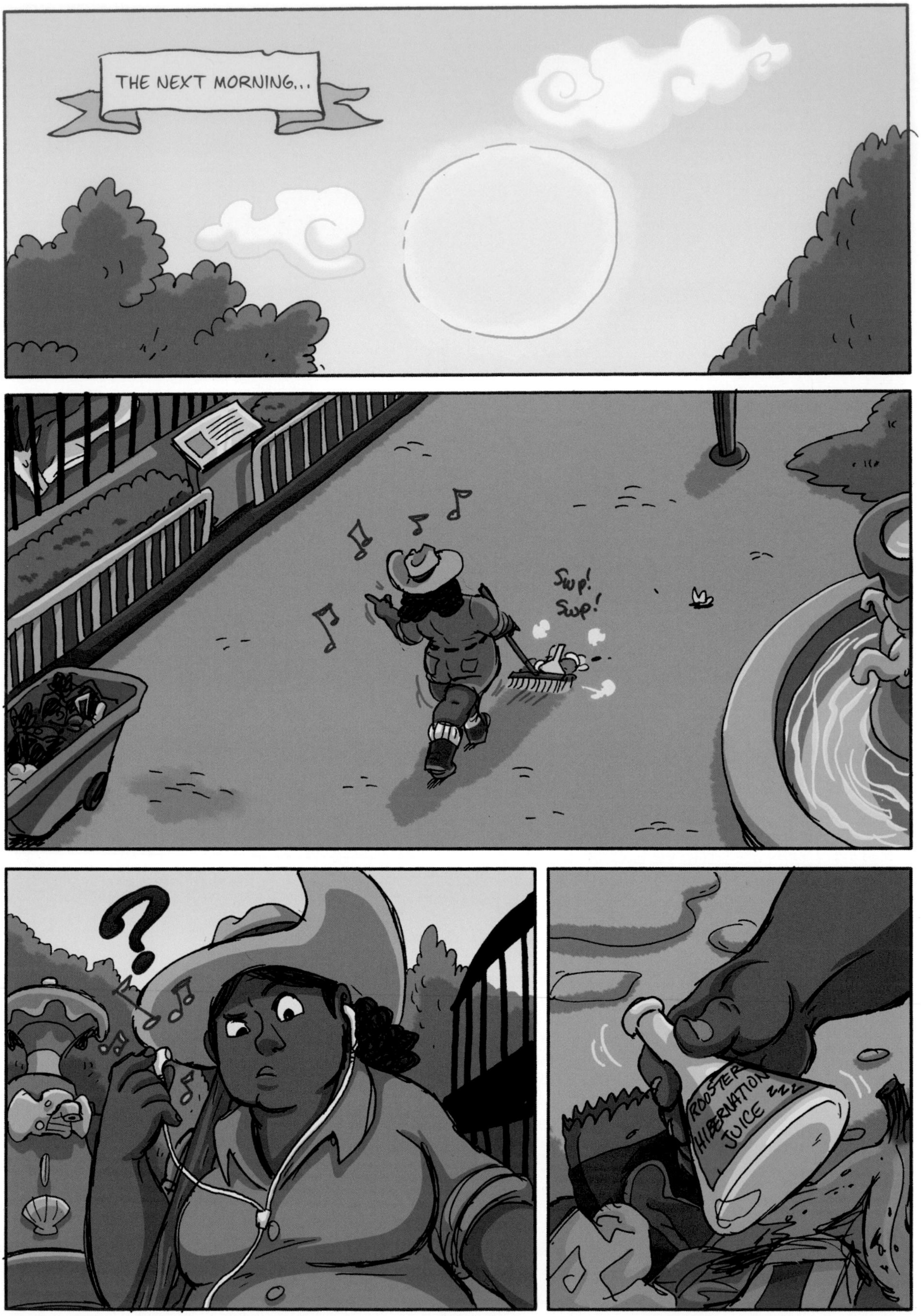
THE NEXT MORNING...
SWP!
SWP!
?
ROOSTER HIBERNATION JUICE
ZZZ

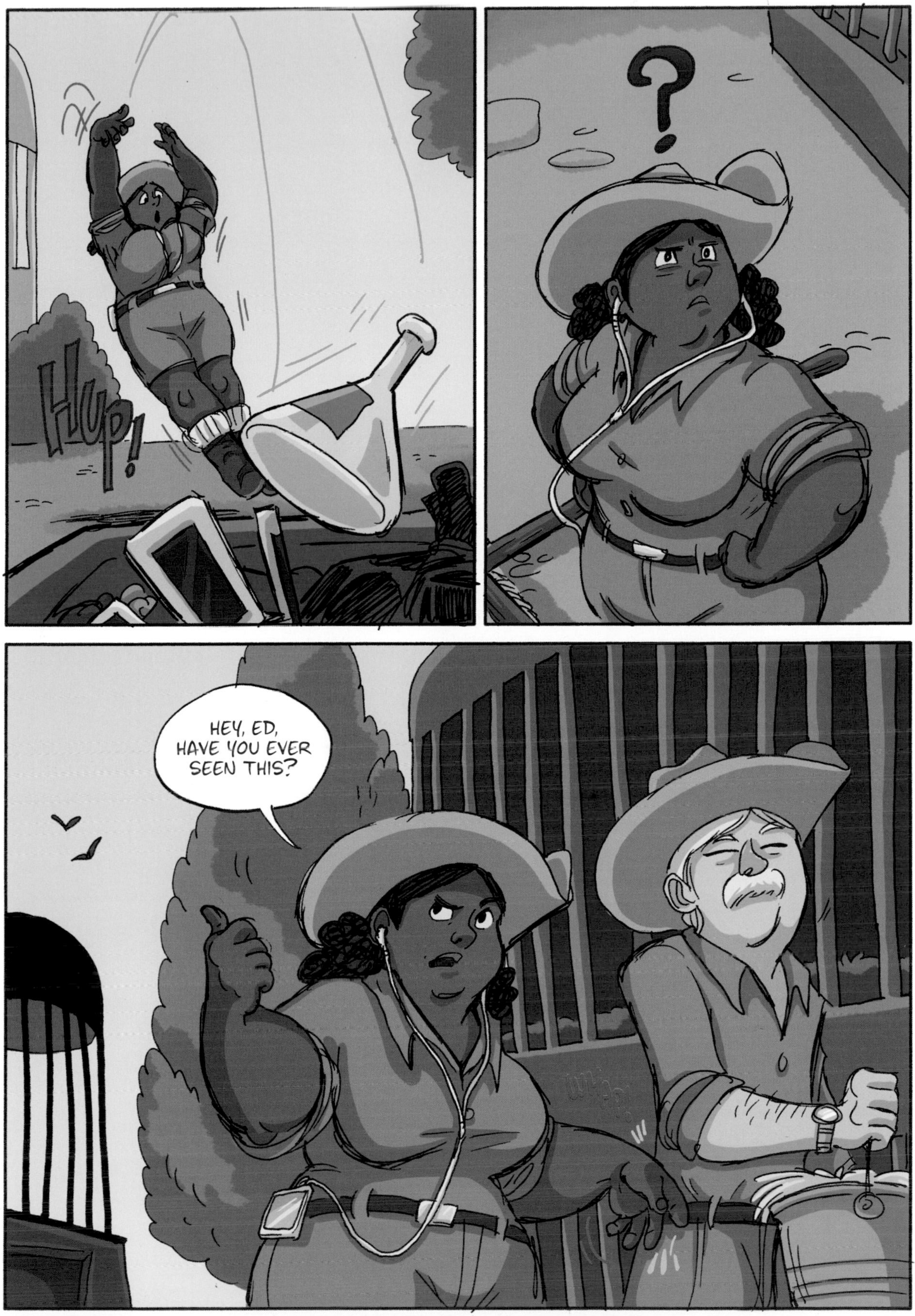
HUP!
?
HEY, ED, HAVE YOU EVER SEEN THIS?

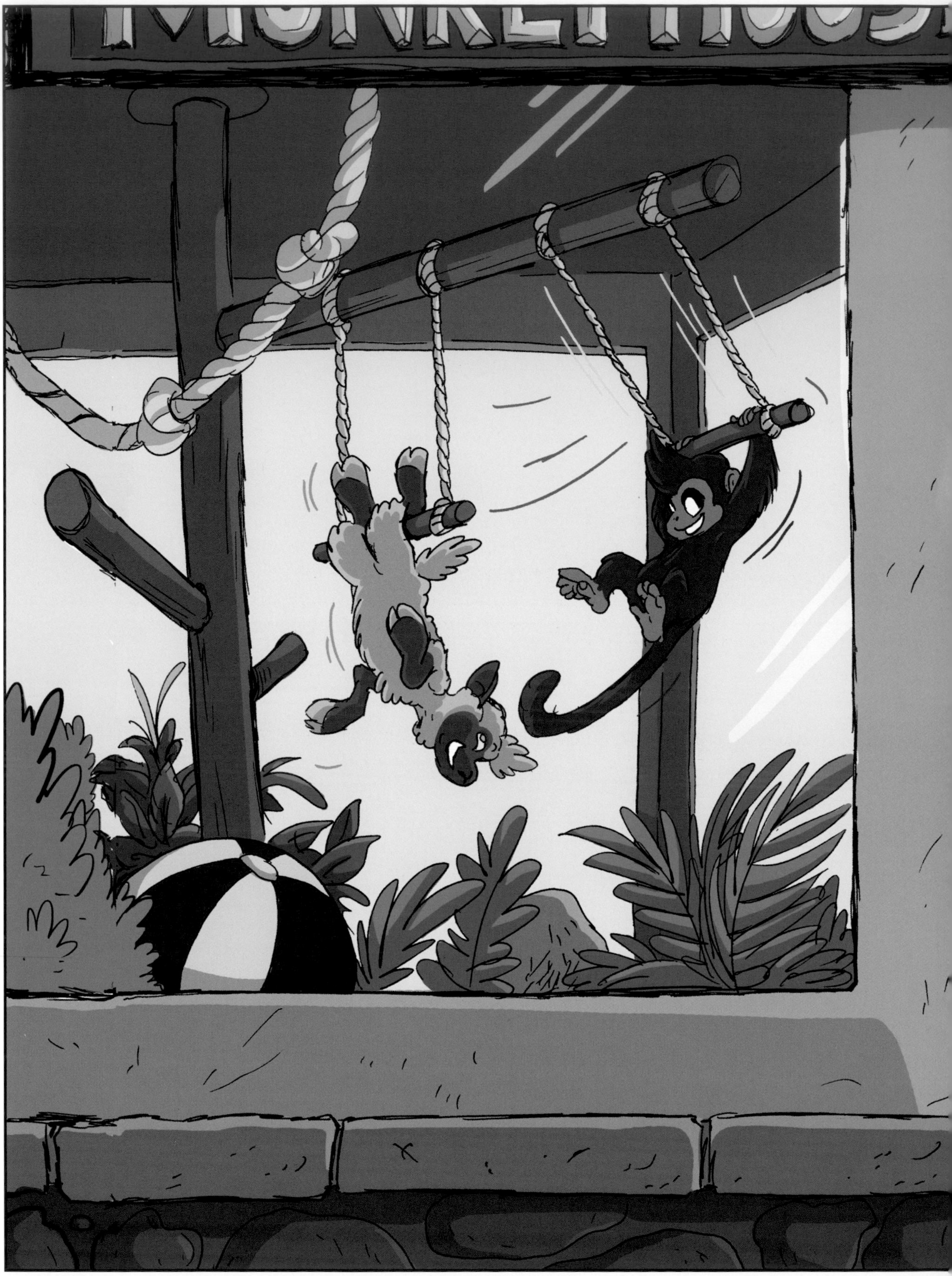

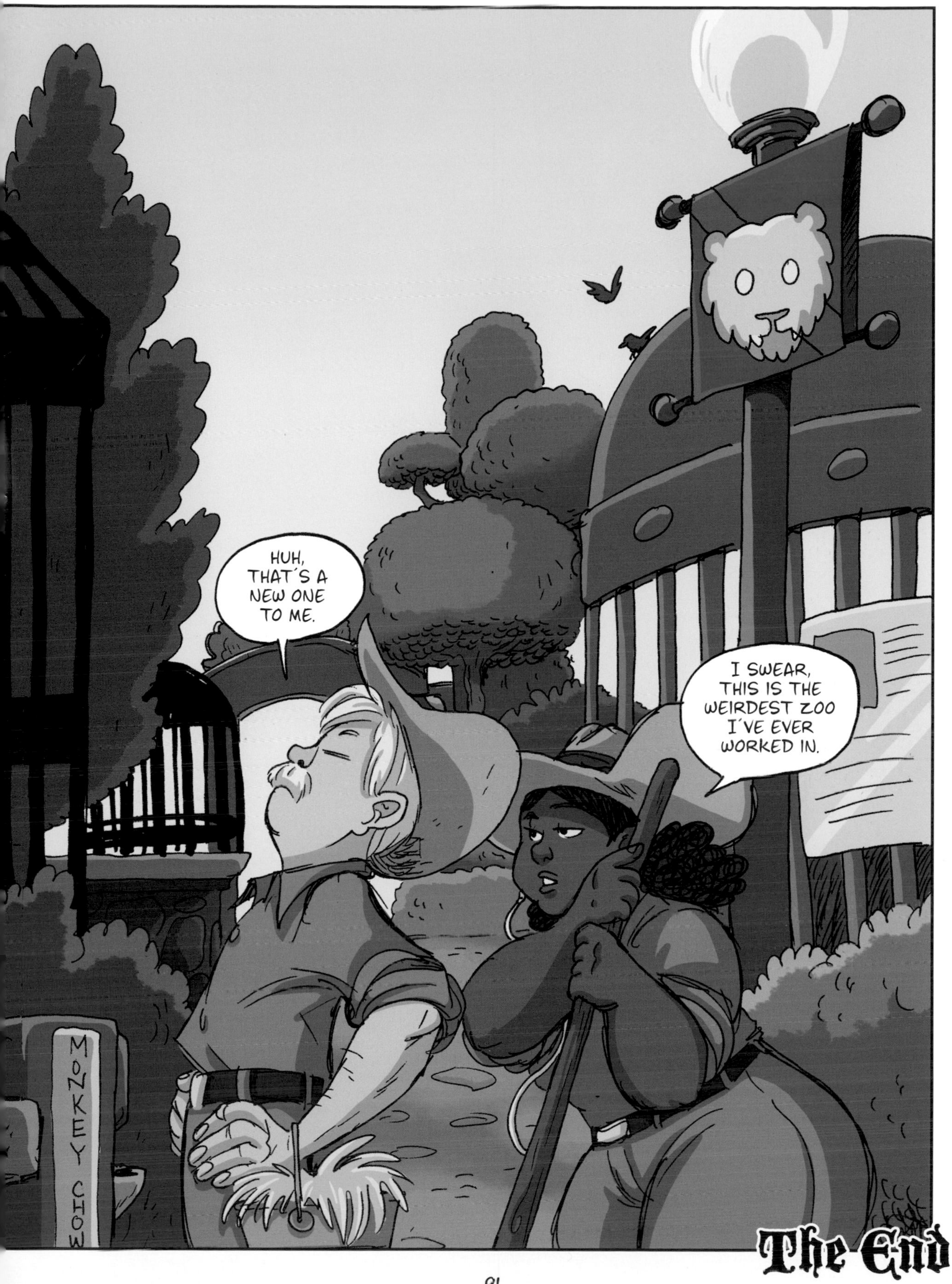
HUH, THAT'S A NEW ONE TO ME.
I SWEAR, THIS IS THE WEIRDEST ZOO I'VE EVER WORKED IN.
MONKEY CHOW
The End

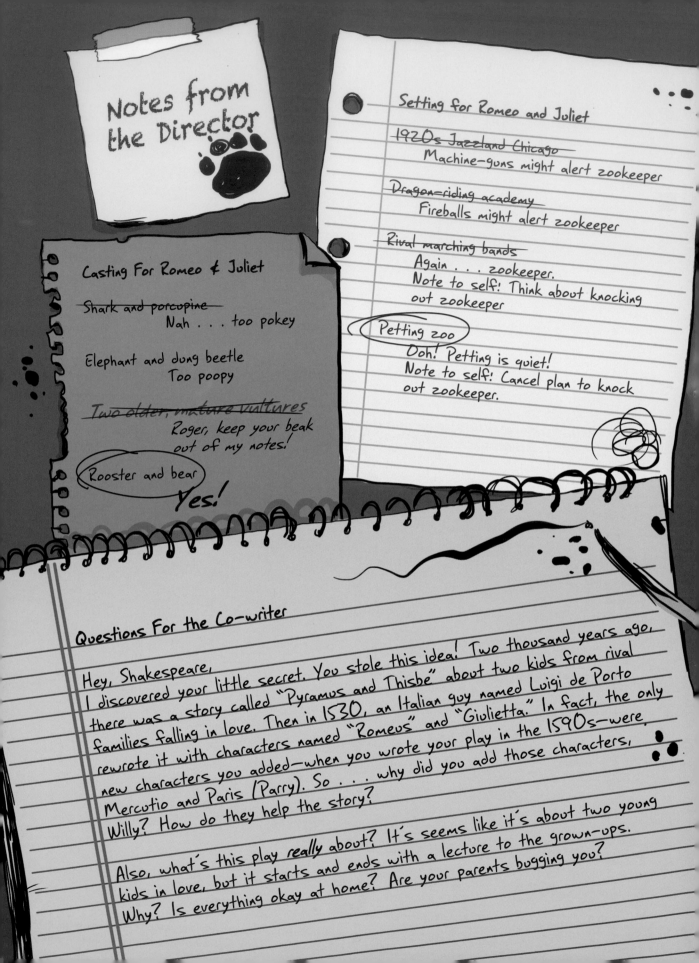

Notes from the Director

Casting For Romeo & Juliet

~~Shark and porcupine~~
      Nah . . . too pokey

Elephant and dung beetle
      Too poopy

~~Two older, mature vultures~~
      Roger, keep your beak
      out of my notes!

(Rooster and bear)
      Yes!

Setting for Romeo and Juliet

~~1920s Jazzland Chicago~~
  Machine-guns might alert zookeeper

~~Dragon-riding academy~~
  Fireballs might alert zookeeper

~~Rival marching bands~~
  Again . . . zookeeper.
  Note to self: Think about knocking
  out zookeeper

(Petting zoo)
  Ooh! Petting is quiet!
  Note to self: Cancel plan to knock
  out zookeeper.

Questions For the Co-writer

Hey, Shakespeare,
I discovered your little secret. You stole this idea! Two thousand years ago, there was a story called "Pyramus and Thisbe" about two kids from rival families falling in love. Then in 1530, an Italian guy named Luigi de Porto rewrote it with characters named "Romeus" and "Giulietta." In fact, the only new characters you added—when you wrote your play in the 1590s—were Mercutio and Paris (Parry). So . . . why did you add those characters, Willy? How do they help the story?

Also, what's this play _really_ about? It's seems like it's about two young kids in love, but it starts and ends with a lecture to the grown-ups. Why? Is everything okay at home? Are your parents bugging you?

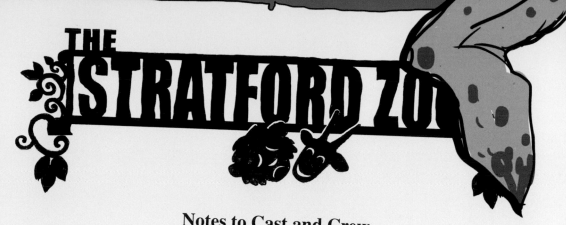

THE STRATFORD ZOO

Notes to Cast and Crew

- I've heard some grumbling from the cast about having to memorize so many lines. Just remember, in Shakespeare's day, actors would perform ten *different* plays every two weeks. So quit complaining!
- Due to the zoo's current lack of bears, Juliet's understudy will be her brother, Reg. This might seem strange, but *Juliet was originally played by a man.* Women weren't even *allowed* on stage until the seventeenth century, over fifty years later.
- After great consideration, I have to deny the cast's request for a cannon. Yes, I understand that Shakespeare used a real cannon in his theater for big entrances and battle scenes, but I feel the zookeeper *might* notice live cannon fire in the middle of the night. Also, those cannons once burned down Shakespeare's entire theater. The zookeeper might notice her entire zoo on fire, too.
- I've decided to cut the twenty minutes of dancing at the end. I know that's how Shakespeare and his actors entertained their audiences after a play, but last week's jig sent three animals to the vet. Some animals were just not meant to cavort. Sorry, hippos. I did appreciate your enthusiasm, though.
- Mercutio and Tibbs: Great energy in the sword-fighting scenes, but it's still a bit sloppy. I want you to rehearse some more tomorrow, for two reasons:

  1) Shakespeare's audience paid to see good fight scenes, so they would boo any actor with poor sword skills.
  2) But more importantly, stage combat is no joke. Actors have lost an eye (or even died!) during sword fights on stage. So your motivation for these scenes is—don't die!

- Some people have asked why we changed a few details from Shakespeare's version. In the original play, the character of the Great Owl (a friar) couldn't contact Romeo and Juliet until it was too late because he was quarantined with the plague. Shakespeare's audience was all too familiar with this. In 1563, the bubonic plague (known as the Black Death) killed over 20,000 people in London alone. That was almost one-third of the city's entire population. And all of this death and disease was *spread by fleas!* I felt that any flea-related plot points would be too scary for our animal audience.

Please Remember:
Check yourself for fleas and ticks after every performance!

To Kusum, of course
—I. L.

For those who draw animals
—Z. G.

First Second

Text copyright © 2015 by Ian Lendler
Art copyright © 2015 by Zack Giallongo

Published by First Second
First Second is an imprint of Roaring Brook Press,
a division of Holtzbrinck Publishing Holdings Limited Partnership
175 Fifth Avenue, New York, New York 10010

All rights reserved

Library of Congress Control Number: 2015937866

Hardcover ISBN 978-1-62672-278-1
Paperback ISBN 978-1-59643-916-0

First Second books may be purchased for business or promotional use. For information
on bulk purchases please contact Macmillan Corporate and Premium Sales Department at
(800) 221-7945 x5442 or by email at specialmarkets@macmillan.com.

First edition 2015
Book design by Colleen AF Venable, Danielle Ceccolini, and John Green

Printed in China by Macmillan Production (Asia) Ltd., Kowloon Bay, Hong Kong (supplier
code 10)

Hardcover: 10 9 8 7 6 5 4 3 2 1
Paperback: 10 9 8 7 6 5 4 3 2 1